The Legal Affair

The Singh Family Trilogy
The Legal Affair

Young Adult Fiction
My So-Called Bollywood Life

ATTENTION: ORGANIZATIONS AND CORPORATIONS

HarperCollins books may be purchased for educational, business, or sales promotional use. For information, please e-mail the Special Markets Department at SPsales@harpercollins.com.

By Nisha Sharma

The Singh Family Trilogy
The Takeover Effect
The Legal Affair

Young Adult Fiction
My So-Called Bollywood Life

THE LEGAL AFFAIR

THE SINGH FAMILY TRILOGY

NISHA SHARMA

AVONIMPULSE
An Imprint of HarperCollinsPublishers

Excerpt from *The Takeover Effect* copyright © 2019 by Nisha Seesan.

Digital Edition AUGUST 2020 ISBN: 978-0-06-285418-6

Print Edition ISBN: 978-0-06-285438-4

Cover design by Nadine Badalaty
Cover photographs © g-stockstudio/iStock/Getty Images (couple); © Tinpixels/iStock/Getty Images (beard); © Arnon Polin/Shutterstock (bracelet)

Avon Impulse and the Avon Impulse logo are registered trademarks of HarperCollins Publishers in the United States of America.

Avon and HarperCollins are registered trademarks of HarperCollins Publishers in the United States of America and other countries.

FIRST EDITION

20 21 22 23 24   HDC   10 9 8 7 6 5 4 3 2 1

*To Smita Kurrumchand, a badass
babe who came to the US when she was
eighteen, and built a life for herself with
guts, hard work, and a generous spirit.*

*Smita, I always knew that I was writing
Raj's story for you.
(Minus the husband parts.)
I hope she inspires you to continue to be an
unapologetic badass boss babe.*

Chapter One

Rajneet

RAJNEET KAUR HOTHI was eighteen the last time she was played for a fool.

She'd just stepped onto American soil at JFK Airport with a freshly stamped F-student visa and all of her belongings in two large suitcases. Her new roommate, a girl she met on an apartment listing site, was supposed to pick her up.

But Kelly never showed. Raj had waited for five hours at the baggage terminal, the last two in terror, before realizing she was completely on her own. She couldn't call her parents in Punjab. Her father had already been so angry with her for wanting to study in America. He wouldn't even take her to the airport.

Her mother had been quiet and reserved during their goodbyes. Raj had sworn that she'd never go running back to them because that would give them even more power over her. Instead she'd wiped her eyes of shame, squared her shoulders, and spoke to security. They'd taken pity on her and directed her to the nearest, most affordable hotel.

The next day, Raj had discovered the apartment she'd paid a deposit for didn't exist, and Kelly's number was no longer in service.

Since that moment twelve years ago, she'd trusted a very small, vetted group of people. She'd carefully screened and cultivated that group and protected them as fiercely as if they were family.

That short list used to include Robert, the man she'd married right after her college graduation ceremony.

She never thought he'd betray her.

In the shadowed backseat of the car, with New York City sidewalks passing by outside her windows, Raj looked at her phone to read the new message from Mina.

MINA: DIVORCED? WHAT DO YOU MEAN YOU'RE GETTING DIVORCED?

RAJ: We'll meet next week. I promise I'll explain everything.

MINA: I'm so mad at you for keeping secrets. I need to know everything.

RAJ: I promise.

After the last text, Raj tucked her cell back into the square gold clutch in her lap. She wiggled the fingers of her bare left hand, then addressed her soon-to-be ex-husband who sat on the limo bench across from her.

"Mina knows about our divorce now."

Robert glanced up, then back at his phone. "Did you tell her?"

"I had to. She learned today that you took a job with WTA."

"Why does that matter?" he asked.

"Oh, I don't know, darling. Maybe because it's the conglomerate that made a hostile takeover attempt for her boyfriend's family business?"

"Raj . . ."

"I can't believe I was dumb enough to think that my husband, a man I've known since college, could do this to me. What's even more astounding is that right under my nose you used that information against me and jeopardized Mina's happiness. Here I thought Mina has been just as important in your life as she has been in mine."

Robert's stony expression started to slip, and Raj felt black joy spark to life inside of her. Focusing on him with her usual intensity always made him uncomfortable.

Good, she thought.

Other than the stress lines around his mouth, though, Robert appeared polished in his custom-fit tuxedo. His nails were neatly manicured and diamond cufflinks winked at his wrists. His angular jaw was clean-shaven, and he appeared the epitome of a wealthy gentleman.

"Did you really expect me to continue acting as your chief legal officer after you served me with divorce papers?"

"Of course not. I also didn't expect you to stab me—your friend, wife, and colleague—in the back. How could you do this after all we've been through together? How could you steal information from my office and purposely use it to hurt me?"

He rolled his eyes, something that Raj knew he did to piss her off. "You mean how could I go to the biggest technology company in the world, a company that would pay me twice what your midsize security staffing company is paying me, and accept a position?"

Raj crossed her legs and the slit in her black velvet gown parted to reveal bronzed, shimmering skin exposed to midthigh. Her hair was styled in barrel curls that draped over one bare shoulder, to match the vintage Dolce. She worked hard to show everyone that she was okay. That she was better than okay. Then she received Mina's text.

And damn Robert for shaking her cool right before she had to make a public appearance.

"You're a thief and a liar," she said as calmly as she could. "And I would make you suffer, if that didn't mean spending more time in your presence during a drawn-out divorce."

Robert pressed a button on the panel above his head and the privacy glass quietly raised behind him to block out their driver. "You know I hate threats. Raj, you'd do the same exact thing in my position. You keep secrets all the time. Hell, how long did it take you to confess to Mina about my new job? See? You even lie to her."

Because his accusation hit home, Raj felt herself stiffen even more. "I keep secrets because I'm in the business of keeping secrets. But I don't tell lies. Especially to those people in my life who have my loyalty. That used to include you."

"You're the one who asked for a divorce, and you're talking loyalty?"

She scrambled forward until she was practically nose to nose with him, breathing the same fire. "I asked for a divorce because you wanted to have a baby and you know I don't want one," she bit out. "At least, not right now, and definitely not with my business partner."

"And that's the real reason, isn't it?" His face turned a molten red. "Even though we've been together for so long, you don't want a kid with me. Because your maternal instincts are fine, dammit. You're always volunteering at that animal shelter and raising money for them."

"Oh my god." She pinched the bridge of her nose. "A dog is not a child, Robert."

"It's pretty much the same thing, Raj."

"I can't believe you're—You know what? Never mind. I gave you an *out* so you can have that family you want. And then you screwed me. You fucking screwed me."

He jabbed a finger at her. "No, what I did was waste years of my life with a woman who never wanted me to be anything but the convenient partner in a contract that wasn't in my best interests."

The limo slowed to a stop in front of Lincoln Center. Raj straightened in her seat and adjusted her sweetheart neckline as the driver rounded the car to open her door.

"I won't waste my time telling you that you knew what you were getting into when you signed that contract. And luckily, the agreement is now broken. You can have a child with a woman who shares your vision for your future and work wherever you want. Don't slouch tonight, darling. It's the last time we do this as a couple. Let's try to make it memorable, okay?"

The door opened, and floodlights temporarily blinded her. Lincoln Center glowed at the top of the broad expanse of steps that were blanketed in a vibrant red carpet.

The fundraiser for the Gen One Foundation was nothing like the scene at the Met Gala every year, but that was to be expected. The public never understood that business could be more entertaining, cutthroat, and sexy than Hollywood glam.

Raj adjusted the slit in her gown again so her shoes and then her legs made an entrance first. She grabbed her driver's hand, winked at him in thanks, and waited for Robert to step out behind her. They moved in sync, like they'd done for years. She slid to the left just as he lifted her hand, kissed her knuckles, and tucked it under his arm. His blotchy skin had returned to its smooth, pale complexion and he had an unimpressed expression on his face now.

She smiled serenely at the cameras, already hating the fact that she would no longer have a convenient partner to stand by her side during events like these. She was fine on her own, but it was nice to have companionship to combat anyone who wanted more than business from her, and to deal with the loneliness that haunted leadership.

Raj waved to a few familiar faces as she and Robert made their way up the stairs and waited for their cue to stand in front of the vinyl backdrop. They posed, smiled some more, and then Robert stepped away so that Raj could pose on her own.

Once inside, they followed the marked path to the Grand Promenade and entered under a canopy of pale pink and purple flowers dripping from the ceiling and the second-floor balcony. A twelve-piece jazz band stationed in the center of the portico made upbeat music that echoed through the space.

"I need a drink," Robert said. He stepped away from Raj's side. "What's our table?"

"We're at Kia's table tonight. The one up front and center to the raised platform."

"I'll meet you there." Without another word, he walked away.

"Ms. Hothi!" Raj turned to see who had called her name. A woman with flaming red hair and an iPad tucked against her hip grabbed Raj's hand. Her enthusiastic shake felt like she was pumping water from a well on a dry day.

"Thank you so, so much for the incredible work you and RKH Collective have done for the Gen One Foundation. With the money your company helped us raise, we'll be able to save so many women who have found themselves in this country without any support or job skills needed to take care of themselves and their families."

"Thank you, sweetie, but I know what the foundation does. I'm on the board."

The woman paused, as if she hadn't been prepared for her speech to be interrupted. "Yes, of course. I'm Maggie, the *head* executive assistant at Gen One Foundation. You'd probably recognize me from the foundation quarterly calls. I came over because Kia would love to thank you before dinner. Do you have a moment?"

"Lead the way."

Raj followed Maggie at a leisurely pace until she reached the high table in the corner of the portico. Kia sparkled in her black gown with white print and diamond clips in her braids. She held court with three men Raj had met previously: the CEO of a major bank, a chief diversity officer at a marketing agency, and a member of the UN.

"Ma'am," Maggie said, cutting off the CEO midsentence. "As you requested, I've found Ms. Raj Hothi for you."

Kia's mouth pursed but she nodded at Maggie. "Thank you. Would you check to make sure all of our speakers are here? Text me if there is an issue."

When the EA left, Raj crossed her arms and smiled at the other woman. "I admire the patience you have with your staff."

Kia burst out laughing. "She doesn't make the best first impression, but she's the most competent assistant I've ever had. Gentlemen? It's been a pleasure. Why don't you go and enjoy yourselves? Have a drink. We appreciate your presence tonight and your interest in supporting Gen One."

Raj said hello, presented her cheek for air-kisses, and waited until she was finally alone with Kia. She leaned down to embrace the woman.

"How long before we're interrupted?"

"The longest I've gone tonight is five minutes," Kia replied.

"Mmm-hmm, then you better tell me what's on your mind."

Kia's smile slipped and her expression became wistful. "I wanted to tell you before I announced it tonight at the podium. I'm leaving the foundation."

"Oh my god." Raj was rarely surprised, but Kia had managed to catch her off guard. "Why would you leave? Gen One Foundation is your life. Is it the committee members again? "

Kia shook her head. "The committee members are fine. I've only shared the news with my advisory group and they are doing everything they can to get me to stay." She let out a deep breath. "Selassie has cancer."

"Oh, Kia."

She held her head high like the regal queen she was, but Raj could see tears shimmering in Kia's eyes. "He's going to be fine. The doctors caught it in time. He's got a long road of treatments, though. He's spent so much of his life supporting me. It's time that I support him."

"You two are lucky to have each other." Raj tucked her clutch under her arm and held out her hands, palms up. Kia gripped them. Raj hoped that the older woman could borrow whatever strength Raj had left to spare.

"If there is anything I can do to help you, please let me know. Do you know who your replacement will be?"

"That's what I wanted to talk to you about. I'd like for you to become chairwoman of the board and CEO of the Gen One Foundation."

Raj had to work at controlling her surprise. That was the last thing that she'd expected Kia to say to her. "I'm . . . humbled that you would think of me."

Kia rocked back with laughter. "No, you're not. You're shocked as hell, honey. But that's okay. You have some time before I give my recommendation to the board. A month or two, tops."

"Kia, I can't run the foundation. Gen One is a full-time job. I have my own business."

"This is what you've always wanted, Raj. How many times have we talked about your love for philanthropy? Between Gen One and your other charitable efforts with the New York City animal shelters, you should be leading your own foundation, and that's what I'm offering you. You're also young, resilient, and you don't put up with the bullshit. Gen One will flourish under your leadership."

"That's a hard sell, Kia, but—"

"But nothing. The organization was started to help save lives. The job training workshops we do, the language classes, the networking seminars. You've experienced it in a very real way. *This* is your comfort zone and one of your passions. Your company isn't your passion. All you have to do is accept the offer."

RKH Collective may not have been her passion, but it was her greatest accomplishment. The idea of letting it go felt like a sharp dagger through her heart.

But Kia was right, too. Raj loved working with Gen One, just like she loved working with her animal shelter projects. They were two things she handled personally.

"I'll . . . think about it," she finally said.

"Good." Kia squeezed her fingers one last time and stepped back. "I do have a word of warning and a word of advice for you if you're going to take the position."

"I'm listening."

"I know that you and your husband are . . . discreet," Kia began with a thin smile. "We have known each other for a long time, so I'm aware of how you live your life, and honestly, it's your life to live. But there is a reason why you and Robert are so quiet about the way you conduct your marriage, isn't there?"

Raj felt the hairs on the back of her neck rise when she realized where Kia was going with this conversation. "Coming from India, working in a male dominated field, I am forced to accept that we still live in a patriarchal society. I am judged for my actions because I'm a woman."

"And a woman of color at that," Kia said.

"Exactly. Men won't give me their money if they disapprove of my lifestyle. I don't like it, but I've had to be discreet, because honestly, discretion is a small price to pay for success."

"Donors of the foundation are also very conservative. The deeper the pockets, the more judgmental the person. You have to show the world you're practically a saint if you want to keep the money rolling in. Being discreet isn't nearly enough if you want the job."

"Are you sure you want me to take this job, Kia?"

Kia nodded. "If the donors find your secrets, you'll be asked to step down. But I know that despite everything I'm telling you, you're the best person for the job."

Someone called Kia's name, and Raj turned to see three women weaving toward them.

"It looks like our five minutes is up," Raj said. She pulled her clutch out from where she'd tucked it under her arm. "Good luck with your keynote tonight, darling."

"Raj," Kia said, resting a hand on her bare arm. "I'm not judging you. But because I know you'd do the same for me, I want you to know all the angles before making a decision."

"Thanks, Kia," Raj said, and kissed the woman's cheek. "If you see your husband before I do, tell him to save me a dance tonight."

Kia barely had a moment to say yes before she was swept away to the other end of the portico.

"You look like you need a drink."

Raj spun on her heels to see a man holding two tumblers of whiskey. Not just any man, but one who immediately captured the interest of the devils on her shoulders.

Because his pictures didn't do him justice, Raj was not prepared for Ajay Singh, the middle of three sons and future CEO of Bharat, Inc. His dark, close-cropped beard and the thick hair slicked back off his face made him look a little wicked, while his slate-gray-and-black tuxedo with an open collar fit snugly enough to make Raj wonder just how hard he was under all that fabric.

Her best friend's boyfriend's brother was delicious to look at, which surprised her since she'd never found Punjabi royalty to be interesting before.

Relax, Rajneet. He's just a man. A gorgeous Punjabi man. You've sworn off those since you left India. Too many expectations, too many entanglements.

He handed her a tumbler and clinked his glass to hers.

"I didn't expect the Singh brothers to be here," she said as she looked up at his towering height and saluted him with her glass. "Usually your father does the publicity, right?"

His gaze narrowed and he stepped closer. "Do we know each other?"

"No, not really. But I know *of* you, your brothers, and your father, Ajay Singh."

"Then I'm at a disadvantage."

"Most men are when it comes to me."

"Is that so? Then you must have experience at leading."

Raj saw the shimmer of heat in his eyes. The way he looked at her had her pressing her thighs together.

"I never thought the future CEO of Bharat would let a woman lead anywhere," she said. "It's the Punjabi blood, no? You all prefer to be in charge."

"I like to think I've evolved. Are you going to tell me who you are before you lead me somewhere interesting tonight?"

He reached out and twirled one of her curls around his finger before letting it fall against the swell of her breast.

Oh my. The surprises kept on coming. She'd never been propositioned by any man, so directly.

"Well?" he prompted. "A name."

"Rajneet. Rajneet Kaur Hothi, but Raj to my friends."

"Raj . . ." The heat in his gaze turned razor sharp.

"That's right." She swirled the whiskey in her glass then tossed it back. *She was finally enjoying herself tonight,* she thought, as she swallowed the smooth liquor and ran a fingertip over the corner of her mouth. "If you think my name sounds familiar, it should. I'm the one who just saved your company from a hostile takeover."

Chapter Two

Ajay

RAJNEET KAUR HOTHI.

Well, shit.

Ajay watched as she shifted the empty glass from hand to hand while he connected the dots. He'd assumed that the person who helped his security team block the hostile takeover by WTA was a man.

That was his misstep.

When his brother's new girlfriend had made the recommendation, he hadn't cared who Raj Hothi was. He just wanted the work done. Now he wished he'd asked more questions. It wouldn't have changed his mind about hiring her, but maybe he would've asked for in-person meetings.

"You're the last person I expected to run into, Raj Hothi."

"Why? Because I don't seem charitable?"

"No, because I'd prepared for a boring night. Fundraisers are about shaking hands and pretending to like everyone until the dessert course is over."

"And now?"

Her husky laugh wrapped around his dick like a vise.

He tossed his whiskey back, just as she'd done. "And now," he said slowly, "I'm glad I came."

"Because of me? Do you like what you see, Ajay?"

Raj had to know she looked stunning, and not because of her dress or her diamond-encrusted heels or her big, luscious hair that he wanted to wrap around his fist. It wasn't even the deep golden brown of her skin that had Ajay itching to touch and stroke. It was her blinding confidence, and a woman that confident pressed all his buttons.

"I think you know the answer to that."

"I do. And because I'm feeling charitable tonight, can I give you a word of advice?"

Ajay mimicked her stance and leaned against the railing. "Please."

"Never attend an event, business or pleasure, unless you're aware of all the major players in the room. You'll put yourself at a serious disadvantage."

"And you're one of those major players?"

"I'm one of the more dangerous ones you have to worry about."

Ajay moved closer to her. God, she smelled delicious. Like cardamom rusk: tough and sweet with a hint of spice. He wondered if she also melted in heat. "Why is that?"

"Information."

"You have it, or you use it?"

"A little of both. My staffing company specializes in security services."

"Yes, that's right. RKH Collective. We're still using your services to clean up the mess that WTA left. My chief of security, Sri, only sings your praises."

"Thank you. After working with Bharat, I am thinking of branching out beyond staffing into technology."

"Cybersecurity?"

"And wearable technology. We're still developing a business strategy. Then we'll be more dangerous than ever."

Ajay leaned in and was thrilled when he saw her pupils dilate and her lips part.

"Tell me, Rajneet. What information do you have on me?"

Her shoulders relaxed a fraction. "You're an easy one. Ajay Singh, middle Singh brother, COO of Bharat, Inc., as well as interim head of HAZ Industries, a conglomerate of businesses from vineyards to real estate owned by the illustrious Singh Family."

"So far, you're on the money."

"I'm not finished. You're also the next in line to take over as CEO of Bharat once your father hits the magic number of sixty-five and is forced to retire at the end of the year. You don't do interviews, conferences, keynotes, or social media. And, unfortunately, speculation has it you're the reason Bharat's gradual profit growth is now suddenly flat."

The last bit of information stung.

"You know," he said slowly, "I normally don't care about public perception. People are talking about me, about my dad and Bharat, and I can't change that. All that really matters is the respect of my family, the board, and my employees."

The corner of her mouth curved up. "That's admirable of you."

"But," he said, holding up a hand, "there is something about you that makes me want to convince you that I'm more than a short dossier."

There was that flash in her eyes again. The same one he saw when he'd leaned in close for the first time. Her voice was low and husky. "I may be open to being convinced."

"I'll have to take my time."

Her expression was a study in surprise, confusion, and then . . . interest. "Mmm-hmm," she said slowly. "That does sound interesting."

Ajay almost swore when his phone vibrated in his pocket. It was audible enough to make Raj step back.

"You may want to check that." She straightened and moved away from the railing.

"No, it's fine."

"It's not. Most likely Mina or one of your brothers. Answer it, Ajay. And remember my advice, will you?" With a slow wink over her shoulder, she sauntered off, weaving through tables and clusters of guests until she disappeared in the crowd.

Ajay pulled out his cell and saw that it was his oldest brother, Hem, calling. How the hell had Raj guessed that one?

"Bhai. What is it?"

"Ajay, you need to brace yourself. Robert Douglass may be there."

"Robert Douglass?" The name was all too familiar. It hadn't been that long since Bharat's shareholder call when they discovered their dirty board members. WTA's representative, Robert Douglass, was a grade-A asshole and the perfect representative for the tech conglomerate that had purchased Bharat stock in secret, infiltrated their board, and now created chaos with their market shares.

His brother let out a breath. "You know Mina's best friend, Raj?"

"Yeah, I just met her."

"Well, Robert Douglass III is her *husband*."

"What are you talking about?"

"Douglass apparently left Raj's company to go to WTA and we don't know how much Robert was able to find out through her. Mina just made the connection when I told her that WTA, specifically Robert, was on the last shareholder call."

Ajay gripped the portico railing hard enough for his

knuckles to whiten. He'd stood there like a fool, drooling over Rajneet Kaur Hothi, while she knew exactly who he was and what he was doing.

She must have been laughing at him the whole time.

"She's getting a divorce."

Hem's words sliced through this rage.

"A divorce? From Douglass?"

"Yes. It looks like Raj may have asked for a divorce after Robert quit her company and started working for WTA. We don't have the full story yet, but Mina will most likely get it next week."

"No," Ajay said. "I'm going to get it now."

"Brother, don't do anything rash."

"Have I ever?"

"No, but there is always a first time."

"I'll call you later." Ajay hung up his phone and pushed his way through tables looking for the liar in question.

He made it halfway across the dance floor before he saw her.

She was speaking with a group of familiar-looking suits. He would draw attention if he approached her now, and he couldn't give a damn.

Raj's eyes widened a fraction at his approach, but she kept speaking to her audience even as he sidled next to her and rested a hand against her lower back.

"—there is a market need for the work. Everyone, I'd like for you to meet Ajay Singh, of Bharat, Inc."

"The technology company," an older Hispanic man with a cloud of snow-white hair replied. He stuck out a hand to shake. "I know your father. I own GridX Power. Jose Rivero."

"Mr. Rivero. Of course," Ajay said. Returning the shake, he flipped through his mental files. "My father speaks highly of the work you did after hurricane season last year. You were able to get Florida's grids back up and running before anyone else."

Mr. Rivero beamed. "We serve our communities the best we can."

"It shows. Mr. Rivero, everyone, I hate to steal Ms. Hothi away, but we have some unfinished business."

"Ajay, we can discuss it later," Raj said.

"Sweetheart," he said with a saccharine tone. "We need to talk. *Now.*"

"I don't think—"

"Do you want me to talk about how you played me in front of spectators?" Ajay asked in Punjabi. "Because, as you said, there are already rumors about me in the media. What's one more?"

Her irritated expression iced over. *Good*, he thought. If she was as angry as he was, neither of them would pull their punches.

"Excuse me. We have a small, friendly *business* matter to address."

"Emphasis on the *friendly*," Ajay said, and winked at Mr. Rivero before leading Raj toward the exit.

"What do you think you're doing?" she hissed as she matched his long strides. "I thought you were smarter than that. You just insinuated a relationship when—"

"You're married. Oh, I know. You were right on the money. My brother was the one who called me. I prefer to get the answers to the rest of my questions from you."

They were almost at the exit when his eyes met the glare of a man who stood in a corner, surrounded by people who looked just like him. Something about his expression made Ajay slow his pace.

"Is that your husband?" He motioned to the man with his chin.

Raj paused, and her spine stiffened under Ajay's hand. "Yes, that's Robert."

Ajay turned and gave Robert a brilliant smile. He waved from across the room as if he was greeting a long-lost friend.

"Stop that," Raj hissed and marched forward without him.

They circumvented the stragglers having quiet conversations in the lobby before turning left toward the theater. They rounded a corner and made it halfway down the corridor before they were alone and far enough away that no one could hear them.

"What the hell was that?" Raj said. Her accent, which hadn't been noticeable at all earlier, was now thick in her voice. She pronounced her *T*s like his parents did when they spoke English.

Ajay stepped forward until they were inches apart. "What games are you playing?"

"Do you think intimidation works on me?" Raj said, arching one long eyebrow. "I eat men in suits like you for breakfast, Ajay Singh."

"Your company's fired," he replied.

She gaped at him. "That's a stupid move. You need me."

"No, I don't. I don't need another mole."

"Another mole? Oh, that's rich. You had one of the most incompetent teams ever, while my people saved your ass. They would never—"

"But your husband would," Ajay said. "And yes, I heard you're getting a divorce. But you never told us that you had someone from WTA in your house while you were working with our information, Raj. Which is why I can't trust my business with yours, nor will my company."

Her nostrils flared. "My business has nothing to do with my marriage."

"Oh?" Ajay leaned down until their noses almost touched. "Can you swear to me that your husband didn't get hold of any information about my company while you were helping us out?"

He saw a flicker in her eyes and knew it was guilt. He suppressed the urge to swear again. "What does he know?"

"Nothing that isn't already public," she responded. "I took care of it."

"You took *care of it*?" Ajay roared. His voice echoed down the empty corridor. "Do you have any idea what this company means to me, means to my father? He started Bharat with nothing but a dream and determination. We almost lost *everything* to WTA because we had a mole in our company. Then you almost screwed us again, and all you can say is that you took care of it?"

"You don't have any idea who the hell you're talking to," she shot back. "Your father isn't the only one who stands on a mountain built of dreams. That's why I put my own money, my own people into helping *your* company when you were the fools who got yourselves into the mess in the first place. Hell, your chief of security was so inept that it took my team a day to produce what he couldn't in months. You think I'd help anybody, Ajay? No, dammit. I made sure Bharat wasn't affected by my mistake and I made up for it tenfold. I take care of my own, and then I gave you more than you deserve."

They were both breathing heavily. The fire burning in her eyes matched his temper, and no matter how hard he tried, the longer he looked at her, the more he seethed. He'd let Rajneet Kaur Hothi take advantage of him for the last time.

"And to think, despite our short conversation, I thought you actually were interested in playing with me, not playing me."

Ajay tucked a soft, thick curl behind her ear, his fingers lingering at the curve of her chin for a moment, before he stepped away and pulled his cell out to call his chief of security

"Sri," he said when the man answered the phone. He locked eyes with Rajneet.

"What can I do for you, boss?"

"Terminate all RKH Collective contractors immediately. We have a breach."

"Sir?" Sri's voice held a note of surprise. "Is there something wrong?"

Ajay felt a niggling of irritation. His head of security was always available, and did what he asked, but there had been a lot of mistakes in the last few months that should've been caught. This was one of them.

"It appears as if the owner of the company is married to WTA's shareholder representative." Raj glared at him but didn't try to stop his conversation.

"I'll get on it right away. That was an oversight on our part, sir."

"The company was a recommendation. We won't make the same mistake again."

"Yes, sir," Sri said.

"And after you're done, talk to our new SVP of legal about what can nullify our noncompete agreement with the company. Then reach out to the consultants and offer a job at double the salary to work for us directly. Be honest. Tell them that their boss didn't act in good faith. If we have to publicize this bullshit to hire those contractors, let's do it. Communications can help."

This time Raj gasped. She reached out to snatch the phone from his hand, but Ajay was already hanging up.

"You son of a bitch," she said, shoving at his shoulder. "What gives you the right—"

"You did," he replied, and tucked his phone away. He took a few steps backward before turning on his heel. "I'm neither easy prey in business nor your personal fuck boy, Raj. Don't underestimate me again."

He didn't bother seeing if she'd follow him this time. He had to go back to the fundraiser and make an appearance.

He was there for Bharat and for his father. His family legacy was the most important thing in his life and no woman would ever change that.

Chapter Three

Rajneet

RAJ DROPPED HER bag on the foyer console table with a loud thud, and slipped into her heels. She was going to be late for her lunch with Mina.

It had been a week since the fundraiser, and she was still dealing with a loss of revenue and employees thanks to her conversation with Ajay Singh. He'd gotten under her skin, and now that she was missing four of her top employees, she was reminded of him every time her human resources team sent her a new hire for approval. She had a bunch of projects on her plate, and backfilling roles was not supposed to be one of them.

She had to explain herself to Mina, too. She hated

explaining herself, even to people she considered her best friends.

"Kaka, was my dry cleaning delivered?" she called out. The cavernous four-thousand-square-foot brownstone echoed in silence. She waited another moment before she repeated her question in Punjabi.

Her frail caretaker popped up at the end of the hall. He had a spatula in his hand and a dishcloth draped over his shoulder. His pagadi, tied in a very regal fashion, matched the color of his beige sweater vest.

"Always shouting, just like when you were a wild little girl," he said as he hobbled forward. "Yes, yes, your clothes are in that apartment you call a closet. I asked the dry cleaners why they shrank all of them, but apparently that was your size. If your grandmother could see you now."

"If my grandmother could see me, she'd laugh at my fortune." Raj approached Kaka and leaned in to give him a smacking kiss on his bearded cheek. "You should be packing. Your flight for India leaves in a few hours."

"What do I need? My family is there to take care of me."

Raj felt a pang of guilt. She'd called Kaka right after she'd gotten married and asked the man who'd taken care of her family's home since she was a little girl to come and take care of her in New York. She made sure he had ample time to visit his grandchildren and brothers and sisters in Punjab, but she was too selfish to let him go so he could return to India permanently. The thought of living without the one constant source of love in her life frightened her.

He guessed her train of thought because one minute he was scolding her, the next he was cupping her cheeks and kissing her forehead. "You'll be fine, gudiya," he said gruffly.

"I know. I'll still miss you."

A timer buzzed softly in the distance and Kaka's eyes went wide. "I forgot the bloody kheer I made." He dashed toward the kitchen.

He'd made her kheer. Her favorite sweet rice pudding. Knowing Kaka, he'd probably stocked her freezer with a bunch of other things, too.

"I'll taste the kheer when I get back from lunch, and then we'll head to the airport!" she called out.

She had twenty minutes to get to the restaurant where she was meeting Mina. Luckily the restaurant was near the animal shelter where she volunteered on weekends, so if the meeting went poorly, she could pop in and cuddle with the dogs.

She was never allowed to have a pet back in India because her parents always said that animals in the house were bad luck. After she moved to the U.S., school, marriage, getting her business off the ground had taken up so much of her time that all she could do was play with the puppies at the shelter periodically. There had also been Robert's allergies. Now that he was going to be out of her life, and she was starting over, she'd finally get that dog she always wanted.

With images of warm snuggling dogs in her head, Raj grabbed her bag and opened the front door. She almost ran straight into her ex-husband. Robert stood on her stoop with a fist raised, ready to knock.

"Is there a reason why you're knocking on my door during the workday?"

His mouth pursed. "Is there a reason why you're home during a workday?"

"I don't believe that's your business anymore."

He leaned forward, peering into the house. "And you're alone? You're usually swarmed with assistants and staff."

"Not your business, Mr. Douglass. Your turn."

"I'm on my way to a client meeting nearby," he said as he ran a hand down his silk tie before adjusting his Windsor knot. "I decided to stop here to get the last of my boxes. Raj, you are keeping the company, the house, and most of the money. Surely you can afford to also retain the housekeeper to open your door."

"Don't be salty, darling," she said, flipping a lock of hair behind her shoulder. "You knew the terms when you signed the prenup. My business, my money, my property. Besides, you will be receiving a nice little settlement."

He rolled his eyes. "A tenth of our joint savings is nothing and you know it."

"Well, good thing you have your trust fund, then." She patted his cheek and stepped aside so that he could enter.

"Are you still mad at me?"

"Yes," she said. "But you know that. I'll be nice, though. How do you like your new life, your new apartment?"

He looked around the foyer as if he hadn't seen it a million times when he'd lived in the house with her. "It's actually more to my taste than I imagined. I've only been there for a few days now, but I have to say, the view from Battery Park is definitely a beautiful sight to see in the morning."

"I envy you. This brownstone feels more and more like the investment we originally purchased it for. You said you left some boxes here?"

"Yes, and since you were so hasty in changing the keypad codes for the doors, I had to knock. I'm missing a few things that I'd packed away from college. Do you think Kaka can get them for me and bring them out to my car?"

Raj shook her head. "Kaka is busy. He's leaving for India in a few hours."

"Again?" He blanched. "Christ. I know that you grew up with him helping you in your family's house, but he's taking advantage of you."

"My house, my rules." She hated when he criticized the way that she treated Kaka. Robert would never understand how Kaka had protected her and continued to do so even though he was in his seventies now.

Her ex-husband held his hands up in surrender. "I'll get the boxes and get out of your hair."

She stepped to the side and waited while he and his driver crossed the foyer and descended the spiral staircase to the lower level. They returned two minutes later. Robert held one small filing box, while his driver had three stacked on top of each other.

Raj held open the door for them to exit, hoping there would be no more small talk, but she wasn't that lucky. He paused and leaned against the doorjamb.

"Oh, before I go, my assistant got a call from your brother a couple days ago."

Raj froze. "My brother?"

"Yes. I don't know how he got my number. Probably those mob connections of his."

Raj rolled her eyes. "Not everything my family does is mob related."

"Yeah, try to sell that to the next idiot. Either way, I didn't speak to your brother directly. I just know that he's been trying to get in touch with you, and he can't get through."

That was because after the last time he'd visited, she had blocked him on pretty much every phone line she had. Guru must've been desperate if he reached out to Robert.

"Just ignore any other calls you get from him. I'll handle it."

"Sounds good. I never liked him or the rest of your family."

"I doubt they care since they didn't like you, either."

Robert grinned. "A relief, if you ask me. Now if only you'd stay away from another Indian family."

Of course he'd bring it up. "If you're fishing for information . . ."

"I saw the way you looked together last weekend," he said. His tone was as grumpy as that of a child who'd been denied a favorite toy. "People saw you leave the hall together." Color flooded his cheeks as he scowled at her.

"We were having a conversation that was none of your business."

"Well, it's become my business if you want to lead the Gen One Foundation. My name is going to come up, Raj. I work for WTA now, and if you're involved with Bharat, our relationship, past and present, will be dissected."

She knew he was right, but in that moment, she couldn't care less what people said about her or her sham marriage. "See you in three months, Robert."

He let out a sigh. "Fine. Be that way. See you soon, Raj."

She watched as he handed the last box over for his driver to put in the trunk before he ducked into the backseat of the black sedan.

"Three months," she said again. Three months and then her divorce would be official. It wasn't fast enough, in Raj's mind, but it would have to do.

RAJ WAS STILL thinking about her conversation with Robert when she arrived at the Thai place downtown. What could her brother possibly want from her now?

She'd gone to extremes to separate herself from her

father's drug-trafficking empire. It was a lucrative business in Punjab where there was a drug crisis, but that wasn't the life Raj had wanted to live.

Now that she was on the verge of a divorce and looking into pursuing a philanthropy career, Guru could come back into her life and do so much more harm to her reputation. She'd have to figure out his motive, his angle, and effectively cut him off. He'd bested her the last time he visited by giving her ultimatums, and when she wouldn't agree, destroyed all ties between Raj and the rest of the family, including her mother.

The driver had pulled to a stop in front of a charming building with arched windows.

"Here we are," he said.

"So soon?" she mused.

He gave her a startled look over his shoulder. "Ma'am, it took us twenty minutes to get to Midtown."

"Ah. Okay, well, I'll text you when I'm done. It shouldn't be more than an hour or so." She slid out of the car, and a few steps later, stepped into a dimly lit restaurant. The seating area was filled with deep violet loveseats clustered in groups of two and four. Long white marble tables matched the crystal and white chandeliers. Most of the lunch crowd had left, but a few suits were lingering over empty dishes.

Mina sat against the left wall, her nose practically pressed to the screen of her phone.

This was family, Raj thought. She realized that she'd been strong enough to survive the loss of her brother,

her mother, and the rest of her blood relatives, but Mina was the one person who could devastate her by ending the relationship.

"Don't be an asshole, Raj," she murmured to herself as she walked to the table.

Mina looked up as Raj approached. Her icy expression behind the black square frames of her glasses could lower the temperature in the room.

Hell. So much for understanding, Raj thought.

"Fashionably late, as always, right?"

Silence.

"Mina, I'm sorry I didn't tell you about Robert's new position," she said, as she slid onto the couch facing Mina.

Her best friend set her phone aside and crossed her arms over her fitted maroon dress. One perfectly threaded eyebrow winged up.

Great. Raj wasn't the best at apologies, but because her relationship with Mina meant more to her than her pride, she had no other choice than to be honest and open . . . even if it felt like jabbing needles in her eyeballs.

"It happened quickly," Raj started. The words felt uncomfortable coming out of her mouth. "Robert and I worked together, we lived in the same house, but we had completely different schedules, different lives. You know that. He comes and goes when he needs to and so do I. A little over a month ago, he came to me and said that we were now in our thirties and it was time to think about having kids."

Mina's mouth fell open. "But you don't want kids."

"Yeah, not with him anyway. We had a contract, not a marriage. A friendship, even, but that's as far as it went. I reminded Robert of the terms of our agreement and . . . well, he quit." Raj shrugged, even though the betrayal still stung.

"So you knew he went to WTA?" Mina asked.

"No, not at first. I thought he was just sulking and that he planned on joining his father's business. Then a week after I started helping you find out who leaked information from your boyfriend's company, I got a security notice. I had left my computer unlocked, and Robert accessed files from my home office."

"Shit, Raj."

"That's when I found out that Robert had gone to WTA, basically bartered my information for a job, and used me. I asked for a divorce, then I put my own money into helping you find out what was going on with your boyfriend's company."

The waitress approached the table with a cheerful greeting and began filling their water glasses. "Do you ladies need another few minutes before ordering? I can always put in a couple drinks for you."

"Wine please," Raj said. "White, dry, and crisp." She rattled off three brands she preferred.

"I may not be staying here long enough to finish a drink, so skip me," Mina said. Her expression was even more glacial than before. The waitress must have picked up on it, because she hurried away without another word.

"You should have fucking told me," Mina hissed as she leaned across the table. "We're best friends, Raj! Do you know how bad this situation is?"

This was not going well. Raj should've been better prepared. She knew that Mina's sense of honesty and honor was as saintly as Guru Nanak's. If she hadn't been so distracted by Robert's early morning visit, she would've focused more time on crafting her apology.

"Mina, I know I made a mistake, but I also know that I was trying to help you. I should've said something, though. I'm not used to being in that position."

"That doesn't change the fact—"

"I know," Raj interrupted. She felt raw and exposed. "I know it doesn't change the fact that I didn't tell you. I haven't told you a lot of things, and I realize how wrong that is. You're important to me and it's like a series of bad mistakes that I'm paying for now. I'm trying to do what's right, Mina. Please. Tell me you at least see that."

After a long minute, Mina let out a sigh and reached across the table, palm up. Raj felt a flicker of hope and held on to the outstretched hand.

"How are you doing?"

Raj let out a breath and felt Mina squeeze her fingers. "I'm. . . . relieved."

"You promise you won't hold secrets like that again?" Mina said in Punjabi.

"Fine, fine. Changa, yaar."

"Good," Mina said. "Now all you have to do is ask my man for forgiveness."

"Excuse me?"

Mina grinned, and it was the first smile Raj had seen from her in a long time. "I don't want you to be at odds with Hem. As soon as I can arrange it, we'll get together so you can apologize to him directly." She held up a hand to call the waitress and asked for two menus.

"You're just being mean now," Raj said.

"Yup," Mina replied without hesitation. "Just because I forgive you doesn't mean I don't expect you to grovel."

"Okay, I'll grovel and even buy you dinner. Just let me know when."

"Deal."

"Deal," Raj said, and just like that, her world felt right again.

The waitress came over, handed them menus, and placed Raj's glass of wine on the table.

"Thank you, darling," Raj said. She smiled up at the waitress. The poor woman was going to get a huge tip

"Uh, sure. I'll give you a moment," she said.

"No need." Raj honed in on the curry section. "I'll have the green curry with chicken. And whatever your scale is for heat? I want twice as spicy, please."

"Same," Mina added and handed over her menu.

"Let's talk about you now," Raj said when they were alone again. "I feel like I've done my part in oversharing. Tell me how things are. Do you like the new job? I know leaving your mother's old firm was hard on you."

"Not as hard as I thought it would be," Mina said.

"It was no longer my mother's firm, and now that I'm working at a functioning practice, it's . . . amazing. It's a whole different environment."

Raj had met Mina years ago at a women's leadership symposium, and it had been clear from the start that her friend had something to prove. Her uncles had taken over the law firm that Mina's mother started before her untimely death, and Mina was determined to take it back. Thankfully, with Hem in her life, now she was focused on herself instead of revenge.

Raj swirled the wine in her glass. "I know your father took the job as SVP of Legal over at Bharat. Does he like it?"

"I mean, he started this week, but so far he's thriving. I haven't seen him this jazzed in forever. It's nice. I feel like we've gotten closer since we no longer work for my uncles."

"Being assigned the Bharat case was the best thing that could've ever happened to you."

"Without a doubt."

Raj looked down at her nails and started to pick at her cuticle. "Do you work with the other Singhs, too? With Ajay?"

"Ajay? I see him sometimes, and there is Sunday morning breakfast at his mother's house . . . Wait. Why do you ask?"

"I met him at the fundraiser. That's where he fired my company. I deserved it, granted, but he was . . . unexpected."

"Unexpected? How? Wouldn't anyone in his position do the same . . . Oh my god." Mina beamed from across the table. Her whole face was vibrant with surprise and joy. "You *like* him!"

"What?" Raj blanched at the idea. "Good god, no. He's an unsharpened business drone and a Punjabi, at that—I've spent half my life avoiding Punjabi men."

"That's because you're still thinking about the type of men in your family that you grew up with in Punjab. The kind that thought binary male-dominant gender roles were law. The Singhs are not like that. True, they're . . . well, protective, but they're not disrespectful and sexist. Which is surprising considering the kind of money they have, and the industry they work in. And out of all three brothers, Ajay is the most reasonable and level-headed."

"Mina, he took my employees! Besides, he seems like a pushover. An attractive pushover, but way too soft."

"That is the biggest load of bullshit you've ever tried to serve me. The guys you sleep with at the club, the Ice Palace, are pushovers. They're controllable. You choose those random hookups because you'll never have to expend energy in getting to know them and sharing a part of who you are. Ajay Singh would never let you control him like that."

"You've lost every bit of sense in your thick head if you think Ajay Singh is for me."

"The truth is biting you in your ass, Raj."

Raj had only had one conversation with Ajay, but he'd done something that very few people could do: surprise her. He was about to be given his father's business on a silver platter, but he was as passionate about it as if he wanted to earn his job, too. Once her anger had cooled and she could look at their interaction from an objective view, his passion, his intelligence, and of course his barely contained sex appeal in that custom tuxedo was . . . appealing. Regardless, Raj had no time for that nonsense. She didn't need a man to keep her company when she already had plans to get a dog.

After taking a sip of her wine, she schooled her expression. "Mina, you're reading into this only because you're happy now. You want everyone to be happy."

"No, I'm selective with my good wishes. You deserve happiness, Raj. The more that I think this through, Ajay can give that to you. He's sweet, and he's proved everyone wrong about his capabilities as a leader. Since his father's illness, he's . . . well, you know. Very much *in charge*. Women in the office don't know whether to stare at his pretty face or run and hide."

If Raj had been given the option to have a Brazilian wax or have this conversation, she would've chosen the wax job. This moment was even more uncomfortable than asking for forgiveness.

"Ajay is quite attractive, but he's younger than the men I prefer—"

"He's *your age*."

"That's really not the point. I put his company at risk. That's not smart business, and you know it."

Mina took Raj's wineglass from her hand and took a sip. "You're about to become a single woman. You have plenty of options. You can be a little reckless and have a fling."

"Actually, I can't. Not if I want to lead the Gen One Foundation."

"What? Are you serious?"

Raj told Mina about the job offer and the warning she'd received about her lifestyle, as well as about Robert's impromptu visit to the brownstone.

"That's a lot," Mina said quietly. "How much time do you have before Kia announces you as her choice for successor?"

"I don't know. Maybe a month or two?"

Mina grabbed Raj's wineglass and, when she saw that it was empty, put it back on the table.

"I bet a ton of people, many of whom you know, would be interested in buying your company."

"Buy my . . . You mean sell RKH?"

Mina nodded, her ponytail bouncing. "You could sell the business, your brownstone, the main office, which is where? Long Island City? That way, you can take the Gen One job if you want it—"

"Or I can start something new."

"Exactly."

The idea was appealing. Raj had gotten offers over

the years, but she hadn't been ready to give up the reins. Now that she was starting a new phase in her personal life, it almost felt right to start fresh in business, too. She just didn't know if she wanted to lead Gen One. more importantly, she didn't know if she wanted to leave the business she'd started from nothing, and the people that supported her to get there.

"Mina, I don't want my reputation ruined or my employees screwed over. They have always been the most important part of my company."

"You'll find the right buyer. I'm sure of it."

Two giant white bowls were placed on the table in front of them. Raj leaned forward and smelled the fragrant curry dish. She picked up her spoon, coated the tip with creamy, pale green sauce, and licked. Mina mimicked her actions across the white table.

"It's . . ." Mina started.

"Not spicy at all," Raj said, looking down at the tiny purse at her side. "The Thai place near your condo is so much better."

"Yeah, you're telling me."

Mina spooned white rice into her bowl. "You know who may have really great advice for what you can do? Ajay."

"You are not giving up about this Ajay thing, are you?"

"Nope!" Mina spooned up more of her curry. "Selling your business is a perfect conversation starter. Tech companies need security services, right? I'm sure Ajay has come across information about other tech companies looking to diversify their portfolios."

Raj froze. Mina's words had sparked an idea, a pretty excellent idea, that began to rapidly form in her mind.

Bharat wasn't growing, but if they acquired a profitable business tangentially related to their services . . . well, that would get the market excited. Their stock price would rise.

And WTA wouldn't have a chance in hell of taking over.

Shit, she was going to have to apologize again, but this time to Ajay. That was the only way she'd get close enough to him to convince him to go into business with her.

"So? What do you think?" Mina asked.

"I'm going to take some time to reflect on my options." *Along with a few other things.* Raj pointed to Mina's bowl. "Does yours even have a pepper or something in it?"

"Nope," Mina said. "I bet Ajay is spicy, though."

"Shut up, Mina."

Chapter Four

Ajay

AJAY RARELY SLEPT without his phone next to his pillow. That way, when his four a.m. alarm went off, he heard it. Except he'd been so distracted the night before that he'd forgotten to go to bed with his device, and when he finally woke up, the bedside clock face read 8:01 a.m.

There was no way it was eight. He hadn't slept in that late since . . . god, when was the last time he slept in?

He sat up, and his laptop, which had been tucked next to his hip, almost crashed to the floor. His reflexes were the only thing that saved his precious machine.

"Fuck me," he mumbled as he set it aside and rubbed his hands over his face to try to clear the rest of his sleep-fogged brain.

The room was awash with a soft morning glow. His automatic blinds hadn't even alerted him to the time of day.

The Stuart Hughes suit that he'd shed when he walked in the door was strewn across the wide chaise angled in the corner. The air still smelled like sandalwood from the cleaning service.

Spending the night at his bungalow at Bharat Mahal had helped clear his thoughts.

It apparently helped with catching up on sleep, too.

Ajay pulled back the covers and stretched, easing his sleep-sore muscles. Hopefully no one was tending the gardens, otherwise they'd get a show. He walked naked downstairs wearing nothing but his silver kara, the bracelet that he never took off. After some searching, he located his phone under a stack of files on the kitchen island.

"This is what happens when you take a break," he said as he watched the messages load on his screen. He had over a hundred emails, sixteen voice mails, and forty-seven texts. He checked his assistant's texts first.

RAFAEL (6:45 AM): Sir, please call me as soon as you are able. You had a conference call at 6:30 you missed.

"Shit," Ajay muttered. That call was supposed to be with the distribution center in India that they were hoping to purchase. He scrolled to the next message.

RAFAEL (6:57 AM): Sir, your brothers are looking for you. I told them you were staying at your bungalow on the Singh family compound.

RAFAEL (7:15 AM): Sir, Hem is on his way to the family compound and should be there at approximately 8 a.m. I've rescheduled your morning meetings and calls before 9 a.m. Your brother Zail landed this morning from California and is also on his way. Please contact me.

"That'll show me the next time I want to sleep in," Ajay said.

RAFAEL (7:34 AM): Ajay, do I need to call your mother to go out there and find you? Am I clearing your schedule for the entire day? Your cousin Bhram is trying to reach you and is unable to do so, as well. By the way, I keep getting lilies at the office. I'd appreciate it if, during your conversation with Bhram, you told him to stop.

Before Ajay could call Rafael to let him know he was awake, his doorbell went off in a series of rings.

His brother. Always punctual.

Punjabi swearing came through the thick wood door loud and clear. "Oye! Are you dead? Answer the door!" Hem shouted in Punjabi.

"Oye, chutiya, I'm naked!" he said, swearing in the same language. He tossed his phone on the counter and rushed back to his room where he found a pair of boxers and tugged them on. If he answered the door in his birthday suit, Hem would probably whip out his dick and a ruler just to be the smartass older brother.

Less than thirty seconds later, Hem was still pounding on the door when he answered. "What the hell, bhai?"

His older brother rolled his eyes. He'd shaved, his hair was neatly styled, and he was dressed as if he was headed to work. "I came to see if you were alive. I'd think you'd have finished most of your workday already."

"I'm a bit behind today." Ajay stepped back for Hem to enter. "Is everything okay?"

"I should be asking you that," Hem said. "Cha?"

"Yeah, if you're making it."

Hem toed off his shoes and shrugged out of his suit jacket, draping it over the back of one of the barstools. "Are you feeling okay?" he asked as he rolled up the cuffs of his oxford shirt. His kara, identical to the one Ajay wore, glinted in the light.

"Bhai, I'm fine."

"I'm only asking because you slept past four thirty, you're naked, and you grew a beard. I don't think you've shaved since before Dad had his second heart attack."

Ajay sat on one of the barstools and ran his fingers through his facial hair. The memory came flooding back. His father wheezing. The car ride to the hospital following the screaming sirens of the ambulance. The hospital waiting room.

Hem had always been an astute bastard.

"Makes me look older. Besides, I've been busy."

"Don't I know it. You're doing great, Ajay. But take care of yourself, too." Hem started to pull the ingredients out of Ajay's cabinet for the chai. Masala mix. Pot. Tea leaves. It was jarring at first to realize that Hem knew where everything was.

It made sense though. Hem rarely stayed at his place, but his bungalow was identical to his own. Zail's was the same too, but he rarely used it since he was mostly on the West Coast overseeing Bharat's operations. Ajay was the only regular visitor. To learn from his father, he had to be near him.

"Where is Mina?" he asked as he picked up his phone to scroll through some of his emails from the night before.

"At the office." Hem poured loose-leaf tea into a pot of water. "I have to drag her away some nights. It's as if she was starving for something new, something challenging. There is so much work to catch up on at my firm, she's gorging herself on it all."

"That's good, right? You guys are working well together. Did you come out here to check on me or to talk about your new relationship?"

Hem hummed. "I'm here because I wanted to ask Mom for Nani's ring."

Ajay froze. "You're going to marry her."

Hem looked at Ajay over his shoulder. "Eventually. When she says she's ready. I know I am, though, so I'm going to be prepared while I wait."

"I'm happy for you," Ajay said. He meant it, too. His brother looked relaxed. At ease. Almost two years ago he'd left the family compound, left the company, because he refused to fall in line with their father's expectations. Now Hem was where he belonged.

The front door opened and Ajay swiveled to look at his latest visitor. His baby brother, dressed in a flannel shirt unbuttoned at the collar, and sporting a man bun and a freshly trimmed beard, strolled in as if he owned the place.

"Hey." He paused when he saw Ajay sitting shirtless at the counter. "Dude, why are you naked?"

"Seriously? I'm in my own house minding my own business. Why are *you* here? Shouldn't you be on WesCo?"

"Touchy, touchy. I'm here for the Gupta wedding next weekend. The one we're all required to go to."

"Next weekend? Already?" Uncle Frankie was on the board at Bharat, and his granddaughter was getting married in the Indian wedding of the season. Festivities were supposed to start on Thursday and go through Sunday. "Is it Indian or American attire?"

"Both," his brothers said in unison.

"Shit." Ajay made a mental note to ask Rafael to secure the family gift for the bride and to also order clothes. He turned back to Zail. "Why are you here a week early, though?"

"I have a couple meetings to go over the budget for next year. I'm also spending some time with our new

SVP of Legal. I texted you last night about it." He kicked off his chappals next to Hem's and straddled the vacant barstool. "Cha?"

"Yeah," Hem replied. "Everything going okay?"

Zail rubbed his hands over his face. "You know that technology we're working on? The one that WTA wants? Well, we filed a provisional patent application last November. It's only good for a year. If we don't finish the software in the next few months, we're screwed."

"Can't we refile?" Hem asked.

"Yeah, but our competitors can put their own patent applications in then, which would effectively block us from having market control. That means millions of dollars down the drain, and the contracts we have in the pipeline all go away. We'll be in the red."

"The R & D team has been on this for a long time," Ajay said. "What's the problem?"

"We don't have our best engineer anymore, that's the problem." Zail's bitterness was clear in his voice. "Sahar was my right-hand woman and the best programmer in the Valley. We lost her, and we lost our edge."

Sahar Ali Khan had been one of the most brilliant minds Ajay had ever met. He had always been fond of her, but he'd had no choice but to let her go. She'd lied to them and failed to disclose that she was related to an executive at WTA. Since Zail had gone to MIT with her and then worked with her on a daily basis, he hurt the most from her loss.

And now Bharat was suffering, too.

"There is buzz in Silicon Valley that WTA is waiting for us to fail so they can make their next move," Zail added.

"Yeah, I kind of figured," Ajay said. If he was in WTA's shoes, he'd wait for Bharat to fail, too, before trying again to take over the company. "What do you need from us?"

"I need Sahar back, but since you won't agree to that, I need time. I don't know if I'll get that, either. Essentially, we're screwed without Sahar."

As if he couldn't stand the idea of failing, Zail paced the living room until he stood under the pull-up bar that was built into the hallway doorframe. He reached up to grab it and started smooth, easy reps. He had to be over two hundred and fifty pounds of muscle, yet he made those pull-ups look as easy as breathing.

"Your role at the company depends on that patent, too," Hem said, pointing at Ajay. "If the company can't deliver the software, you're going to lose the support of the board and major shareholders when Dad announces his retirement and names you as his successor."

Ajay looked back and forth between his brothers. "I'm going to need a backup plan, then. Something that gets buyers, investors, hell, shareholders out of their seats and cheering."

Hem poured milk into the boiling tea water. The pot sizzled for a second before calming. "How are the rest of the businesses in HAZ Industries doing? The vineyard, the hotels, the clubs, the rental properties? Is there something there we're doing differently?"

"Not a thing, Hem. Everything is status quo." Which meant that it was time to shake things up, Ajay thought. He made a mental note to review their other businesses with the executive team.

Hem rounded the counter and shoved Zail so he let go of the pull-up bar. "Hut, yaar. Move. I'll show you how it's done." He gripped the handles and started to do pull-ups twice as fast as Zail. As he lifted his knees to form a ninety-degree angle, he looked over at Ajay and spoke as if taking a stroll in the gardens instead of lifting his body weight.

"Maybe we can get Dad to take a vacation in California. He could help with the software."

"I don't think he's ready to travel," Zail said. "And his health is still too fragile for us to work on it here."

The sound of sizzling erupted from the stove, and Ajay vaulted out of his chair. He pulled the chai pot off the burner just as it overflowed.

"Dammit, Hem! You're not supposed to leave the pot once you put the milk in."

"Oh, relax," Hem said as he continued to do pull-ups. "It tastes better when tea's boiled like that. No sugar for me."

"Me, either," Zail said.

Great. Not only had Ajay slept late, but his brothers were now busting his balls and making a mess in his kitchen. He loved his family, but this was why he some-times spent nights at his penthouse.

Grumbling to himself, he strained the chai into three cups and dumped the pot and strainer into the sink. His phone rang just as he finished wiping down the counter and grabbed his cup for his first blissful sip. Expecting Rafael, he answered.

"Sorry, I slept in."

"Tsk-tsk, Ajay Singh."

The warm rasp of Rajneet Kaur Hothi's voice filled his ear and went straight to his gut. It heated his blood in a way that he hadn't experienced in . . . god, he didn't even know how long it had been since a woman had him so twisted. He shut that reaction down as quickly as it started.

"What can I do for you, Ms. Hothi?"

"Other than give my employees back?"

He chuckled. "Not a chance in hell." Ajay looked at his brothers, Zail standing with his arms crossed, a thunderous look on his face, while Hem stayed sus-pended midair in a pull-up.

"Are we even then?"

"Hardly," Ajay said. "How did you get this number?"

Her laugh twisted around him like a vise. "I have my ways. I was trying to get hold of your father, actually. I prefer to speak with the person in charge, but you'll have to do."

He wondered if she'd said that on purpose to rile him. If so, it was working. He was already dealing with pressure to be as great as the men who'd come before him. He didn't need this stranger wondering if he was less of a leader, less of a man.

"You're doing a piss-poor job of negotiating for whatever it is you called me for," he said calmly.

"I want a meeting."

"A . . . meeting. About what?"

"An opportunity to secure your spot as CEO."

He jerked up in his seat. The fact that his brothers and he had just been talking about the same subject felt eerily like fate. Not that he believed in fate.

Much.

"You have my attention."

"Not over the phone, darling. This is better in person. I'll have my assistant reach out to yours to discuss the details. Then we'll talk about how Bharat needs to spend some money."

"I'm wrapped up for the next few weeks."

He heard her sigh. It sounded practiced, as if she was expecting his hesitation. "Your patent needs to be filed by November, right?"

"How did you—"

"I deal in information, Ajay. I told you that already. If you want to be CEO, you need either a huge win for Bharat by securing that patent before WTA comes in and blocks you . . . or you need a backup plan. Not to sound juvenile, but that's Corporate Maneuvers 101. I'll have my assistant contact you next week."

She hung up the phone without another word.

Well, wasn't that both irritating and intriguing, Ajay thought. He looked over at his brothers, and before he could tell them what the call was about, Zail burst out, enraged.

"Why didn't you tell her off?"

"Why would I do that?"

"Because she's the reason why we lost Sahar!" He pounded a fist against his chest. "She came forward with this bullshit, faulty information, and we lost the best thing we had."

Hem dropped from the pull-up bar. "Zail, she wasn't the one who lied to us. Sahar did. Sahar knew what was going on and didn't tell us she had a relative working at WTA."

"Because it wasn't true," Zail snapped. "All we had was some vague evidence. Nothing concrete. I went to Sahar myself, confronted her, and she told me that it was a set up. I believe her. We should've all believed her. And now you're getting in bed with the sapa, with the *snake*? No, I'm not going to stand here and let that happen. I won't do it."

Ajay knew that Zail had taken Sahar's loss hard, but this was next level. He took a sip of his chai and sat on a counter stool.

"If I force my way into the CEO position without the support of our shareholders and board members, *and* we can't deliver on the relocation software, then we're going to lose money. Raj wants a meeting because she has a business proposition that could potentially miti-gate our risk. I want to see what she has to say."

"Sounds reasonable," Hem said. "There is no harm in hearing her out. From what Mina says, she's a smart businesswoman who created a successful enterprise out of nothing."

"Fuck this. I'm not going to stand here and listen to you all talk about working with this woman." Zail stormed out of the house without a backward look.

"He has feelings for Sahar," Ajay said to Hem.

"Yeah, and he blames Raj for losing her," Hem re-plied. "Do you think she'll be at the Gupta wedding? We've never seen her at the desi society events before, but Uncle Frankie has invited every South Asian entre-preneur in the tristate area. She must be on the list."

Ajay paused and thought about the way Raj had op-erated so far. "I think she'll show depending on how our meeting goes. She wants something from us. She'll make an appearance at the wedding just because she knows that we'll be there."

Hem grinned. "You're going to play a game of cat and mouse, little brother."

"Yup. I just don't know who's the cat and who's the mouse. I don't know if I care, either. Let's get to the main house."

Chapter Five

Rajneet

UNKNOWN NUMBER: It's your bhai. We need to talk.

RAJ STARED AT the text message for a moment longer before she blocked the number, turned her phone to Do Not Disturb, and tucked it back into her tote. She had no idea how her brother got her contact information, but she'd have to resource someone to find out.

When she left India and came to the US to study, he'd been one of the only people who supported her. He'd argued with their parents that he'd gone abroad to get his education, and she should be able to, as well. But then, when she didn't want to go home to Punjab to fall in line and meet every expectation that had been laid at her feet since her birth, he'd turned his back on her. And after she'd opened RKH Collective, he'd ensured everyone else in her family did the same.

Her car slowed in front of a slate-gray building at the heart of Park Avenue.

"Here we are," the driver said.

"Thank you. One hour."

"I'll be waiting for your text, ma'am."

She stepped out of the car and into the balmy fall air. The weather meant nothing to the dramatic hustle of Midtown. Men and women in suits strode down the sidewalk with wireless earbuds and various sizes of leather bags, creating a frenetic movement that demanded everyone keep up. The sheer energy smelled like money and confirmed what she already knew: she had too much on her plate right now to lose focus on what mattered most to her.

Squaring her shoulders, she strode through the glass doors of Bharat's office building with her tote hanging from her forearm.

The lobby was an architectural showpiece of glass and steel. Twisting pillars formed arches over a wide, oval concierge desk.

"Hello," she said as she approached the first available attendee. "Rajneet Kaur Hothi. Here to see Mr. Ajay Singh in Bharat's offices."

"Just you?" the woman asked.

It wasn't a strange question. She usually brought one

of her assistants or even an executive with her, depending on the nature of the business meeting. She didn't want to alarm anyone at RKH, though, so for the first time in years, she was on her own.

"Just me today."

The woman took her ID, pointed a handheld camera at her for a picture, and printed out a visitor's tag. "Elevators to the far right for floors forty-six to sixty-five. They're expecting you."

Raj made her way up to Bharat's executive floor and stepped into a lobby that was encased in even more glass. A slender man of medium height in a suit and narrow black tie greeted her at the entrance.

"Ms. Hothi?" he asked, tablet in hand.

"That's me."

"I'm Rafael. Ajay's EA. I can take you to him now."

"Rafael, please call me Raj. It's a pleasure to meet you. Lead the way." She gestured toward the open workspace behind reception.

Raj didn't know why she was so surprised that Ajay had a male EA. As someone who hated stereotypes about women in the workplace, she shouldn't automatically believe stereotypes about Indian men, too. She knew enough professionals that she had to stop assuming they were all sexist predictable pigs. Ajay could have a male EA instead of an attractive woman supporting his sexist fantasies. But then again, Ajay wasn't an average Punjabi man and he'd done nothing predictable.

They followed the perimeter of the floor until they

reached the far corner office. The glass walls were covered with a privacy screen, but Raj could hear voices coming from behind the double doors.

Rafael entered first, then stepped aside for Raj.

The skyline was the first thing that she saw. The river, the harbor, and glinting steel stroked in sunlight. In front of it was a large mahogany desk with dual monitors. A matching table was situated in the corner with a Polycom unit and telepresence screens hanging on the wall above it. A couch and two armchairs bracketed a coffee table off to the right of the desk.

Ajay wasn't alone. He stood from his high-back leather chair just as Mina and a man Raj didn't recognize turned to face her. Hem, Mina's boyfriend and the eldest Singh brother, leaned against the side of the desk.

"Sir," Rafael began, "Ms. Hothi is here for your one o'clock. Raj, can I get you anything?"

"No thank you, Rafael. I appreciate it."

He nodded and shut the door behind her quietly.

Raj turned back to the expectant faces and started with the familiar.

"Mina."

Her best friend's lips quirked. "Raj. I want to introduce you to my father, Tushar Kohli. Dad, this is my best friend, Raj."

The older man extended a hand, but Raj brushed it away. "Uncle, family doesn't greet family like that." She kissed his cheek and gave him a friendly hug.

Tushar Kohli patted her shoulder and pulled away.

His lips quirked in amusement. "It's nice to finally meet you."

Raj turned to Hem. She grabbed her earlobes just like her mother used to when apologizing. "Sorry, yaar. I made a mistake and tried to fix it," she said in Punjabi.

"Find a better way to fix it next time," he responded in kind.

"You have my word."

She pivoted to Ajay, who stood, arms crossed, watching her the whole time. The intensity of his stare had her hesitating, but she forced herself to relax. "Ajay Singh."

"Rajneet Kaur Hothi."

"Thank you for making the time to see me."

"You called this meeting. I wasn't sure what it was about, so I have Tushar, our head of Legal, and our outside counsel in attendance. Does that suit you?"

"Yes, that's fine."

He motioned to the couch and armchairs. "Why don't we have a seat so you can tell us what's on your mind?"

She hated the formality of his tone, but she more than anyone knew that there was a certain dance that had to be done leading up to a business negotiation. The small talk, the handshakes, and hugs. It was all part of a build-up.

She sank into the armchair, and when everyone else was seated, she began. "Ajay, your father not only started your company, but he built a reputation over the last thirty years. And now his time as CEO is coming to an end."

There was a tick at the corner of Ajay's mouth, as if he hadn't expected her directness to come quite so soon. He, along with Tushar, Mina, and Hem, remained silent.

"Deepak Singh's health, along with his upcoming sixty-fifth birthday, mean that it's time for him to step down. Since Hem isn't interested in taking over your family company, that leaves you."

"You're not telling us anything we don't already know," Ajay said. "What's your point?"

"My point is that you're recovering from a press nightmare. After WTA tried to take over your company, your leadership is in question, Bharat's pristine reputation is at stake, and your stock prices have stagnated."

"We're aware of the work that needs to be done," Hem said. "We know how bad the situation is. We also have a plan for how to fix it."

"Right," Raj said. "The software that was in development before your head of R & D was fired for being a WTA mole. You have a provisional patent that ends in what, one year? That means that your deadline is November."

Ajay and Hem looked at each other.

Mina laughed. "I told you that she knows everything."

Raj grinned. "It's public information at this point." She leaned forward in her seat and met Ajay's glare. "Your patent is not going to get the market excited enough to increase the value of your shares and to secure support for your position as CEO. You need to do something drastic, otherwise you won't get the support you need."

"What do you propose?" Hem asked.

"Buy RKH Collective. Expand Bharat to include cybersecurity and physical security services."

Pin-drop silence.

"Raj . . ." Mina started. "This wasn't exactly what I meant last week when I said you should sell your business."

"No, but it makes sense." Raj paced to the window. This was harder for her than she'd expected, but she knew it was the right decision for her future. "Bharat has to expand, and the timing is perfect. Not to mention, the type of work RKH does is a natural extension of what you already do."

"Ms. Hothi—"

"Raj, please."

"Raj, then." Tushar nodded. "What exactly can RKH provide that Bharat doesn't have? We can create a dedicated security team on our own if that's an area we want to pursue."

She turned on her heel to look at the expectant faces in the room. "I have a local facility, trained employees, long-term contracts, and a growth strategy. It would take years for Bharat to develop what I'm offering you today."

Her eyes met Ajay's. "You sign the paperwork for a buyout and make the announcement. No one will question that you're perfect for CEO."

"Clear the room."

Ajay had spoken so matter-of-factly that it took her a moment to register his words.

"No, it's fine—" she began.

"Clear the room," he said again.

Raj watched as Ajay shared a look with his family and legal counsel before, one by one, they stood and headed for the door.

"I'm going to make sure Zail is occupied," Hem murmured. "Call me if you need me, brother."

"That goes for you, too," Mina said, pointing at Raj.

Raj and Ajay were alone a moment later.

He strode forward, then stood with her, shoulder to shoulder, facing the brilliant blue sky and glistening cityscape together.

"Why are you selling?"

"You didn't need to clear the room for me to tell you that."

"I did if I wanted you to cut the bullshit."

She straightened. "Are you still pissed at me about Robert?"

"No, but it looks like you're still keeping secrets."

"Watch your step, Ajay Singh. You aren't my only choice for a buyer."

He rolled his eyes, and for the first time in as long as she could remember, Raj was speechless. Had he seriously just rolled his eyes at her? She hated when a man rolled his eyes.

"Answer the question, Rajneet. Why are you selling?"

"It's an opportune time to—"

"The truth."

She faced him, arms crossed. "Cut me off again and I'll cut off more than your words. Understand?"

"Hothi, did you know you get this little sexy accent when you're pissed? Kind of like all of the polish and sheen and *assimilation* can't control you. Your Punjabi roots are showing, and you're a real phataka when they do."

Assimilation. That fucking word grated on her nerves like nothing else ever could. In the same breath he'd complimented her by calling her a firecracker. Ajay, with his comfortable upbringing and his proud Punjabi parents who'd established roots before he could, would never understand what it was like to immigrate to a new country at such a young age, to be a woman who had to speak the language of her older, straight-white-male client base. Just because she had polish didn't mean she'd assimilated. Just because she'd married a man to give her access to her dreams didn't mean she'd suppressed her Punjabi roots.

So many second-generation Indians didn't understand, she thought as she stepped back from Ajay. Her fury was barely contained. "I think we're done here."

"You have to tell me if you want to work with me and my family."

"That's not a business require—"

"I thought you were smarter than that."

"I want to start over!" she burst out. Her hands fisted

at her sides as she tried to regain control of her temper. "Because my divorce is going through in a few months. I have a job offer from Gen One, and I want to screw my ex-husband after he screwed with me, by selling to his competitor, dammit. I also want a challenge again and selling accomplishes all those things. Happy?"

Ajay smiled at her now, and it was so disarming that she stood motionless, even as he reached out and tucked her hair behind her ear.

"I'm sorry. That comment was out of line."

"You said it to piss me off."

"And it worked. I won't go there again, though."

Raj paused. "I . . . appreciate it."

"I can't commit to anything until I meet with my executive team," he said. "In the meantime, we'll get the nondisclosures in place. If and when we decide we're interested, you'll send over your corporate documents and we'll start the review process."

She let out an audible breath.

"I'll have my legal team get the ball rolling on our end. Maybe we'll do business, or maybe we won't. I'm willing to explore the options, though."

Raj grabbed her bag and had crossed the room when Ajay's hand caught hers. She turned and found herself inches from his chest. He'd sneaked up behind her so silently that she hadn't even realized he'd followed her to the exit.

"What's this?" she asked, leaning back against the door. A fluttering in the pit of her stomach spread warmth through her body. She was barely able to control her shiver.

Ajay shifted so that his hands rested on either side of her head. He leaned forward until his nose almost touched hers. His scent, a subtle fresh and clean musk, fogged her senses. He was so much taller than her that it felt like he was surrounding her.

"When is the divorce final?" he asked. His voice was low, and Raj followed the subtle curve of his lips as they moved. She felt hypnotized.

"Three months."

"Three months until you're a free woman?"

"I've been a free woman since I was eighteen. Marriage doesn't change that, you ass."

"I wasn't referring to your freedom as a woman . . . *darling*. You got an offer from Gen One. Knowing as much as I do about you, there is no way you're going to take another lover right now." He inched impossibly closer when he whispered those words, and her skin hummed with anticipation. "You're too worried right now that you'll be caught when all eyes are on you as a potential candidate. But when you're ready, I'm willing."

"I thought you weren't going to touch me. Not after the gala." What was happening to her? How had the tables turned on her so quickly? She straightened, horrified at herself for being sucked under, like a current was dragging her away from solid ground.

He traced a hand down the curve of her cheek. "I think we still have unfinished business between us that

I'd like to explore. Don't you want to see how we are, too?" Ajay stepped back, leaving her unsteady on her stilettos. "Now that we're not mad at each other and all. I'll see you at the Gupta wedding. I assume you were invited."

Her brain kicked in again now that he had given her space. "I've been invited to the reception. Are you going to be there?"

"Frankie, the bride's grandfather, is on the Bharat board. He's an old friend of our father's."

Raj made it a point to decline every Indian wedding she was ever invited to. Spending days exchanging social niceties with women who would rather see her floating in the Hudson was not her strength. However, she'd go to the Gupta reception. Being seen was important for her image now. For her company's image.

And for closing the sale of RKH and starting over.

Raj smiled at Ajay, even though she was still a bit lightheaded from his close proximity. With a little wiggle of her fingers, she opened the door. "It's been a pleasure. I look forward to seeing you and your brothers this weekend."

"Raj?"

"Yes?" she said, pausing to look over her shoulder.

"I have a feeling you'll be seeing a lot more of me. Soon."

Chapter Six

Ajay

RAJ: Are you going to make a decision?

AJAY: Just because you have my number doesn't mean you are permitted to use it at your convenience.

RAJ: Then don't answer. I know how busy you are, Ajay. That's why I'm trying to wrap things up.

AJAY: Trying to get rid of me so soon?

RAJ: Is that why you're stringing me along? So you could spend more time with me? That's an interesting tactic.

AJAY: Is it working?

RAJ: I'll let you know. Send the nondisclosures at least. I'm not a patient woman.

AJAY: Then I'll have to make the waiting more pleasurable for you. Check your inbox. Tushar sent the disclosures.

A PUNJABI WEDDING meant three things: alcohol, bhangra, and lots of matchmaking. Ajay didn't mind the first two, but the third was the reason the last thirty-six hours of his life had been the most miserable he'd had to endure since the last wedding he'd attended with his family. Four events meant four separate opportunities for his mother and her friends to try to force single women on him.

He'd danced with a surgeon who was as interested in him as he was in her, been encouraged to sit and eat with a grad student searching for internship opportunities, and talked to an engineer his brother Zail had dated the year before. Ajay's patience had come to an end.

Since taking over as COO, his lack of time had limited his relationships to mutually satisfying sex and the occasional business dinner. His partners knew that he wasn't looking for a long-term commitment, and they weren't looking for them, either.

Raj would understand that kind of laser focus on work, he thought as he sipped his whiskey in a shadowed corner. She would know the odds and demand nothing more or less than what either of them had to give. The only problem was that after her little business meeting at the beginning of the week, she was now a potential investment. In his line of work, that meant hands off . . .

for now. He couldn't help flirting with her via text, but that was going to have to stop, too.

He surveyed Uncle Frankie's ballroom, which took up the first floor of his Long Island family estate, hoping he'd get a glimpse of the woman who'd occupied his brain space during the week. The terrace doors were open to a cool, breezy night, while the front entrance, flanked by marble statues of Lord Ganesh, welcomed a steady stream of late arrivals. The round tables bracketing both sides of the makeshift dance floor were blanketed with ice-blue tablecloths, and crystal vases overflowed with indigo-colored flowers. A DJ pumped out the heavy bass beats of current Punjabi music and Bollywood songs while a few people took advantage of the open dance floor. Waitstaff in crisp-collared shirts and black vests lingered in the crowd with the last of the fusion food appetizers.

Ajay grabbed a samosa pinwheel from a passing tray and popped it into his mouth.

"Still eating?" Zail asked as he sidled next to him. "After the mehendi event on Thursday night, then the Indian American Idol party—"

"The sangeet."

"They had a professional sound system and lights, Ajay. That wasn't a normal sangeet with old ladies singing folk songs. Anyway, after the mehendi, the sangeet, and today's lunch with silver thaali plates toppling with food, I can't find any room to eat."

"More for me, then," Ajay said. "The food is the best

part of this whole wedding." He eyed a passing tray and decided to forgo the tandoori brie with mint chutney.

"Do you know how much money we're all burning by being here instead of working in the office?"

"To the penny," Ajay replied. "But we still have to make an appearance."

"Next time, I'm going to fake a travel delay. Mom wants you to stop hiding in the corner and come back to the table."

"I'm not hiding, I'm—"

"Looking for Raj. I know." The bitterness was obvious in his voice.

Ajay reached out and clasped his brother's shoulder. "I haven't made a decision yet or talked to Dad about it. We'll have to do this together, anyway. Dad, you, Hem, and me."

Zail's eyebrows furrowed and his frown deepened. "The fact that you're considering it at all is what bothers me. She's why we lost Sahar. That should be enough of a reason not to even give her the time of day."

"Sahar is why we lost Sahar, Zail."

"It was *a setup*," he said through gritted teeth. "The security report is super vague, isn't it? You have a name of her potential relative, and a bunch of possible connections, but no family pictures, no birth certificates, nothing concrete. I'm telling you, bhai. There is no way Sahar's uncle works for WTA. I would've known about it. We went to school together. We worked together. Raj's intel is wrong or she's played you."

"Raj had nothing to gain by getting rid of Sahar. And Sri, our head of security, couldn't find anything that disproved Raj's findings."

"Sri is an idiot and you should've fired him the minute he screwed up."

Zail had never hidden his feelings about Sri. The fact that Raj agreed with him and had said something similar at the gala rubbed Ajay the wrong way. Maybe it was time to call Sri in and transfer him to a different department. It was just that the man was his first hire since he started the department. Since Ajay had brought him on to lead the cyber security team, Sri had always been loyal. Maybe something had changed.

A group of aunties wearing brightly colored saris and anarkalis giggled behind their hands as they passed. Ajay could barely control an eye roll. He looked over at his brother.

"I'm sorry. I know you don't like Sri or Raj, and you believed in Sahar, but there was nothing more we could do. Come on. Let's get back before we're accosted."

They wove through tables and dancers until they reached the secluded corner where Uncle Frankie had put the entire Singh family. Ajay's parents sat at one end of the table while Hem and Mina sat next to them.

Ajay's mother looked regal in a pale cream and gold salwar kameez with a thick gold choker and matching gold earrings. She pointed at Ajay and then at his father. "Come sit next to your papa. He's in a sour mood."

Deepak Singh, the genius businessman who'd created

some of the most groundbreaking location technology in the world, sat back in his chair with his arms crossed over his broad tuxedo-clad chest. "I don't understand why I can't go sit with Frankie. Tusi mainu mara rahe ho. You're killing me, woman."

"Deepak, if you go sit with him you'll want to drink whiskey and smoke cigars. The doctor was very clear about your restrictions. Stop whining, otherwise I really will kill you."

"Dad, we'll have your whiskey for you," Ajay said with a grin. He sat next to the man who'd taught him how to drink. "When is dinner? Do we get to eat right away or is Uncle Frankie going to have, like, ten relatives toast the bride and groom first? Those speeches are so long."

Ajay's mom leaned across his father and gripped his hand. Her wrists full of bangles rang as they hit the table-top. "You can't go until you meet Shilpa Aunty's niece."

"Here we go again," Zail mumbled next to him.

A buzzing interrupted their flow of conversation, and Ajay pulled out his cell phone from his breast pocket. Out of the corner of his eye, he saw that the rest of his family was checking their various devices, as well.

"That's me," Mina said. She reached into a tiny pouch that matched the mirror work on her salwar kameez to retrieve her phone. "Oh. Raj is here."

Even as she said the words, Ajay spotted the woman he'd been waiting to see. Anticipation unfurled in his gut as he took her in. She wasn't as tall as some of the other Punjabi women in attendance, but like always, her heels gave her formidable stature. Her gown flowed around her as she paused at the entrance where Uncle Frankie was still greeting the last of the arrivals. Ajay watched as she folded her hands together as if to say namaste, and then handed over an envelope.

Ajay didn't realize he was standing until Zail said his name in a sharp tone.

"Don't even think about bringing her here to sit with us."

"No, I—" An older man went over to talk to Frankie and Raj.

If he was going to speak with her, he needed to look inconspicuous. The old man next to him would have to do as his excuse. "Papa, I want to introduce you to someone. Can you take a walk with me?"

Deepak Singh's face brightened, and without asking Ajay's mother what she would prefer, he was out of his chair like a shot. "Challo, puttar. Let's go."

Ajay held out his arm for his father to hold.

"Ajay," Mina called out. Her expression was solemn. "She's more delicate than she wants people to think. Be kind."

"This is business, Mina. Nothing more." He led his father slowly across the ballroom to where Raj stood talking with Uncle Frankie and the second gentleman.

"Your mother is hovering," his father said. "I was about to go mad."

"I could tell. Now as repayment, I need you to be on your best behavior."

"I am always on my best behavior, even when I am being used by my grown son to talk to a pretty girl."

"It's not like that."

"Hem gave me a little bit of background, Ajay. I know your mind better than you think. Just remember that your mother is like a vulture when it comes to these things. She's going to ask questions."

"It's nice to know that some things never change."

They approached the trio near the entrance. It took all of Ajay's concentration not to freeze when Raj's eyes met his.

She looked even more stunning up close. Her makeup was muted, and in the center of her perfectly arched brows she wore a simple round rhinestone bindi that matched the trimmings on the purse-pouch that hung from her wrist. Her lips parted slightly as she scanned him head to toe before she turned back to Uncle Frankie.

"Apologies for interrupting," Ajay said as he moved to stand next to Raj. "Uncle Frankie, I wanted to introduce my father to Ms. Hothi here."

The old man's bushy white eyebrows leaped in surprise. "You know each other? I didn't think your circles crossed."

"I didn't think yours did, either, Uncle Frankie."

"Ms. Hothi invested in an office complex in Long

Island City with a few other parties that Peter here put together. We've kept in touch for, what is it, Raj, a year now?"

"Just about. Ajay, I'm so glad that you've brought this incredibly handsome man over." She reached out and gripped his father's hand in both of hers. "The legendary Deepak Singh needs no introduction. I'm so sorry I missed you at the last fundraiser event you were scheduled to attend. Your wife is a lucky woman to have such a dashing hero in a tux at her side." She leaned over and pressed a kiss to each crinkled cheek.

Ajay thought she was laying it on a bit thick, and he was about to say so when he saw his father's face go ruddy with pleasure.

Well, I'll be damned, he thought. She'd charmed his father with a few cheesy words.

"Fundraiser?" Deepak asked. "Was it Gen One? I'm disappointed now more than ever that I missed the opportunity to meet such a lovely person such as yourself then. It's a shame our paths haven't crossed before?"

"The disappointment is mutual."

"Deepak, Raj is in the security business," Peter said. "If Bharat is ever in the market for security services, you should partner up!"

"Most decisions I now defer to my son."

Ajay's heart clenched with love and gratitude.

"Dad, as it turns out, Ms. Hothi and I are already in discussions for an . . . opportunity."

"Really?" Uncle Frankie leaned forward. "Deepak,

what do you think about this? Should the board get involved?"

"Mr. Gupta," Raj said, her voice holding a strain of surprise. "As a board member, do you question all of Bharat's decisions? That's a lot of micromanaging, don't you think?"

"Well, I—"

"I expect my board to support me and know that I am invested in the success of my company. I'm sure Ajay feels the same."

Ajay raised an eyebrow at Raj. "Uncle Frankie will have to soon see me as a leader and not the boy running around his backyard during Holi celebrations in the spring."

"Deepak," Uncle Frankie said, motioning to both Raj and Ajay. "These kids . . ."

Deepak put his hands up. "I know. They know more than we do, which is why I am convinced that Bharat will be in good hands. And Raj, I look forward to seeing what you and my son do together."

The music changed and a slow song filtered through the speakers around the room.

"Oh, that's the second to last song before dinner service," Uncle Frankie said. "If you'll excuse me, I have to get back to my table. I hope you enjoy the reception tonight!"

He and Peter said their goodbyes before walking toward the left side of the ballroom.

"You two should dance," Ajay's father said. He motioned to the couples who had stepped onto the floor. "Take advantage of the music!"

"I have to get you back to the table, too," Ajay said.

"I'm old, puttar, but I'm strong enough to walk across a room by myself. Raj? Come out to New Jersey sometime. My wife is a wonderful cook. We'll talk more about business and your family. Okay?"

Something flickered in Raj's expression, but she held that serene smile on her face. "That sounds lovely. I look forward to it."

With one last pointed look at Ajay, Deepak Singh shuffled back toward his table. Hem met him halfway across the room, and despite what looked like an obvious protest, Deepak leaned on his eldest son the rest of the way to his chair.

"Well?" Ajay said to Raj. "Care to dance?"

She looked around the room and raised a brow. "You're going to call attention to yourself. Everyone is probably going to find out the minute they see us together that I'm a soon-to-be divorcée. Not exactly an aunty favorite."

"Fuck 'em."

"You know I'm only here because I want a deal," Raj said.

Ajay leaned in and, with immense satisfaction, saw desire in her eyes. "If you want me, then you're going to have to work for it."

She looked down at Ajay's arm and then met his gaze before she let him lead her to the center of the dance floor.

There was barely an inch between them, and Ajay couldn't help thinking they fit so incredibly well together. The heat from her hands as they curled over his shoulder and around his palm was deliciously warm. Her hair hung in loose waves to the small of her back, and it brushed over his knuckles. She smelled like honey and spice, and he'd bet if he leaned in to press his lips to the curve of her neck, she'd taste just as delicious.

She tilted her chin up at him as if to ask what he was thinking. Their eyes met as they slowly swayed to the deep timbre of a voice singing a Punjabi love song.

"I wasn't going to do this, you know," he said. "Dance with you. Flirt with you. Be with you. You're now a potential investment."

Her husky laugh was like smooth bourbon sliding through his system. "Darling, no one is asking you to be a gentleman. I often find that when Punjabis act chivalrous, they're lions wearing sheep's clothing. Other than your father when he was defending you, I haven't met any other who has proven me wrong."

"We've come a long way since your childhood in the motherland," Ajay said in Punjabi.

She looked up at him, surprise in her expression.

He spun her in a circle and brought her closer. "Oh yes. I know how to look into someone's bio, too. You haven't gone back since you were eighteen and have very little connection with the Indian community here."

"I can still spot a lion when I see one."

"Soni," he said, knowing that the Punjabi word for

beautiful fit her more perfectly than any English endearment could. "Lion or not, I don't let people play me. I thought we'd established that."

He skimmed his fingertips up to touch the exposed skin between her shoulder blades before sliding his hand down again to rest at the small of her back.

"Ajay, if you're going to lead, then don't hesitate in business, either. Stop letting people like Frankie get away with making comments like that in public. If you don't, he will continue to undermine your authority and other people will start doing the same thing."

He hummed in agreement and felt her falter in his arms for a moment.

"What?"

"You're not going to brush me off? Tell me that you don't need advice from a woman?"

Ajay leaned in until his lips were a breath away from the shell of her ear. "Who am I to turn down sound advice? I need all of the help I can get."

Her breath hitched, and when Ajay pulled back, he could tell that there was heat in her eyes. Her desire only fueled his own.

"Now that," she said slowly, "was a damn good line."

Before he could pull her closer and screw both of their reputations, the song ended and Raj slipped out of his arms. She gave a regal nod and turned to the opposite end of the ballroom.

"I think my table is over on that side," she said.

"I'll escort you."

"No need. People will talk."

"They'll talk anyway."

Ajay tucked her hand under his arm and walked with her in silence. They shared one last look before Ajay turned and crossed the expanse of the ballroom to his family.

His parents eyed him with interest, even as Ajay pulled out a chair and sat down.

Ajay's father leaned over and said, "I like her."

"She's definitely an interesting woman."

"What's the deal?" he asked. "The business deal, I mean."

His father had a twinkle in his eyes. The old man was up to something, but Ajay relented and answered the question, starting with the type of services she provided and ending with the meeting that took place earlier in the week.

"What are you thinking, puttar?"

"Papa, I haven't decided." He lowered his voice. Even though his brothers and mother were distracted by the waitstaff delivering food, he wanted to make sure they couldn't hear him. "I want the family to be aligned on this but Zail is . . . not."

"Being aligned is not always going to be possible and you know it." His father picked up a triangle of naan. "But for what it's worth, I think it's a solid business investment."

"Really?"

"Yes," he said, and then switched to Punjabi. "Bharat

didn't grow to its current size because I made safe decisions. Your gut is telling you this is a good risk, and you
should listen."

Ajay nodded. "You're not matchmaking, are you?"

His father grinned, and the smile was a carefree,
beautiful sight to see. It had been way too long since
Deepak Singh smiled.

"Papa," he said after a moment. "She's still married.
And now we're looking to buy her company."

His father's response was a shrug. "I really like her.
Possibilities aren't just for technology and science.
They're for people, too. Raj Hothi is a smart possibility
for you. Just because she has a past doesn't make her any
less qualified."

"You're getting way ahead of yourself," Ajay said.

"No, you're just not keeping up."

He leaned into his wife's side to take her naan. They
shared a familiar look filled with love.

Ajay began eating the food that had been placed in
front of him even as his thoughts continued to center
around Raj. He was interested, but that was where it
would have to end. He had an obligation to his family,
to his legacy.

Chapter Seven

Rajneet

AJAY SINGH: I'll need financials, corporate docs, everything you got.

RAJ: Did yesterday's wedding sell you? Are we making a deal?

AJAY SINGH: Not yet, Rajneet. But send docs to my counsel, cc me. I want to see what I'm working with and I'll call you tomorrow.

RAJ: My Mondays are usually busy, but I'll clear my calendar for you.

AJAY SINGH: Oh? Your evening, too?

RAJ: It depends on how interesting you're willing to make the negotiations.

RAJ SAT BEHIND her glass desk surrounded with paper-work. Her head of Legal, Harnette, occupied one of the off-white chairs across from her, while her assistant, Tracey, sat in the other. They'd been hovering over their tablets and laptops for the last hour and a half.

"I think that covers it for prepping Bharat," Raj said to two of her oldest employees. "If Bharat needs anything else, then route the request to my cell phone. I'll handle it personally. This is just talk. I don't want to alarm anyone."

She was met with nods.

"Do we have anything else?"

Her assistant nodded. "The animal shelter in Mid-town. They called and wanted to ask if you could come down after the fifteenth. They said that you may be inter-ested in seeing some of the animals that are coming in."

Raj felt her heart jump and pressed a hand to her chest. She'd wanted one for so long, but with getting her business off the ground and with Robert's allergies, it had never been possible. But now . . .

"Was it—" She cleared her throat. "Was it Jill who called?"

"Yes, I believe so."

Jill managed the shelter. She also knew exactly what Raj wanted.

The news had her itching to call Jill for more infor-mation right that second. Instead, she took a deep breath and nodded at Tracey. "Thank you for the message. Please add it to my calendar for the weekend following the fifteenth. Let Jill know that I'm seriously considering this time. Now that is taken care of, why don't you two order lunch? On me. You deserve it."

"I'll take you up on that," Harnette said with a smile.

"Me, too," Tracey added. "Want me to order something for you, too, boss?"

"Sure. Use my corporate card."

Tracey gave a thumbs-up. Before she could stand, the cell phone she gripped in her other hand let out a shrill.

She tucked her phone between her ear and shoulder. "Raj Hothi's office."

Raj watched her assistant's eyes go wide. She shot a look at Harnette, who had also remained seated.

"What is it?" Raj asked.

Tracey pulled the phone away from her ear and pressed the mute button on the screen. "It's security downstairs. They said they stopped a man from entering the building. He wants to see you. Claims he's your brother. Do you even have a brother?"

Raj felt her stomach pitch and nausea roil in her gut. Her first instinct was to have security throw him out, but that would only delay the inevitable. Guru had endless patience. Even when they were kids, he'd been able to wait her out. She remembered that he'd hide in the poppy fields during Holi and then blast her with colored water from a squirt gun when she got tired of hiding.

She refused to hide in her own damn office now.

Raj tapped her red nails against her desk as she debated her options. If she tried to ignore him, he would just wait for her to leave work.

No, ignoring was a coward's way. It was what her mother would do, and she was not her mother. She wasn't going to just let someone walk into her life and make demands that she accepted without argument. No, this was her company, her territory.

"Boss, what do you want—"

"Ask for his name." She knew what it would be, but it was important for Guru to realize that she wasn't going to welcome him into her life.

Tracey unmuted the phone and spoke into the receiver. She paused as security responded to her question, and then said, "Guru Hothi."

"Okay, tell security to send him up. Move my call with Kia at Gen One by ten minutes. Harnette, you can head out, too."

"Raj, are you sure?" Harnette asked. "Tracey and I, or one of your other senior VPs can stay with you."

"No, I'm fine. Guru is an old . . . acquaintance."

They looked at each other, as if trying to determine whether or not to believe Raj's brush-off, before they walked to the door.

"Let us know if you need us," Tracey said.

"Thanks, Tracey."

She watched them walk toward their desks through the glass wall of her office before she turned to her windows. Her view wasn't as impressive as that of the Singh brothers, but she was still proud of it.

"Gudiya."

The endearment was spoken in a rough, deep timbre. She turned slowly, and barely controlled her jaw from dropping.

The last time she'd seen her brother he was thirty and looked like a walking advertisement for how not to wear designer clothes. He was the son of a Punjabi mob boss with a gold spoon tucked between his teeth.

And now he looked like the mob boss himself.

Guru Hothi's leather pants and jacket had been replaced with a fitted gray suit and a pagadi that matched the color of his subtle pinstripes. Gone were the ostentatious watch and layers of gold chains. Instead, his Rolex was a bit more tasteful, and his jewelry was limited to a kara on his wrist, two gold rings, and a diamond stud in one ear. He stroked a hand over a closely trimmed beard.

"I haven't changed *that* much for you to keep staring at me like that," he said in Punjabi.

"What are you doing here, Guru?"

"Trying to chase you down when I have better things to do back in India." He strolled across her office and pulled out the chair Tracey had recently vacated. He dropped into it and crossed an ankle over his knee. "How have you been?"

Seeing him was like a kick in the teeth. He reminded her of everything she'd escaped and everything she missed. "I'm going to ask you one more time before I tell you to get out. What are you doing here, Guru?"

He looked up at her, straight in the eyes, and said coolly, "Mom is dying. She has six months, maybe less. She wants to see you before she's gone."

Raj stumbled to her chair and dropped into it like a stone. The stomach bile rose again, and this time she had to brace her hands on her knees and take a few easy breaths.

"Do you want some water? I can call one of your staff to bring you some."

She looked up at her brother, who was eyeing her as if he was . . . concerned. Which couldn't be the case, of course. No, he'd turned his back on her long ago.

Her mother, the one person Raj had hoped would still love her when she decided to forge an independent future for herself, had turned her back on Raj, too.

Raj could still remember hearing her mother's voice on the phone that last time. The cold rejection had been sharper than a chef's knife. Even though the wounds on her heart had been scabbed over for so long, they still throbbed at the memory.

"What—what happened?"

"Mom has a tumor," Guru said softly. "In her spine, and now there are growths in her brain. She's gone through surgeries and radiation treatment, but nothing is working."

"Why does she want to see me?"

"Because you are her only daughter."

The way he said it, the accusing tone in his voice, had her straightening. "I thought she only had a son.

Isn't that what you told me the last time you came to New York? Isn't that what she told me the last time I called her? You got what you wanted. I'm no longer a part of the family. You can't continue to change your mind, bhaiya."

His expression hardened. Darkened until Raj's spine straightened in an unconscious reaction. "You've been in the US for too long, Rajneet. The life you choose is only worthy if you honor the people who created it for you. You never honored your family."

"And my family never honored me."

Raj knew it was useless to try to argue with Guru about familial obligations, but she couldn't stop herself from fighting back. He'd never know how hard it had been for her to tear her roots out as quickly and violently as a hundred-year-old tree toppling over in a storm. Her traditional upbringing, her legacy, was as rich and old as the soil in her family's poppy fields.

And Raj's brother didn't have the same pressures that she'd had as a Punjabi woman. He'd been able to run wild growing up. No one expected him to account for his time, to be home at a certain hour, or to get a degree as a résumé builder for marriage.

No. She was not going to waste her breath fighting him on binary gender roles and cultural responsibilities that her family refused to let go.

"I'm sorry that Mumma is sick. I'm sorry she's suffering and she's dying. I . . . I've always missed her. But when I refused to use my company to help you grow the family's drug trade, she cut me off just like you wanted her to."

"This is her dying wish."

"Her guilty conscience is not my responsibility."

"Even Papa has come around and would like to hear from you," Guru said. He leaned back again and steepled his fingers in front of him.

The news shocked her nearly as much as the news about her mother. "What are you talking about?"

"Papa misses you, as well. When he retired from the business, he got soft. And then Mumma got sick. The bottom line is that I run the family now. I make the decisions. If Mumma wants to see you, then I will do what I can to make it happen for her."

"Are you going to try to drag me back to Punjab again?" Raj asked bitterly.

"No, but I am going to be staying in New York until you agree to go."

Raj's jaw dropped. "You cannot be serious! Who is going to oversee the . . . trade?"

He scoffed, and the hard lines in his face deepened. "The family business always made you uneasy. It's opium, Raj. You can say it. And I have people who are overseeing things while I'm here. You have nothing to worry about when you come back."

"Won't people find out about your dirty little secrets if you're not there to keep them all quiet?"

"What dirty secrets?" He spread his arms out as if looking for someone to challenge his statement. "You've been away for a long time, Raj, but I expected you to at least keep tabs on us. We've been outsourcing opium to pharmaceutical companies in Europe and the US. Nothing dirty about that, nah?"

"Wh-what?"

"There is more profit in pharma. We're legal now. Mostly." His grin was quick and reminded her of the boy that he used to be. "There are still a lot of people who want what we have. We play nice in the sandbox, but almost all of our money is clean. Now, as a peace offering, I can purchase your ticket, and you can be in and out of India in twenty-four hours. When would you like to leave?"

She was losing ground. She could feel it sliding out from under her. The freedom that she loved so much was disappearing like it used to when she was a child.

Except she wasn't a child anymore. She wasn't going to fall in line.

"Guru, I can't just pick up and leave. I own a business. I'm in the middle of—"

"A divorce, I know."

Her shoulders straightened at the disapproval in his voice. "I also own a company. And, like I said, my family's guilty conscience is not my responsibility. I have a negotiation in progress, so if you'll excuse me."

His eyebrows formed a V, and his gaze narrowed. "With a South Asian tech company?"

"It's time you leave, Guru!"

Even as she stood, horrified at the way she'd shouted,

Guru sat smiling at her. "You never used to worry about yelling before. You were always screaming and yelling as you ran all over the farmhouse when you were a kid."

"Those days are over now."

He stood, straightened his tie and jacket. "I guess so. Our mother is on a timeline. I'll give your assistant my phone number. Try not to block this one. And don't take too long to decide. Even though I'm taking business meetings and working remotely, I need to get back to India. Commit."

"I'm not committing to anything and your bullying me is not going to work." She saw her assistant standing at her desk through the glass wall of her office and shook her head. Dammit, she was still yelling.

"You always were quick tempered," Guru said with an amused smile. "The Punjabi princess that was the family phataka. A firecracker." He buttoned his suit jacket and moved toward the door. "I can't force you to come. Obviously. But we'll be seeing a lot of each other until you decide to do the right thing. This is for Mumma, Rajneet. Business shouldn't get in the way."

With that parting message, he slipped out of her office, left a card on Tracey's desk as he passed, and disappeared through the lobby double doors and out to the elevators.

When she was sure he was gone, Raj dropped heavily into her chair. Her heart was beating fast, and her skin felt clammy.

"Hey," Tracey said from the door. "Are you okay?"

"Yes. Yes, of course."

"Okay. First, Ajay at Bharat called. He asked if you could call him back."

"Fine."

"And your next call is on the line. Kia from Gen One. Do you want me to hold her off?"

"No." Raj brushed her hair back over her shoulders and straightened in her chair. "No, I'll take the call. Just tell her that I need a minute."

Tracey nodded. "Will do, boss." She shut the door behind her.

Raj looked at the blinking light on her desk comm unit and closed her eyes. If Ajay was still on the line, then maybe, just maybe, she'd talk to him. They'd pick at each other and she'd feel better, because he'd give her exactly what she needed. They hadn't known each other for long, but she was sure he'd know what to say. Punjabi families could understand family pressure like hers. Ajay would understand. But not Kia. Not anyone else.

"Pull yourself together, Rajneet," she muttered, even as she felt the tears burn in the back of her throat. Memories of her mother flashed in her mind like a merry-go-round that she couldn't stop. Her hand shook as she reached for her cell phone that sat in a cradle at the corner of her desk and opened her photos. Her fingers hovered over the albums link for a second before she clicked on it and scrolled until she reached the last few pictures she'd taken in Punjab.

Her mother's face stared back at her in one of her

favorite images. Their cheeks were pressed together, and their smiles were almost mirror images of each other.

God, she looked so young, so hopeful.

And her mother. After spending years staring at that picture, Raj was sure that there was trepidation in those eyes.

Raj sniffed and brushed away the lone tear that escaped. She looked down at her wet fingertip, and it snapped her out of her fog-brained thoughts. What was she doing? She had work. She immediately closed her photo app, tossed her cell phone aside and dabbed at her eyes.

Pushing all thoughts about her brother, her mother, and old memories aside, she reached out with a steady hand and answered Kia's call on her comm unit.

"Hello, Kia. How are you, darling?"

Chapter Eight

Ajay

AJAY'S PHONE BUZZED as he stepped out of his private elevator. The name that flashed across the screen had him smiling.

"You promised you'd clear your Monday calendar for me," he said when he answered. She had been on his mind, a distraction from the work he needed to accomplish. He wanted to listen to her smoky voice, with that cultured, barely there accent he hadn't heard since he danced with her at the wedding. The fact that she had him waiting put him on edge.

"It's been a long day, darling," she replied.

Ajay had expected her to take the bait, to say something pithy, but he could hear her exhaustion. "Anything I can do to help?"

"Besides buy my company? No. If you have a minute, we can talk. Or you can just send your questions to my attorney if you prefer."

"There are quite a few. Starting with what kept you busy all day when you're trying to sell. Not a good look." Ajay toed off his shoes and dropped his bag on his dining table. The automatic motion lights sensed his presence and a warm glow spread through his living area and kitchen. His two-story floor-to-ceiling windows sparkled with views of the New York City skyline.

"I told you the first time we met. I don't play games," he said.

"Ajay, just ask your questions so I can leave my office and go home."

Now he was sure something was wrong. He opened his stainless steel fridge and spotted some vegetables and a packet of chicken thighs. Even as another one of Raj's sighs echoed through the receiver, an idea formed in his head.

"Why don't you come over?"

"Come over? Where?" The surprise was evident in her voice.

"To my penthouse. Have you had dinner?"

"No, but—"

"I'll cook. Are you a vegetarian?"

"No. Ajay—"

"Good," he said. "I was hoping for chicken. Just a

simple chicken masala. None of the oil and butter gravy bullshit that restaurants serve, I promise." He took out a few items and lined them up on his island counter. "I'll send a car to your office to pick you up. Text me your address."

There was that sigh again. It was delicate and said so much. Ajay couldn't help but grin even as he knew she was going to lacerate him.

"I'm not going to have sex with you."

"Of course not," he replied. "I haven't fed you yet."

"Ajay."

"Raj." He put her on speakerphone and took off his jacket. "It's just dinner. Bring your damn computer if it'll make you feel better. But let's have some food and talk about this. I spent the whole day on the phone and on my laptop. I want to spend some time with a beautiful woman in person now, even if it is to do more work."

She waited a beat before responding. "I'll bring dessert." And with that, she hung up the phone.

Ajay grinned as he rolled his sleeves to his elbows. "You've made things more interesting since you've showed up, Rajneet Kaur Hothi. I'll give you that." After forwarding the address she'd sent to his driver, he got to work.

He put his surround-sound speakers to use and played some music on low. There was already a bottle of white from his family vineyards chilling, and it took no time at all for the sounds of garlic, onions, ghee, and cumin seeds to sizzle in a wok on his restaurant-grade stove.

Ajay liked to say that his mother taught him how to cook, but in all honesty, his mother had refused to let him in the kitchen. It was her domain and she did what she wanted. It wasn't until he started working long hours after college that he realized if he wanted home cooking, he'd have to do it himself. And then the art of putting dinner together, even if it was only to feed himself on late nights, relaxed him. It was the perfect transition he needed after a long day.

It didn't hurt his sex life, either.

He'd set the chicken to simmer and the naan in the oven to warm when his phone buzzed.

FRONT DESK: Mr. Singh, we have a Ms. Hothi here to see you.

AJAY: Send her up. Please also add her to the list of approved visitors.

FRONT DESK: Yes, sir.

Anticipation hummed in his veins as he filled two wineglasses. He took one of them to the door with him and opened it just as Raj stepped out of the elevator. She looked elegant in her cream sheath dress with short sleeves and a boat neck. For the first time, Ajay could see the elegant curve of her neck, since she'd scooped her hair up in a loose ponytail. Raj paused when she spotted him, surprise etched in the tired lines of her face, changing to approval at the glass of wine in his hand.

"I hope that's for me," she said.

"You sounded like you could use it."

"I could, yes."

She gave him her large tote to carry and slipped the wineglass out of his hand. Ajay moved just enough so she could enter his apartment. She had to brush past him, and the look she shot him over her shoulder had Ajay grinning. She knew exactly what he'd done.

Ajay waited as she removed her heels and then followed her silently into his kitchen.

"This is . . . wow," she said as she stopped in front of the windows. "My brownstone could never compete with the view."

He put her tote down next to his briefcase and moved behind her. "Even if you had the option of a penthouse, it wouldn't accomplish what you were trying to do."

"Oh?" Her lips pursed, naked of any lipstick. "Do tell what you think I was trying to accomplish."

"No need to get all fiery. A brownstone is a statement home. It's commonly associated with old money, with class and distinction. A penthouse is for the artists and the new-money types. To establish a business in a man's world, you needed distinction, not artistry. My father did the heavy lifting for my family. Created a compound in New Jersey. That's why I could do whatever the hell

I wanted. No one cares where I live or what that says about me. Not yet, anyway."

"That's remarkably . . . astute," Raj said. She put her wineglass down on the counter, then walked over to the kitchen sink to wash her hands. "Is there anything I can do? Please say no, since I'm a terrible cook."

"No." Ajay grinned. "It's almost ready. Not into cooking?"

"No, I brought over my family housekeeper. He does everything for me, including keeping me fed. I'd think you'd have someone like that, too."

"I prefer things this way." He dipped a spoon in the masala sauce, blew on it, then held it out for Raj to taste. "Tell me what you think."

Ajay slipped the spoon between her plump, naked lips. Her eyes drifted closed in pleasure. "Mmm," she moaned. The throaty sound had his dick hardening painfully in a second.

"You made it spicy," she said.

"Too hot?" His voice turned gruff, but he didn't care.

"No. It's perfect. Ajay, you are full of surprises."

Her tongue wet her top lip in a slow, sweeping motion.

His control snapped. He tossed the spoon he was holding into the sink with a resounding clatter and, without a word of warning, yanked her to him and pressed his mouth against hers.

She tasted delicious. Spicy and sweet. Rich and

sharp from the wine. Her mouth was pliant and soft under his as he bowed over her, desperate to consume that first taste. She opened under him, her tongue meeting his even as her fingers dove into his hair and his arms wrapped around her waist. Ajay took, tasting her, drowning, desperate for more.

When she slanted her mouth against his, pressing impossibly closer, he growled and lifted her inches off the ground so his erection could nestle at the juncture of her thighs.

They moaned in unison from the delicious feel of fitting together, before Raj pulled back.

"I said I wouldn't sleep with you," she whispered, out of breath and sounding desperate. Her eyes dropped to his mouth and she kissed him. Once. Twice. Again, with a hint of teeth.

"I haven't asked you to."

"Then you should probably let me go."

Slowly, knowing that he was torturing them both, he let her slide down the length of his body until she was on her feet again.

She stepped back, adjusted her dress, and straightened her ponytail. "Really, Ajay?" She sounded shaky, just like he felt. "You feed me, and that's all it takes?"

"It was the sex noises, actually," he said as he pulled the naan out of the oven and rested the tray on the cooling rack. "Next time you do that, I'll be throwing you over my shoulder and showing you my bedroom."

"Promises, promises," she said.

He gripped her waist and, unable to help himself, pressed a kiss to the curve of her neck before he gently moved her to the side so he could get plates and bowls from a cabinet. "Better keep your distance, woman. Okay to eat with your hands?"

"I won't even answer that insulting question."

"Hands it is."

They washed up, and as Ajay brought the food to the table in front of his windows, he couldn't help but feel a twinge of satisfaction as she kept a wide berth. He was still burning for her, but it was nice to know that her cool demeanor was hiding the same fire.

He topped off their glasses and, with his phone, dimmed the lights so New York could shine. "Now. Tell me what happened today."

Raj froze, a torn wedge of naan hovering over her chicken. "That's not your—"

"Stop right there. Before you get defensive, I'm not asking you because you're obligated to share, because we want each other, but because I want to listen. Maybe that'll help."

Ajay watched her as she scooped up chicken and took a bite. Her eyes drifted closed. "This is really good, Ajay. My compliments to the chef."

"Thank you."

He dug into his food, as well, and for a few minutes they ate in silence.

"My mother is dying."

The words cut through the air like his chef's knife. "Oh, baby."

"I-I'm sad," she said in Punjabi, then switched back to English, as if she realized her slip. "I know logically I'm sad, but I haven't spoken to my mother since I married Robert. My brother, he's the one who told me, ensured that the whole family was cut off from me. I've accepted that."

"Why did your brother cut you off? Because you married a white guy?" He could understand some very traditional Punjabi families with status doing the same thing. Hell, his extended family had cut off his cousin Bhram for being gay.

Ajay saw her hesitation as she sipped her wine. "I'm not going to tell anyone, Raj," he assured her. "This is off the record."

"It's not that. It's just that I don't think I've ever told anyone other than Mina and Robert."

"Told anyone what?"

"My father owns thousands of acres of poppy fields. My family has an . . . operation."

"Poppy fields? Poppy . . . You're talking opium." His stomach twisted. Shit. His uncle had gotten in trouble with the mob because of his drug habit. He would have to call Sri later to find out what Raj's connections were with organized crime, and if she was connected in any way to the group that had harmed his family. "Does your father still do opium?"

"My brother has taken over, but from what I understand, it's mostly legal now. They're a supplier for pharma companies."

Well, thank the gods, Ajay thought to himself. He wasn't a fool. He knew the reason it mattered so much was because he wanted her, and her connections to his family were already complicated enough. "I'm assuming it wasn't always legal, though."

Raj took a bite and chewed before answering. "This is incredible, Ajay. You've surprised me."

"Thank you, but you're changing the subject."

She laughed, and her ponytail slid over her shoulder. She looked so young now. It was a layer of Raj's personality that Ajay ached to see, and now that he'd witnessed the vulnerability, he wanted to do everything he could to help her. To protect her.

She'd probably knee him if he ever admitted that. Instead, he topped off their wine and waited for her to finish.

"Growing up, things were . . . dark in my home, even if they kept the drugs and guns out of sight from me and my mother. All I was expected to do was finish my twelfth standard and then get married. My parents had been so controlling my whole life. I had security at all times. Going to school, coming home from school, even at weddings we attended. My only escape was books, and I studied hard. I wanted freedom. I never wanted to be at the mercy of someone else's checkbook."

"So you convinced your parents you should go to

college. Except instead of going home after you finished, you found your escape with Robert Douglass and got married instead."

The corner of her mouth twitched. "Yes, you could say that. My plan was to switch my student visa to an H visa. I had a few job opportunities lined up that were willing to sponsor my H. I was at the top of my class, and I wasn't worried about the work. My family, however, worried me. They would fly to the US and drag me home, H visa be damned."

"Sounds like something my family would do in similar circumstances."

"Robert's, too. He screwed around for most of his childhood and then for the first two years of college. They had a very specific life planned for him, too, because they didn't trust him to make sound decisions on his own. They were worried about their reputation."

"And Robert didn't want that?"

"No, darling," she said with a laugh.

"How did you meet the bastard anyway? He was in classes with you?"

Raj nodded. "We'd met through a study group, and after I told him that he didn't have a chance in hell with me, we became friends. It was an odd friendship, but he was always respectful after that. Years passed until a few weeks before graduation. He wanted to go to law school and prove himself, while I was sweating, thinking about my parents showing up on my doorstep. That's when we struck a deal over cheap beer and nachos in the West Village."

Ajay burst out laughing. "Raj, you are not the cheap beer and nachos type."

"I was when I had no money," she said. "And Robert used to play along."

Ajay slid another naan onto her plate and took one for himself. "You borrowed his money to start your company, and he went to law school. Then he started working for you, right?"

"Pretty much. And then my brother showed up." She took another bite of food. Ajay tried to ignore the way her eyes drifted closed when she chewed. The way she savored something he made for her was going to be the vision he revisited in the shower later that night. Her sensuality was like a drug he had to consciously ignore so he could pay attention.

"Your brother," he said.

Raj nodded. "I had kept in touch with him and my mother. It was brief, and the conversations were hard, because they hated what I'd done. My father was completely out of the picture, but Mom still loved me. Anyway, Guru found out about my security business and said it was time to show loyalty to the family that gave me the opportunity to live free in New York."

"He wanted you to use your business to help their drug trade."

"Pretty much. At that point, drugs had become an

epidemic in Punjab, and drug trafficking had peaked in profits. They wanted my loyalty. I refused. My brother cut me off. And then—" Her breath hitched. "Then my mother cut me off. Guru didn't want anyone in the family to have any connection with me."

"I'm so sorry." He'd have to find out more about her brother, too. The thought of someone hurting Raj like that was . . . unacceptable.

She was being honest with him, sharing a part of herself that he didn't think she'd be open to delving into. Whatever her reasons were, he'd honor her trust. And then, maybe later, he'd be able to beat the shit out of her brother for hurting her.

"I put it behind me," she continued. "That's why I was a bit shocked when my brother said she wants to see me one last time."

"To assuage her guilt. Since she's dying."

"Exactly. He ruined my perfectly good mood, too. I'm thinking of getting a puppy, and the shelter that I volunteer at may have one for me."

Ajay didn't think she could have surprised him any more than she just had. "A *puppy*?"

"Yup. I've always wanted one. Just my dog and me."

"Ugh, you're the type to torture a poor pooch by dressing it up, aren't you?"

"Of course," she said with a laugh.

He asked her more questions about her future puppy, about her childhood, about her mother, and if she knew whether or not she wanted to go home and say good-bye. He'd have to revisit her confession about organized crime connections later.

"Want some more wine?" Ajay asked after they finished their meal. "Saffron Fields limited stock."

"Yes. It'll probably go great with dessert." She dug into her tote bag and pulled out a Tupperware container.

"Is that . . . is that kheer?"

"It is. I told you I'd bring dessert. I just happened to have this in my office. Remember that housekeeper I told you about? Kaka made me a ton before he went back to India for a couple weeks."

"You've just topped my masala chicken with rice pudding."

Her smile was so arresting that Ajay had to turn away from her and busy himself with grabbing two spoons, otherwise he'd do something stupid like ask her to stay the night. Stay for the weekend. Stay for . . . well, however long she wanted.

And wasn't that a scary thought? The back of his neck prickled with unease as he let it sink in.

He handed over a spoon, and they dug into the kheer together, taking sips of the wine between bites.

"Thank you," she said when they'd practically polished off the container.

"For what?"

"For being a friend tonight."

Her words rubbed against him like sandpaper. Hadn't she just told him how she met her soon-to-be ex-husband?

There was no way he was going to let her pull the same bullshit with him. "I'm not your friend, Raj."

Her eyebrow raised delicately. "No?"

"No." He reached out and cupped her chin, holding firm even as she pulled back. "Don't you dare treat me like you treat that asshole, Robert, or put me in the same category as Mina. If we're going to be involved, I want more than that. I think I've made that clear."

"I'll only give you what I'm ready to give, Ajay. And if that means friendship, then that's what you'll take."

His anger began to boil, even as she pulled away from him. "I never thought you'd be a coward, Raj."

"Excuse me?"

"You just unloaded. You're regretting it. So now, to protect yourself, you're trying to keep me at a safe distance."

She paled, then shot to her feet. "I think your feelings are hurt and you're reading into things a bit to save your poor ego."

"And I still think you're a coward." He stood, as well, nose to nose with her. "We've wanted each other from the first moment that we met. And now you're backpedaling. Is it too much to share both your body and your mind with me?"

She grabbed her tote, her hands fumbling as she looped it over her shoulder. "I think we're done here. Thank you for dinner. Send my questions to Legal, will you, darling?"

He followed her to the door, close behind. "Dammit,

what did you think was going to happen between us? We'd just casually fuck, I'd buy you out, eat you out, and we'd go on our merry way?"

She whirled on her heel to face him, anger in her eyes. "If that's what I wanted, then yes, that's all that would happen. You don't get to push me, to bully me into more than what I'm willing to offer."

"And you don't get to run scared from something that could be great for both of us, or assume I'll fall in line like that puppy you've always wanted."

She yanked open the door, shoes and bag in hand. "Ajay Singh, you'll fucking roll over like I expect you to or you could kiss anything between us goodbye," she said, and slammed the door behind her.

Chapter Nine

Ajay

AJAY KNEW IT wasn't a good look for him to be leaving the gym at eleven on a Friday night. He was practically the only one in the facility in his building, and when he returned to his penthouse, his plans were to get back to work. He'd been going to lift weights and run every day since his fight with Raj on Monday. If he didn't burn off the anger somehow, it would spill over to his employees, and that couldn't happen.

How much she affected him was irritating, he thought, as he dressed in jeans and a sweatshirt. He quickly made himself a cup of chai and sat at the dining room table with his laptop. What was more important for him to remember was that Raj might have family connections that could hurt everyone, not just his uncle.

He checked his watch. He'd put off his conversation with Sri for way too long.

AJAY: I know it's late, but I need to ask you a few questions. If you're not available, please schedule time with Rafael on my calendar for tomorrow.
SRI: I can talk now, sir.

Ajay put in a video call in response. Sri's bald head glistened under recessed lighting. His deep-set brown eyes were shadowed behind thick lenses.

"Sir," Sri said. "How can I help?"

"I know you have a full plate. I need you to do some additional digging for me. A side project."

"Yes, sir?"

"Rajneet Kaur Hothi. I need to know about her background."

"Owner of RKH Collective?"

"Yes. Tell me about her family. What do they do? I want to know everything. Okay?"

"Yes, sir."

"Great. Thanks, Sri. Any updates on your other projects?"

Ajay's head of security shook his head. "Not yet, sir."

The amount of time and space that Ajay had given the man, including the additional resources, should've been more than enough for him to at least figure out WTA's next move.

"I need you to provide daily progress updates to Rafael, Sri."

Sri balked, but managed to control his expression. "Sir?"

"I want progress, Sri."

"But sir, daily progress updates will take time that I don't have."

"You'll have to make it," Ajay said. "This has gone on for a while now."

Sri cleared his throat and pulled at the collar of his sweatshirt. "Yes, sir."

Ajay hung up without another word. He'd barely gotten control of his irritation before another incoming call notification popped up. He answered and a video chat box filled his screen. "Bhram. Kidha, bhai? How are you doing?"

"Vadhiya, vadhiya." Bhram looked freshly shaved and showered. He sat against the predawn light in the UK. "I thought I'd catch you before I went to gurdwara."

"Gurdwara? Shit, is it a holy day or a cultural holiday? Am I going to have to get back to New Jersey tomorrow morning?"

"No, fool, but if you're only going to the temple on holy days, your mother is going to find out and kill you. I've been going with Gopal Uncle. Now that he's out of rehab, he's staying here in London with me. We go to gurdwara, eat in the kitchens, and then volunteer in the food pantry."

Ajay winced. Not only had he neglected going to gurdwara for a long time, he'd also forgotten that his cousin had been taking care of his father's brother.

"If Gopal is doing better with you, then don't send him back to India just yet. Our fight with WTA isn't over, and they may exploit him again. He's a weak link."

"I know, brother. I didn't call to talk about our uncle, though."

"Fine. The answer is no, I cannot pass a message to Rafael in math class. You're going to have to be a big boy and ask him to the school dance all on your own."

"Up yours," Bhram said, lifting a middle finger. "I can woo Rafael on my own. He's just going to take some more time to convince that I deserve a second chance."

"Good. Now if you're done, I have actual work to do, brother."

"I'll let you get to it, but I found out some information that you may want to know. A connection of mine who works in California has a partner at WTA. He said that WTA hasn't been able to complete the location software that is supposed to compete with ours. I know that Zail is under the gun to meet the patent filing deadline, but it looks like that's the only challenge he'll have. WTA is not a threat."

Ajay's mind raced as he processed the information. "That means Sahar didn't go work for WTA, even though that's exactly where we assumed she'd go."

"Bingo. If the intel was right, and she was going to work for WTA, then she would've helped them complete their project before ours. Has your security team been able to keep track of her and verify the relationship in WTA?"

"No, actually." It hadn't been until Bhram said her name that he realized he hadn't asked Sri for follow-ups on that project in particular. Sri should've been able to easily secure that information. His head of security had definitely become a liability. His gut was telling him to let the man go, but there was too much at stake right now to make any hasty moves in one of his most essential departments. He'd also been the one to trust Sri from the beginning, and he hated being wrong. Hopefully with the daily status updates, he'd prompted Sri to move faster to get answers.

Ajay scrubbed a hand down his face before focusing in on his cousin again. "I'll connect with Security. Right now, I'm setting up for a major acquisition."

"Acquisition?"

Ajay told Bhram about the project, about Raj's connection to the company through her ex-husband, the information she'd provided about Sahar. And because Bhram was family and another brother to him, Ajay admitted how much he wanted Raj. When he was finished, Bhram let out a low whistle.

"That's a lot, Ajay. But then again, you always put a

shit ton of pressure on yourself. If you really want to do this, though, I support you. I just think that you need to work fast. You have to make the announcement at the quarterly board meeting, which is in, what, three or four weeks? Sitting by yourself on a Friday night reviewing corporate documents isn't going to be enough. You should get the answers straight from Raj."

"I have Legal on it."

"Not enough." Ajay shook his head even as Bhram said the words. "Your instincts are sharper than all of ours. You read people just like your father can. Talk to her about the business to get the best sense of how to approach this acquisition. And who knows? Maybe it'll solve your itch, too."

"If she'll talk to me."

"Ha. Now you know how I feel. At least in your situation, Raj wants you to buy her company, so eventually she'll have to come around."

"Thanks for the advice, Bhram."

"You got it. Now I'm off to gurdwara. Don't be a jerk and go visit Guru Nanak soon. You need an answer to a prayer to get through the next few months."

"Thanks, asshole."

"You're welcome."

After Bhram's parting shot, the screen went blank. Ajay sat in the silence of his penthouse for a long time. His chai had gone cold, and the email on his screen went unread. He remembered his cousin's advice and picked up his phone.

AJAY: I'm reviewing your files. Your sales projections don't add up.

RAJ: You're still considering my company after Monday?

AJAY: You think that I'm foolish enough to let sex get in the way of business? No, *darling*. I'm exploring every opportunity for profit and buying yours looks like a good one.

RAJ: I'm glad to hear that. Have your EA call mine to set up a call. My attorneys can answer you.

AJAY: You want us to buy the company, you talk to me personally when I want an answer.

RAJ: I guess that's fair.

AJAY: Good. Let's talk now?

RAJ: I'm unavailable now.

AJAY: Plans on your Friday night?

RAJ: As a matter of fact, yes. I'm on my way to the Ice Palace. This conversation will have to wait for some other time, Ajay. Email me those questions.

Ajay jolted when he read the words on the screen. The Ice Palace was one of the hottest clubs in the Meat-packing District. He barely went out, and even he knew that. Everyone who was anyone wanted to be seen there. More importantly, the Fire Lounge was an exclusive VIP room for private parties. There was no doubt what went on behind those closed doors.

His gut churned at the thought of Raj going to a club

and having meaningless sex. Sex with someone who wasn't him.

"Yeah, that's not going to happen," he grumbled, and strode toward his bedroom. He dialed Rafael's cell as he began digging through his closet.

"Yes, sir," Rafael said.

"I need to get on the VIP list for the Ice Palace. Tonight."

"Uh . . . sir?"

"Tonight, Rafael."

"Ajay . . . you normally don't go to places like the— Oh. I understand now. Give me ten minutes. I'll have your driver meet you out front in the same amount of time."

"Thanks, Rafael."

Ajay hung up the phone and ripped off his clothes in a fury. With each passing minute, his anger continued to bubble.

"There is only one reason why she told me what her plans are, and that's because she wants to get a reaction out of me. Well, Raj, you're about to see my reaction. If you want to fuck, then I'm your man," he said under his breath. "I am the only person you're going to mess around with from here on out, dammit."

Fifteen minutes later, he was on his way to the Ice Palace.

I hope you're ready for me, he thought to himself as anticipation burned through his veins. Raj had underestimated him for the last time.

Chapter Ten

Rajneet

RAJ HAD BEEN out of sorts all week long. Between her brother showing up, preparing her company for sale, and thinking about the way things had ended with Ajay, she couldn't focus.

No matter what Ajay thought, she was not a coward. His words still rang in her ears as she replayed their argument in her head for the millionth time. She preferred noncommittal relationships so she could focus on her business. It had been her mistake to open up, to share more than she'd intended to. He'd caught her at a weak moment.

And just as she was ready to relax at the Ice Palace,

he'd texted her again, reminding her that he was still a force she had to eventually deal with.

Raj crossed her legs and the center slit of her long black dress parted to the tops of her thighs. Her foot tapped in the air to the music, and the heel of her strappy YSL stiletto sparkled, shooting small rays of light at every beat. The muted music vibrated through the red leather sectional underneath her, and the strobe lights on the other side of the two-way mirror behind the sofa brightened the Fire Lounge.

It was a small space, but it had a canapés cart, a fully stocked bar, and a private bathroom in the back with necessities discreetly tucked in drawers. She'd reserved the room for the entire night, a privilege only available to her as a private investor in the Ice Palace nightclub.

"Whiskey neat, Raj?" Harrison asked, holding up a bottle.

"Yes, darling."

She watched her chosen lover for the night as he moved across the room. He had a lean frame, an angular jaw, and a thick cock when fully erect. She'd slept with him before and knew that he made sure she came before he claimed his own orgasm. More importantly, he did what he was told. With him, Raj never had to worry about who controlled the situation.

"I didn't think you'd call this weekend," he said as he passed her the whiskey.

"Oh? Why is that?"

"You've been busy. Rumor has it that you're considering an offer from Gen One to run the foundation."

Raj took a sip of her drink and rested her arms along the back of the sofa. "Oh, that little rumor is getting around if a lawyer up in Connecticut has heard it."

Harrison grinned at her, winked, then backtracked to the canapés. "I usually hear things when people with a lot of money are making big moves. So? Any truth to it?"

Raj shook her hair back, thrusting her barely covered breasts out for him. She was enjoying the whiskey and the way her body felt in her favorite dress. Images of Ajay came to mind along with the feel of his kiss and the strength of his hold. She grew damp with the memory and shifted in her seat.

Was she making the right decision? Cutting him off and choosing another lover before they'd had an opportunity to explore what was between them?

Yes. The answer had to be yes. This was the only way.

She looked down at the long lines of her body, her curves that had filled out over the last few years, and smiled at the scene she must have made. Arms spread, legs naked, completely open to being taken. Damn that Punjabi asshole for making her so hot.

"Harrison, I think it's time to stop the chitchat."

He shot her a look of surprise but put down his drink and the plate he'd begun to pile up with the free food. "Your wish is my command."

He'd taken two steps toward her when the sound

of a fist hitting the steel entrance door echoed over the music.

"Who in the world could that be?" Harrison asked. "Did you invite someone else to play with us tonight?"

She shook her head. "No one knows I'm here, except . . . hell."

Her heart pounded and her pulse raced at the thought of seeing him again. Did he know she was with another man? Would he start a scene? She wouldn't put it past him. She had taunted him when she responded to his text, and she should've known he would react.

Oh well, Raj thought. She'd just have to switch gears. To be honest, Ajay was the man she wanted anyway. Harrison was only a willing substitute. Her arousal ramped up.

She stayed in her position, whiskey in hand, arms outstretched, and legs bare. Every part of her was both relaxed and humming with anticipation.

"Get that for me, will you?"

Harrison shrugged and answered the door.

Raj couldn't see who he was speaking to or make out their words. But she could read Harrison's expression. He balked and then, without a backward glance, left the room.

Ajay stepped through the opening.

"How did you get through my security?" she asked as he locked them inside.

"I told them to move, otherwise everyone would

know who I was there to see. Even your security knows that you like your discretion."

"Mmm-hmm." She swirled her whiskey, then took a sip, hoping that her nerves weren't apparent. "I didn't tell you where I was so you could interrupt my fun, Ajay. But since you're here, what can I do for you?"

He shrugged out of his jacket, tossed it aside, and unbuttoned the cuffs of his sleeves. "I think the question is, what can I do for you tonight?"

Her breath caught. "Is that why you came? Because you couldn't stand anyone else touching me, so you've come to offer yourself? You can't stop me from sleeping with whoever I want. I thought we covered that."

He swaggered toward her as he finished rolling up his sleeves. "No, I can't." He took the whiskey glass out of her hand and drank the rest of the contents. "But I can make you so fucking crazy that you only want to sleep with me."

Ajay tossed the glass to the side where it shattered against the wall.

Oh my.

"Spread your legs, Raj."

"I don't know if you're the type of man who can deliver on your promises," she said, her voice steady even as she began to ache for him, her body humming. "I'm not your vanilla sex kind of girl. This Punjabi kudi prefers a certain . . . style."

"Then style you shall have."

She laughed, shaking her thick, loose hair back before she scooted forward so her hips rested at the edge of the seat. She wanted him, had been driven to the Fire Lounge because she couldn't stop thinking about him. And honestly, she was grateful he was here. Raj just hoped she was doing the right thing for her heart if she broke her own rules and let him in.

"How about we make this a little more interesting?" she asked.

"What did you have in mind?"

"A simple wager." She watched him as she parted her knees. Her black thong was on full display, and her bare pussy lips peeked out the sides of the fabric. "If you can truly give me an experience that no one ever has before, we'll play this your way."

"This?" He raised an eyebrow.

"Us. You and me. If you want to be lovers, I'll try. If you want to be exclusive, I can promise you that. Or if you want to revert back to friendship, well, you know that's where my preference is. But I'm willing to give you more if, and only if, you can prove you're good enough for me," she said. "But if you're not, and baby, I've had truly exquisite sex before, then you accept friendship and we move on. Is that fair?"

He gracefully dropped to his knees between her legs. "Is there a time restriction?"

The question had her heart pounding. "I'll be generous. How does an hour sound?"

"You should've given me less than that. You're

making this too easy for me." He cupped the back of her neck. "Challenge accepted."

Ajay pulled her forward until their mouths crushed together. He held her hostage with tongue and teeth, and the shape of his lips as they moved over hers. She moaned against him as she tasted the amalgam of rich spiciness that she'd always equate with Ajay. His wide shoulders were hard and muscled under her hands as she pulled him closer.

She was going to lose.

Ajay's hands raced up the sides of her thighs, gripped her thong, and tore.

"I want to taste you," he said breathlessly when they came up for air.

"Then taste." She leaned back against the sofa and lifted one leg, then the other, until they rested on his shoulders.

He ran a finger down her slit and rubbed his beard against the inside of her thigh. "God, you're so fucking soft. Your cunt is soaking."

Without warning, he slapped the palm of his hand over her clit. She jumped, yelping as a shock of pleasure jolted through her body.

Before she had time to recover, Ajay was spreading her and licking the entire length of her pussy with his hot, firm tongue. Raj's eyes rolled back as she gasped under the onslaught of his mouth and the rough sensation of his facial hair. She couldn't think, couldn't breathe, as he continued to torment her. He pushed a finger inside her, then two, pumping slowly as he worshipped her clit. Her hips rolled forward in tandem with his movements. Her orgasm built at an alarming rate.

Then Raj's legs tensed, her belly quivered, and his pumping became quick and erratic. She felt the chaos inside of her reaching a precipice as her fingers buried in his hair. Ajay moaned against her, then sucked her clit hard.

She toppled over the edge and came in a rush. Her legs slipped off his shoulders as she lay spent, slumped against the sofa. When was the last time she'd come that hard thanks to oral sex? And who was this man who could find her clitoris with ease, when most of her lovers usually required direction in the dark?

"Well," she said, gasping for air.

He wiped his mouth against the back of his hand. "We're not done yet."

"I'll say," she said as she looked down at the sizable tent in his pants. She was still trembling from the force of her orgasm. She doubted she'd have another one within the hour, but she sure as hell was willing to try.

Ajay's eyes lifted and then focused on the window behind her. Raj turned to see a woman's back pressed against the glass. A man stood in front of her, his hands running up and down her hips.

"Do you like what you see?" Raj asked breathlessly, her body still humming with pleasure. She reached out and undid his belt. "That's the perk of this room. You can watch other people. This is the back of the club, so a lot of couples choose this spot right in front of the mirror. You'd be amazed at what I've watched. It's surprisingly easy to see, considering the lighting."

She unzipped him and pulled out one hell of an impressive erection. Whoever had started the rumor that Indian men lacked in size had obviously never slept with one, especially a Singh. Ajay continued to watch the couple kiss and dance against the window as Raj stroked him from root to tip. Her crimson fingernails traced over his balls, then she cupped him at the base before she took him into her mouth.

Ajay grunted, then sweetly, carefully, brushed her hair off her face. "Look at me when you suck my dick," he said gruffly.

The bluntness of his words was like an aphrodisiac to her. She moaned as she licked him, gently massaging his balls at the same time. She felt him shudder and reveled in the power she possessed.

She began touching herself, excited that she was giving him the same pleasure that he'd given her. To her surprise, she felt another orgasm burning inside of her. She coaxed it with quick fingers against her clit.

"Soni, the show is about to get interesting," he said with clipped, breathless words. "I'd hate for you to miss it." She pulled back and looked over her shoulder at the window. The girl was now facing the glass, her palms and forehead pressed against the two-way mirror. Her blond hair billowed around her shoulders, and her expression was that of lust. The man had one hand down the front of her miniscule skirt, a move only visible to the mirror. The rest of the crowd pulsed and danced around them without a clue as to what was happening.

"She looks beautiful," Raj said.

"You'll come when she does."

"Excuse me?"

Ajay pulled her to her feet, then turned her to face the mirror. The couple on the other side were moving their hips and one pink nipple popped out from the woman's top.

"Do you like what you see?" Raj asked. "Does her nakedness arouse you?"

"No." He pushed the straps of Raj's dress off her shoulders until the fabric pooled at her feet. She was all but naked except for her excellent shoes.

"This is what I like to see," Ajay said. "This is what arouses me. This is what has me jacking off every night, fisting my cock."

She hadn't wanted anyone as mindlessly as she wanted Ajay then. She was willing to beg for it, but she schooled her voice and reached up to pinch her nipples, moaning at their sensitivity. "I think it's time you fucked me, otherwise she'll come before I do."

"Yes," he said hoarsely in her ear. "You can see it on her face. He's going to take her, and she knows it."

Before Raj could make the next move, Ajay maneuvered her so that she was kneeling on the couch in front of the couple outside.

"Put your hands where hers are."

Raj had never done this before, even though she'd watched discreet sex from the Fire Lounge countless times. She did as she was told, though, until the only thing separating her from the blonde was the window.

The other man fumbled with his slacks.

Oh god.

Raj heard the tear of a foil packet behind her and then felt Ajay's hands on her hips. As the blonde jerked around, her legs wrapping over her man's waist, Ajay thrust into Raj, hot and hard. He filled her up until a scream bubbled from her throat. She tossed her hair back, arching against Ajay, urging him on.

"Yes," she gasped, crying out for more.

He reached around and slapped her clit again until she screamed. Then he set a punishing pace, fucking her until she could barely hold on. The couple outside jerked together then collapsed against the mirror, their bodies shuddering and heaving in time with the music.

"Don't stop," Raj chanted. "Don't you dare."

Ajay fucked her faster, taking her voice, and her pleasure, until she had nothing left to give him, nothing she could afford. Shock and blinding ecstasy consumed her when Ajay gripped her hair, holding it tight as the orgasm rushed through her body.

Her legs quivered, and she would've collapsed if Ajay hadn't held her up, an arm banded around her waist.

With one, then two last thrusts, he claimed his own orgasm.

They lay on the couch like shipwreck survivors, gasping for air, waiting minutes, ages, for their bodies and minds to catch up with their racing hearts.

Ajay was the first to move. He pressed a kiss to the curve of her neck, then untangled himself from her and walked to the bathroom. Raj heard the trashcan close and the sound of running water over the music.

She raised an eyebrow as Ajay returned with a towelette. "Is that for me?" she said, her voice husky from her screams.

"Yes." Raj spread her legs again, letting him run the cool towelette over her, cleaning her. She closed her eyes, enjoying the feel of his touch and regretting how quickly he finished.

Ajay tossed the towelette aside, then picked up her dress, holding it out for her. "This was remarkably easy to take off you."

"That's the point," she said. "I won't lie and admit that I'm glad it was you who removed it." She stood, wobbling on her heels for a moment before her legs could support her.

"It goes over the head."

He obliged and helped her tug it into place. Then, with a twinkle of wickedness in his eyes, he massaged her breasts underneath the thin covering. "I didn't focus on these nearly enough. I have time left, don't I?"

"I think I'm spent," Raj said. She tilted her chin up, lips pursed, until he grinned and pressed a brief kiss to her mouth. She needed the kiss, the moment of affection from him—something she'd never needed from any of her other lovers. It was jarring, but she'd evaluate her feelings later.

"Does this mean I win?" he asked.

"Don't be so smug about it."

"I think I deserve a moment of smugness." He wrapped his arms around her waist and cuddled her closer. Raj felt warm and frighteningly touched by the gesture.

"Now that you've won, what are your plans?"

"Well . . ." He motioned toward the glass where the couple had once been. "Coming back here with you would be nice. But for now, I'm thinking we should explore food together."

"Food."

"Yes. I'd like to take you on a date. For Indian food."

"Tonight?"

Ajay shook his head. "Tomorrow is soon enough."

She felt a conflicting mix of relief and disappointment. On the one hand, she wouldn't have minded taking him into her bed, but on the other, she realized that her hormones were probably driving that emotion. She'd never had a man in her bed before. She preferred to keep them out of her personal space. She reached up and stroked his beard.

"Fine. Tomorrow. An Indian food date. It better be worth it, Ajay."

He grinned, pulling her close. "Soni, basa tusi itaraza karo."

Just you wait.

Chapter Eleven

Ajay

It had cost Ajay to be a gentleman, but he took Raj home, kissed her until his head spun, and returned to his penthouse alone. He hadn't known Raj that long, but he could already tell that she was a cautious woman who would appreciate some time to process what'd happened between them. If he'd spent the night, there was a very good chance that she'd push him away again.

Fortunately, it was less than twenty-four hours before he headed toward her brownstone again. He cruised uptown in his Bugatti with the early-fall breeze filtering through his window and twilight sparkling over the city. He rarely drove, since he preferred working during his commute, but he hoped Raj would enjoy the privacy.

He turned up the house music on his radio as he reminisced on the way Raj had looked when he saw her at the Ice Palace. She was magnificent. From the moment he walked into the Fire Lounge, he'd known that any doubt in his mind about her didn't stand a chance against how much he wanted her. She'd taken his breath away as she sat framed in the lights pulsing through the window, with her bare legs crossed, her arms spread out on the back of the sofa. He was infuriated by the thought of someone else touching her, but his only option was to make his case and convince her that he was the only man for her.

For now, anyway.

Ajay was lucky that there was a hydrant right in front of her brownstone entrance. After pulling into the small opening, he rounded the car just as she exited her building.

He'd imagined she'd wear something elegant and chic like her office attire, but what emerged was something so much better.

Her feet were covered in open-toed ankle boots, and her legs were encased in slim-fit jeans. Her gorgeous head of thick hair was tied up in a messy topknot, which went with the strappy floral blouse and the tiny black rectangular purse that hung low on her hip. She stood at the top of her stairs, smiling down at him. The smooth, sultry expression had his pulse jumping.

"Do I pass muster for first-date attire?"

"Come down here and ask me," he said.

She took her time, leisurely descending her short staircase. Her feet grazed the sidewalk before he swooped her up in a kiss.

There she is, he thought as he sank into the feel of her. When her hands slid over his shoulders and into his hair, he knew that if he didn't stop now, they'd end up in her house for the rest of the night.

Ajay leaned back and wiped a thumb over his bottom lip. "I look forward to more of that later."

"Maybe I do, too," she said smoothly, but he could tell by the rise and fall of her chest that she'd been as affected as he had. Good.

"Come on. We're going to get stuck in traffic as it is, and we don't want to miss some truly excellent chole."

"Is that the type of Indian food we're eating? Punjabi food?" she asked as she slipped into the passenger seat of his low-slung car. She ran a hand over the plush interior. "This is a damn nice vehicle for a casual date where we're both going to eat with our hands."

Ajay looked down at his clothes and grinned. "I would've swept you away to the Hamptons in this thing if I could. The weather is always gorgeous this time of year. But we'd have to clear our schedules and our EAs would probably have killed us."

She was still laughing as he pulled away from the curb and drove toward RFK Bridge. "They'd make it happen, but then do something truly heinous to get back at us later, like reschedule all our canceled calls for six in the morning."

"Rafael has definitely done that to me before," Ajay said. "He hates when I cancel."

They talked about business for a few minutes as Ajay maneuvered through Saturday-evening traffic. He reached out and took her hand once he made it to FDR Drive.

She jolted as if he'd electrocuted her.

"What?" he asked. "What's wrong?"

"I think you should probably tell me your terms," she said, glancing down at their joined hands.

"I'm not following."

"Ajay, although I've been married, any intimate relationship I've had with a man has been physical and discreet."

"Discrete? Is that what you want from me, too?"

She let out a breath. "I . . . I don't know. I'm still not divorced, and I'm looking to start a position with Gen One. Maybe. While you're at the verge of taking over as CEO."

"And it gets complicated. Okay, I understand what you're saying. We can remain discrete for as long as our current circumstances exist. As for us, I expect you to come to me for whatever you need."

"Whatever?" she said with amusement in her voice.

"Yes. And for as long as we're doing this, I expect your honesty. I'll give you the same."

She let out a deep breath. "You need to qualify."

"I need to qualify honesty?"

Raj nodded. "To be frank, I can be honest with what I tell you, but that doesn't mean I share all my secrets."

"I want your secrets," he said. He wanted everything. He'd spent half the night and most of his Saturday thinking about what drew him to her. Her confidence, her intelligence, the chemistry were all a given. But maybe her complexity was part of it, too. Ajay knew that he was quickly becoming addicted to uncovering her pockets of sweetness.

"That may be a deal breaker," she replied.

"I'm willing to compromise," he said, squeezing her hand. "No lying by omission. Just admit whether or not you're ready to share information and we'll review on a case-by-case basis."

"Deal," she said. "Monogamous?"

"Without question."

"Sleeping arrangements?" she continued. "I work late or work from home, and since our last security breach—"

Ajay snorted.

"I can't get a lot done if you're present."

"That's fair," Ajay said. A knot in his chest tightened. He wanted to deny her this one thing because it meant that she didn't trust him, but he didn't blame her. Her husband and friend, someone she'd known for years, had taken advantage of her. It would take time before she could see that he wasn't like Robert. Ajay shot her an easy grin. "Sometimes I'm in New Jersey, so my schedule is also a bit rigid. Tonight?"

"Maybe," she said. "Kaka, my housekeeper, comes back from India early in the morning. I want to be there to welcome him home."

Kaka. Her family. He had to admire her loyalty to the people she prioritized in her life. Hopefully he'd be added to that list.

They shifted gears to talk about work, their shared charity passions, and Raj's interest in Gen One. They were neck deep in market discussions by the time Ajay pulled into a small private parking lot in Astoria. He slipped the lot owner a hundred-dollar bill, then linked his fingers with Raj's as they strolled toward the restaurant.

"You know, Hem took Mina to a place down here for their first date."

Raj hummed. "Mina told me. Dosa Hut. But you said we're eating chole, not dosas."

"I did. Do you like chole?"

"Yes, but I have a Punjabi housekeeper who makes the best. This is going to have to be pretty spectacular."

He slowed in front of a small shop with counter service. "This will not disappoint. I came out to Queens almost every weekend when I was in college just to eat with my friends."

They wove through tables packed with patrons until they reached the counter that had one old register, packets of supari—a mix of fennel seeds and sugar crystals— and a large tip jar.

"We'll take two orders of bature chole, Uncle," Ajay said in Punjabi. He squeezed Raj's hand. "Do you want a lassi or cha?"

"Garam cha."

After paying, they took their order number in the form of a plastic card and sat near the front window against the wall. Ajay stretched his long legs out so that his knees bracketed hers before he leaned across the table.

"What are you thinking?" he asked.

"This place smells like my mom's kitchen—" Her face went blank and Ajay could see her putting her mask back on. Raj's smooth, flawless composure reflected back at him. "We should be making use of the time. What do you want to know about RKH?"

"Don't do that, Rajneet."

"Don't do what, darling?"

Ajay leaned back and watched her for a moment. She looked so much younger like this. Her lips were bare, and she was lacking the exquisite jewelry that usually winked at her earlobes and from her neck. He wanted more, though. More vulnerability, more honesty, and more of the real Raj. "My family's company is personal. It was built by people with passion." He switched to Punjabi. "Your polish is sexy, but I need to see beneath the veneer. I want your passion."

The struggle was visible on her face. She didn't want to show herself, but she was a smart woman. She could read him, his resolve, and knew this was important.

"My mother . . ." she continued slowly ". . . used to make the best bature chole ever. It was the one thing that the staff wasn't allowed to help her with. She'd create this yeasted dough that would puff up into a dome, and then pinch off perfectly sized pieces, roll them out flat, and then drop them into this sizzling oil. The minute I heard that sound, it didn't matter where I was in the farmhouse, I'd come running."

Farmhouse, Ajay thought. Farmhouses in Punjab were often palatial. It made sense that her family, with its drug trafficking roots and poppy fields, had a lot of money.

He remembered what he'd asked Sri to do the previous night. If he was going to get into a relationship with this woman, he needed to trust her. It might be in his best interests to pull the project from Sri for now. He'd have to remember to take care of that when he got home.

"You miss your mom's cooking," he said.

"I do. Mom's chole were made from a generations-old recipe," she continued. "To make the chickpeas, she'd be cooking them for two days. Washing, rinsing, draining, and then stewing them in her special sauce. To this day, I don't know what masalas she used. Not that it would do me much good. Who knows if she still cooks, with her health . . ."

Ajay squeezed her hand. "Whether she cooks or not, it doesn't change the fact that you still didn't get the skill from her, right?"

Her lips twitched. "I guess so."

"Then I guess I'll have to do all the cooking. Except chole. Maybe we'll leave that to true experts. Honestly, this place might not make chole as memorable as your mother's, but I bet they're pretty close."

"Mmm-hmm."

She'd crossed her arms and leaned on the table. A wistful expression, one of memories reflected in her eyes.

"How long has it been?" he asked.

"Twelve years last month. I came here when I was eighteen."

Ajay slid his hand across the scarred vinyl-top table, palm up. She looked down at it and then back up at his face, amused. Once her fingers were locked in his hold, he asked the question that had been plaguing him since the gala.

"Did you ever have feelings for Robert?"

She shook her head. "We had a mutually beneficial arrangement. I hated being a cliché, a stereotype of an Indian woman who married for a green card. But I had my reasons, and I was going to make it with or without Robert. He just ensured that my family wouldn't interfere."

"I'm not one to judge," Ajay said. "People think that getting a green card is as easy as getting a driver's license. So many of our international employees who transfer end up having to wait fifteen years or more for their green cards."

"It doesn't stop people from making crass assumptions," Raj said. "That's why Robert and I decided to live together, to pretend we were happily married, while remaining discreet about the nature of our relationship."

"Any rumors now that you're getting divorced?"

"I've heard a few. Most are off base, and the rest are harmless. As long as they don't affect my reputation and my company, I couldn't care less about rumors."

Two cups of steaming chai were placed in front of them. Ajay watched the unfiltered delight brighten Raj's expression before she bracketed her hands around the mug. She leaned down to smell it, eyes closed, lips slightly parted. The joy on her face made his heart clench.

"Tell me about RKH. When and how did you come up with the idea?"

Raj shrugged one delicate shoulder. "A mix of listening to my father complain about security breaches and a class project in my senior year. After I married Robert, his grandmother, the only woman who liked me, became a mentor. She worked for decades in the Douglass family company, and she helped me with contacts, connections, and developing a little bit of polish that I needed, before she passed away a few years ago."

"Why do you think you got along so well?"

Raj shrugged. "She was an immigrant, too. Granted, Greece isn't exactly the same as India, but similar enough that we both enjoyed each other's company at all mandatory family get-togethers. She was always laughing and had a horde of pets. She is the reason I started working with the shelters in Manhattan. When she died, most of her money went to those shelters, and her last remaining pet, a sweet old hound, was taken in by one of her nephews."

"But you wanted her hound?"

"Of course," she said, a wistful expression on her face. "But Robert has an allergy. Thankfully, that's no longer a barrier."

Before he could second-guess himself, he gripped both cups and slid them to the side.

"What are you—"

He stood, scraping his chair back with a loud, defining screech, leaned over the table, and pressed his mouth against hers. He could feel her surprise and her shock, and used her lowered guard ruthlessly to his advantage by slipping his tongue between her parted lips.

She tasted like sin and redemption, both twining through his body, tightening in his gut, and fogging his brain. He took the kiss deeper, pulling a small sound of pleasure from her throat.

Her hands came up and her fingers stroked his cheeks through his beard. He felt her respond now, her lips softening, sipping from his mouth as if she was also hooked on the same drug he'd discovered in her. Her teeth nipped at his bottom lip, and he groaned in pleasure.

Raj was a treasure, and he'd barely opened the box to discover all of her. Even as his fingers dove into her tidy hair, urging her mouth closer, the sound of someone clearing their throat cut through his lust-fogged brain.

He slowly pulled back, registering the confusion in Raj's eyes, before he sat in his chair and turned to the older Punjabi uncle. The uncle looked more irritated at them than embarrassed as he held a tray overflowing with food in his hands, tapping one foot impatiently.

"Sorry," Ajay said, as if he was being scolded like a child.

Smooth, Singh. Your conditioning to apologize is surely going to win over the lady now.

Raj's mask was fully in place as she adjusted her hair in that calm, classy way that she had, and looked anywhere but at Ajay and the man who placed their food in front of them.

"So," Ajay said when they were alone again. "That's becoming a habit that I'm enjoying. I hope you don't mind."

Raj adjusted her puffed bature in front of her and leaned down to smell the dark brown chole topped with shredded ginger and parsley.

"You're a brave soul if you want to kiss me again after this much onion and garlic, Singh."

The corner of her perfect mouth curved, and he couldn't help but smile in response. "You're worth the sacrifice."

Chapter Twelve

Rajneet

MONDAY

AJAY: We never talked about business.

RAJ: That's because you were either feeding me or screwing me.

AJAY: You can't blame me for that. You're irresistible.

AJAY: Tomorrow night?

RAJ: Late meeting. Wednesday is good.

AJAY: Have a conflict. I'm dealing with our Europe properties. It'll go on forever. Thursday after eight?

RAJ: I'll get back to you.

TUESDAY

RAJ: Thursday is a no-go.

AJAY: I can clear my schedule for Friday?

RAJ: No, I have an off-site.

AJAY: This weekend?

RAJ: . . . Maybe.

AJAY: What? What is it?

RAJ: I'm supposed to go look at a puppy on Saturday.

AJAY: At the shelter you volunteer at? Is this the puppy that the woman who you work with called about?

RAJ: Yup. Apparently said puppy has had shots, has been spayed, and is ready for visitors.

AJAY: Then let's go see it. Tell me what time you want to go, and I'll clear my schedule.

RAJ: You want to come with me?

AJAY: Yes.

IF SOMEONE HAD told Raj three months ago that she was going to meet Ajay Singh, go toe-to-toe with him after her husband went to work with Bharat, Inc.'s biggest competitor, then start an affair with the man, she would've laughed. But now, after their first time in the Fire Lounge, one date, and a few hours in her bed, she was a believer.

Ajay clasped her hand in his as they walked toward the shelter. The feeling was new, but not wholly unexpected. Ajay liked holding her and touching her in public despite their promise to remain discrete.

She was coming to enjoy the feeling.

"Were you ever allowed to have a dog growing up?" Raj asked.

"Nope," Ajay replied. "My parents were very old school. They believed that dogs belong outside. They shouldn't be trapped. Even though, I bet if they had a dog now, it would be treated like royalty."

"We had dogs on the farm, but they were never allowed inside," she said as she led Ajay to the front of the Midtown dog shelter. "If it wasn't for Robert's grandmother, I wouldn't have known how great dogs are as companions instead of just farm animals."

"Are you excited?" he asked, a tinge of amusement in his voice.

She couldn't help but grin up at him. "More than ever."

Raj pulled open the double doors of reinforced steel and checked in at the front desk before entering the adoption room where dog pens lined the walls. The puppy room was to the left and the cats were on the other side of the floor. The familiar smells of animals and cleaning agents filled her nostrils.

The bigger dogs began barking from their pens. Some of them circled in front of the doors, and others stood on their hind legs to get her attention.

"We're supposed to wait here for Jill," she said.

"That's the woman who runs the shelter?"

"That she is." Raj pulled away from Ajay's side and rushed toward the larger dogs, her heart hurting as it did every time she saw them. "I know, babies. I wish I could take you all but you're way too big for me."

"You would adopt them if you could, wouldn't you?" Ajay asked.

Raj glanced at him over her shoulder as she crouched down in front of a senior poodle mix. "Of course."

She went down the row and petted each dog, aware that Ajay followed close behind, standing next to her sometimes as if he was ready to step between her and the pen. She knew very well that he wanted to make sure she didn't get bitten but was trying to hide his intentions by pretending to be supportive instead. Men were so easy to read sometimes.

"Gen One is your next move," he said, breaking their silence. "But what about opening up your own foundation?"

Raj let Ajay help her get to her feet. "What do you mean?"

"I mean, Gen One has a very narrow focus. With your own foundation, you could do things like this." He motioned to the rows of shelter animals waiting for new homes. "Soni, you love being here," he said in Punjabi. "Your face is glowing. Wouldn't you want to help out just as much with the animal shelters you're involved in?"

"Sure, but I can still do that and also work for Gen One."

"But not with as much attention and focus as you'd be able to on your own, right?"

"That's true." She circled until they stood in front of the door they'd entered from. "What brought this on?"

Ajay tucked his hands into his jeans pockets. "I see you like this, and then I think about how you were at the Gen One gala. I can't help but think this is where you belong, not at a conservative organization."

She felt her heart clutch. He saw so much. Or maybe she let him see a part of her that she should be more careful with. It was too fast, too soon for her to be feeling so attached to Ajay Singh. She turned her back on him and approached one of the shepherds on the far wall who was dancing on her hind legs, begging for attention.

"Gen One is my gateway into the work that I like to do."

"It's a worthy cause, no argument. But are you sure it's a gateway or a step farther from your goal? Even if you work for another company, heading up a large private foundation, you could do this kind of work. Bharat, for example, has a foundation that my mother directs. She recommends causes and we just supply the money."

Raj gave him a rueful smile. "Well, I'm not going to do any philanthropic work if I can't sell my company. You still haven't given me a decision."

"Fine," he said, holding his hands up in surrender. "I know avoidance when I hear it. I'll let it go."

"Thank you."

"As for buying you out, I still haven't connected with my brothers and father. It'll be a few more days before I can get you an answer."

"Good. My employees are on edge because the office gossip mill is buzzing with the rumor that I'm selling. Then there is Kia, who isn't helping. She's already acting like the outgoing CEO of the foundation."

Before Ajay could respond, a woman wearing a lanyard and a utility belt, and holding dog leashes, stepped out of the puppy room. Her eyes lit up when she saw Raj.

"Why, hello there, stranger!" she said with her arms stretched wide.

Raj wrapped her arms around Jill for a fierce hug. Jill was one of the few women she really enjoying being around. She had dedicated her life to working in animal shelters across New York and was a genuinely warm and caring human. In Raj's eyes, that classified Jill as a modern-day saint.

"I got your message about coming after the fifteenth," Raj said. "I'm here and I brought my . . . friend. This is Ajay Singh."

Ajay held out a hand for Jill to shake. His gaze turned razor sharp. "It's boyfriend, but the word is still hard for Raj to say since she's in the process of finalizing her divorce. She's getting used to it."

"What happened to discrete?" Raj said in Punjabi.

Ajay shrugged, doing a poor job at hiding his smile.

"Oh god, Raj," Jill said, her hand covering her mouth. "I figured when your assistant called me and said that you were seriously interested in coming in to see the dog I thought was for you, it was because your husband was going to take allergy shots or something, not because you're getting a divorce."

"It's fine," Raj replied. She shot Ajay a dirty look. "It was time. And I'm glad, honestly, that it worked out the way it did, because you seemed pretty confident this puppy was for me."

Jill nodded, and motioned for them to come with her. "I know that we've always been on the lookout, uh, former husband's allergies aside, but nothing really fit in terms of what you were looking for despite the thousands of dogs that have come through since you started working with us. I can see now that it wasn't meant to be. The timing wasn't right. The stars may have aligned finally."

"What makes you think so?" Raj said. Her heart began pounding. She'd wanted this for so long that she'd hate it if Jill was wrong about this dog.

"I've been doing this for a while," Jill said. "I have instincts."

"Then I trust them completely."

Ajay chuckled behind her.

"What?" she asked before entering the puppy room. "What's so funny?"

He grinned at her, his broad shoulders shrugging. "I just wonder what your employees and colleagues would say if they saw you like this."

"They'd think I'm about to get a puppy," she responded.

"No, they'd think you're soft. And sweet."

Raj glared at him in response before she followed Jill through a door that had a stop sign and the words *Close doors behind you at all times* printed on it. They entered the narrow room with a row of small pens lining each wall. Blankets covered the tops of the pens, and the sounds of mewing and high-pitched barks echoed around them.

"We got a few transfers from a kill shelter down south," Jill said softly. "I saw Khunda's picture and didn't even wait to call you."

"Khunda?" Raj said, stunned. "How do you spell it?"

Jill showed Raj the card with the spelling.

Raj looked up at Ajay. "This is a Punjabi word, except it wouldn't be pronounced khun-dah, but khund. It means sugar. Who named her? Usually the names are something ridiculous like Sunny or Tuxedo."

"No idea, but I think if her name is a word in your language, a sweet one at that, it's another sign." Jill opened the last pen on the bottom right. She reached inside and pulled out the tiniest Short-hair Chihuahua that Raj had ever seen. The puppy had a long snout, unlike the tiny pointed nose she'd seen on most Chihuahuas. Her coat was pure white except for the large tan ears that were almost the size of her head. Her entire body fit on the palms of Jill's hands.

"Khunda, meet Raj," Jill said. "Raj, meet Khunda. She's about thirteen weeks."

The puppy was shaking hard in fear. Her tail was

tucked tightly between her legs, even though Jill was cradling her as gently as she could. "She's very submissive and needs a lot of love and affection. You can give that to her."

Raj put out a hand for Khunda to smell, and when a tiny pink tongue peeked out to lick at her finger, she gently took the puppy in her hands. The puppy barely weighed three pounds, Raj thought, as she tucked the quivering bundle into the cradle of her arms.

Khunda's shaking slowed, and she buried her little tiny head into the crook of Raj's elbow. She felt the tiny body expand with each breath, and then gently relax with release.

In that one instant, she knew that this puppy was hers. Raj could feel the tears well in her eyes. "I finally found you," she whispered. "You need me, and I need you."

"Oh, baby," Ajay said softly behind her. "She's perfect."

He looked at Raj with such intensity that she had to turn away. She didn't know what he saw in her at that moment, but she didn't really care, either. She was holding her new family member. Khunda was for her.

Raj stroked one tiny ear and cleared her throat. "Jill, what do I need to do to bring her home?"

Jill clasped her hands in front of her chest and bounced on her toes. "Well, we have to do a final checkup. Then there is an interview, application, and reference check. However, since you're a long-time donor, we can fast-track that for you. You may be able to have her as early as next week."

It seemed way too long to leave her dog at the shelter, but she knew that the process had to be followed. "I just want to cuddle a little longer," she whispered. "And then we'll get started."

It took ten more minutes before she was able to give Khunda back to Jill. The puppy had fallen asleep in her arms, and Raj didn't want to let her go. After one last, longing look at the puppy in her pen, she went into Jill's office with Ajay and filled out the required paperwork. Another fifteen minutes later, they were standing outside on the sidewalk.

"Congratulations," Ajay said, dropping a soft kiss on her upturned mouth. "You are going to be a dog mom. After seeing you in there, Raj . . . I know Khunda is right for you."

"Thanks for coming with me," Raj said. She couldn't have been more surprised at how much it meant to her that Ajay was there to share her first moments with Khunda.

"I wouldn't have had it any other way," Ajay said, stroking a finger down her cheek. "It was . . . enlightening. Want to go to lunch to celebrate?"

Raj felt her phone buzz in her purse and pulled it from her crossbody.

The name *Roshan* flashed on the screen.

"I need to take this," she said. "One second." She moved farther down the sidewalk before she answered.

"Roshan."

"Raj. It's good to hear your voice."

"You, too, traitor," she said with humor. She looked up at Ajay who was busy checking his own phone a few feet away.

Would he know the name of Raj's former employee that worked on his securities team? More importantly, did Ajay realize the magnitude of skill he now possessed. Roshan had been one of her top people. He'd also been the first to jump at the offer for more money. "Are you looking for another offer?"

Instead of taking the bait and teasing her back like the old friends they used to be, Roshan's tone cut through her expectations of small talk.

"I found something at Bharat. I was going to call Sri first, but Raj, I don't trust him."

Alarm bells flashed in her mind. "Why is that?"

"He's not very . . . transparent with the information he finds. I'll have to tell him eventually, but I figured that you might have some insight."

Raj stepped out of the way of moving pedestrians and leaned against the side of a building. "Tell me," she said.

"Sahar Ali Khan wasn't the mole."

"Wait, what?"

Roshan let out a deep breath that rushed through the phone like a wind tunnel. "Bharat had us continue to look into Sahar, her whereabouts, any information that may have been leaked, even after she was terminated from the company."

"She's ghosted."

"Completely," Roshan confirmed. "She's not working at WTA like we expected. Her condo went up for sale days after her termination and sold pretty fast. Real estate is hard to find in the Valley, so it makes sense. All of her things were put into a storage container, and her mail was forwarded to her mother's house in Peoria, Illinois."

"Roshan, that doesn't mean she wasn't responsible."

"No, and Sri knows that, so we kept looking. This morning, something came up while I was putting in a few extra hours. Are you ready for it?"

Raj glanced over at Ajay. "Yes."

"The so-called relative at WTA? He doesn't exist. Let's just say that if we didn't have Bharat's resources, I would've never found out that the employee ID for this relative is a fake. You, your team, everyone was duped."

"Oh no," Raj said, pinching the bridge of her nose.

"That's not all. The relocation software that WTA wants is all housed in a depository. Only Sahar and one other person had access to all of the depository. We thought Sahar was downloading the source code for the software. I went back and checked the history, and her key was used to access the depository and download all the source code twenty-four hours *after* she was walked off the premises. Raj, she couldn't have gotten back into the depository if she tried. It had to be someone else."

"Shit."

Roshan laughed. "I don't think I've ever heard someone say 'shit' with so much class before."

"It's a gift. Roshan, someone else got into Bharat's servers. I'm pissed that my consultants fell for WTA's trap, but I'll deal with that later. Right now, we have to tell the Singhs."

"I'll call Sri and ask for a meeting."

"Let me talk to Ajay first," Raj said. "I'm the one who fed them information through Mina, and I had you looking under my direction. I should be the one to come clean with the news first. I'm responsible."

"Responsible for what?"

Ajay's voice had Raj turning around to see him standing next to her. "Raj?"

"Hold on," she responded. "Roshan? Stay available. I'm going to see if I can address this with all the Singhs today."

"Roger that. Text me when it's time to loop in Sri."

"Will do. And thanks. For trusting me and calling first."

"Hey, it's the least I could do. You hired me when no one else would."

She hung up and looked over at Ajay. If it had been any other man, she would've told him to mind his own business. But this was Ajay, and his company, his family, were everything to him. More importantly, she couldn't hide the truth from him. She'd committed to honesty when they started . . . whatever it was that was growing between them.

"Ajay, that was Roshan Patel."

The glint in his eyes sharpened. "New employee.

Reports to Sri. Came from RKH Collective but now works for me. Why is he calling you?"

"A sense of loyalty. And he doesn't trust Sri."

"Dammit, Raj, you should've called me over before he even opened his mouth. It's a violation of his privacy contract to share any information with you and grounds for termination."

"Good," she said, crossing her arms over her chest, facing his growing anger like an Olympian. "Fire him and I'll take him back. Ajay, you need to realize that two people now are telling you that your head of security, Sri, is useless. One of those people is your *girlfriend* who owns a security company."

Ajay's lips thinned. "He's my responsibility, not yours. You've made your feelings clear."

Ajay had so much to learn, starting with when to let go of the deadweight. His father must've protected Sri or something for Ajay to act this way.

"Look, are you going to listen to what I'm about to tell you or not?"

He nodded, his body tense with anger.

"The information my company found for Bharat, Inc. was a set up. We were fed false information. Sahar Ali Khan isn't your mole."

Ajay hesitated. "Roshan said this?"

"Yes. He and the rest of Sri's team know that Sahar hasn't been found yet, nor has she been in contact with WTA."

Ajay looked over his shoulder, and then back at

Raj. "My cousin told me. Apparently, Sahar disappeared."

"It gets worse. Roshan was reviewing Sahar's access history, and he found that her key was used to download data twenty-four hours after she was fired."

Ajay's face turned thunderous. "Motherfucker."

Raj nodded, almost expecting Ajay to throw a punch. She wanted to do some damage, herself.

"Roshan said that he found the information after doing a deep dive in data that we didn't have access to as consultants. Even then, I'm sorry that I had any part in this."

He paced, running his fingers through his hair and messing up his perfectly combed style. "My father and brothers have to know. We have to triage."

"My advice is to keep it from Sri. I mean it, Ajay."

He stared at her with that piercing intensity she first saw at the Gen One gala. "Fine," he finally said. "Let's go. We have about an hour's drive."

"Excuse me? Where are *we* going that's an hour away?"

Ajay ushered her forward with a firm hand on her back as he led her in the direction of his car. "We have to get to the Bharat compound in New Jersey. This news is better in person."

Raj dug in her heels until Ajay stopped and faced her. "I am *not* going to your family compound." A flutter of nerves and panic swarmed her belly. His parents lived there. Specifically, his mother.

"Roshan called you. You've been involved from the beginning. Also, I could use your insight. Come on."

"Ajay, wait," she said before he could start walking. She motioned to her cropped jeans, her sandals, and her halter blouse. "It's not Punjabi-parent appropriate."

She could see the distraction in his eyes and that he didn't even bother assessing her clothes. "What, do you think my parents care if you show up in jeans? They're not going to expect you to wear a damn Patiala salwar with a bindi and paranda in your hair."

She crossed her arms.

"Raj, tusi mainu marana ja rahe ho. Fine. We have to get going now, then. Your place is out of the way, and I have to let Hem and Zail know we're having a family meeting."

"I don't have to be at a family meeting," she said, the panic in her stomach growing stronger. "Just drop me off. Call me if you need me."

Ajay pressed a hard, firm kiss against her mouth. "I think we both are going to come to the same conclusion sooner or later."

"What conclusion?"

"I'm going to always need you. Now come on. We'll talk on the way."

Chapter Thirteen

Ajay

THIS WAS NOT how he'd planned on spending his weekend, Ajay thought.

He'd just had a life-altering experience, watching Raj hold a puppy, his heart clenching at the pure joy on her face. He'd been sucker punched with the realization that he was in grave danger of feeling more than attraction and lust for this woman.

This was uncharted territory and his red-alert button was beeping uncontrollably in his head every time he looked at her.

And dammit, instead of focusing on Raj, he had to work. For the first time in his adult life, he wasn't prioritizing his father's company. He wanted to be with a woman instead.

If that didn't make his red-alert button blare an even more deafening alarm, he didn't know what would. It was vital now for Ajay to get his feelings under control. There was too much at stake for him to fall in love with a woman just because she looked like a goddess holding a puppy.

He brooded as they went back to Raj's brownstone for her to change, and then back to his penthouse where he dropped off his car. His driver picked them up shortly after and started the trek to New Jersey.

"Are your brothers going to meet us at your place?" Raj asked.

"Hem, Mina, and Mina's father, Tushar, will be there."

Raj sat on the bench seat across from him, scrolling through her phone and nodding absently. "You got lucky with Tushar. He's been great to work with. He's already reviewed preliminary corporate documents."

"But not Sri."

She paused in her scrolling to glance at him. "No. Not Sri."

Ajay had known Sri was a liability for a while now. Not because of Raj, but because of the man's failure to provide current information. Why hadn't he shared the intel about Sahar during one of his daily status updates?

"Can I ask you something?" he said to Raj.

She raised a brow. "If you're done being pissy."

"What? I was not being pissy."

"Mmm-hmm," she said, watching her phone. "You know, I'm only coming along because I feel a sense of obligation. My company started this project for Bharat, and even though RKH was removed, I follow through. You could be a little more grateful about it. I don't have to be here."

"Okay, fine. I was being pissy." He didn't have to tell her that he was actually pissy about the way things were between them, and not about the phone call she'd received from one of *his* employees. "Sorry."

"Apology accepted," she said.

"Great. I need your input."

She sighed, which only made him grin.

"What is it?"

"Let's say Bharat is hemorrhaging because of this mole who is selling our trade secrets. Hypothetically."

"Right. Hypothetically."

"We addressed Sahar, thanks to your company, but now we learn that we haven't found the actual culprit. Other than fire Sri, what would you do?"

Raj put her phone aside. "You can't really get anything accomplished if you don't fire the people who are making bad calls. If you don't fire Sri, nothing else you do will be of any value. Why are you so adamant about keeping Sri in the first place?"

Ajay rolled his shoulders, hating to admit how much he'd been at fault from the beginning with his head of security. "Because Sri was my first big hire at Bharat.

When I started working as COO, I wanted a security department, so I personally handled the staffing. It was a big job to get that team set up. My father trusted me completely to do it right."

Raj shrugged. "So? You made a call that at the time you felt was right. People change. Circumstances change. You can't blame yourself if Sri didn't turn out the way you'd hoped. Look at me. I hired my husband, and I never thought he'd screw me."

Ajay grinned, took her hands, and dropped kisses in the centers of her palms. "What you're saying is that it's not me."

"Are any of your other businesses in trouble?"

Ajay thought about his family's vineyard. It was better than ever. They were now thinking about opening up a boutique B and B on the premises. The properties in Europe were thriving, and the other luxury investments were producing profits at exponential rates. He'd been personally responsible for making decisions about every project under the HAZ Industries umbrella.

"Bharat is the only one," he finally answered.

"Then no one is going to question your decision to fire Sri except you," she said, and leaned forward to give him a quick kiss.

"Yeah. Okay." He felt marginally better but couldn't decide if it was her words or the kiss that did it. He let her get back to her emails and knew that he had to use the rest of their travel time to work, too.

THEY'D ATTENDED TO business for the rest of the drive to New Jersey. Raj worked on her phone, Ajay on his laptop. She asked him his opinion on various investments, and he asked hers as he thought about his impending CEO nomination and the patent application that still needed to be addressed. As weird as it sounded, sharing so many things in common and talking to Raj in the same language was comforting. He felt closer to her in some ways, and it was another layer of her personality that he felt intimately connected to.

The car turned into the long driveway, and Raj shifted forward until she sat at the edge of her seat to look out the window.

"Impressive," she said.

Ajay grinned. "That's the point."

They pulled in front of the main house, and Ajay led Raj up the stairs to the front doors. After they kicked off their shoes on the entranceway mat, they walked barefoot down the tile corridor, past the arched opening, and into the expansive living room. His father staggered to his feet from his spot at the end of the long cream-colored sectional in front of a TV with international business news playing on low. His smile was bright, even though there was still worry in his eyes.

"Puttar? We weren't expecting you today. Is everything okay? You brought company."

Ajay rushed forward to grab his father's arm. "Why don't you sit down?"

"Nonsense. We have a guest!"

"Well, this handsome gentleman looks even more dashing since the last time I saw him," Raj said smoothly. She crossed the room as quickly as Ajay had and took his father's hands. "You can greet me just fine from this wonderful couch you've been sitting on. Just like your name suggests. A king on his throne."

Deepak laughed, his cheeks turning ruddy with pleasure.

"Hullo, beti," he said, referring to her as daughter.

"Why don't you get comfortable? We'll go dancing later when you're up for it." She gently urged him back onto the cushions even as she gave him a quick wink.

"It's so lovely to see you, despite what can't be the best of circumstances if my son has dragged you here on a Saturday for work."

Ajay met Raj's eyes and saw the understanding in them. He hadn't told his parents about their brand-new relationship. He and Raj might be in their thirties, but he was an Indian man. His mother would make his life hell if she knew that they were dating. Hopefully Raj understood Ajay's reasons for self-preservation with his family despite his eagerness to share the news with others.

The sound of the front door opening echoed down the hall. "Hello?" Hem called out.

"They must've been right behind us," Ajay said. "We're in the living room, guys!"

Hem and Mina walked in moments later.

"You know, I'm going to look forward to nailing this bastard. He keeps ruining my weekends," Hem said.

"Puttar?" Ajay's father gripped his wrist. "What is Hem talking about?"

"It's a bit of a story, Papa," Ajay said. "Raj, why don't you— What? What is it?"

All her charm seemed to slip. He wondered what he'd done, then he realized that she wasn't looking at him, but at someone over his shoulder.

His mother had entered the room, her hands clasped in front of her. "Hullo," she said.

Mina was closest to her, so she reached out and gave her a quick hug. "Aunty, I smell something delicious."

"Daal and rice," his mother said and pinched Mina's chin with affection. "More than enough for my future daughter-in-law. We'll have some soon."

Ajay could smell it now, too. The rich scent of spice wafted through the house, and his hunger warred with his focus on Raj and his concern for his father's legacy.

He looked back at the woman who'd complicated his thoughts for the last month. For someone so easy with people, she remained quiet. She'd instantly charmed his father on two occasions now, but seemed to hide behind a wall with his mother. Ajay remembered that her own relationship with her mother was strained, especially since the woman was dying. He wondered if that was affecting her mood.

He looped an arm around his mother's petite frame. "Rajneet Kaur Hothi. This is the first love of my life. Mumma, Raj is Mina's best friend, as well as CEO and founder of RKH Collective, a company that Bharat is looking to purchase."

"Ah, a smart woman," his mother said in English. She held out a hand to shake. "Welcome to my home, Rajneet."

Raj stepped forward to take the offered hand. "Sat Sri Akaal, Auntyji." She shook, and then pressed her hands together in front of her chest. "You have a beautiful home and beautiful children, too."

Ajay's mother's eyes instantly filled with tears. Raj's calm expression turned to panic, and she looked at him, as if begging for him to do something, to do anything.

"Don't worry about the crying," Mina said as she came to the rescue. "She did that to me, too, the first time I spoke to her in Punjabi. Well, sort of. That day was a bit different than today."

Ajay's mother nodded vigorously, then pressed a hand to her chest. "I have such lovely sardarnis in my house now. It feels like home."

"You've been a US citizen and calling New Jersey home for over thirty years," Ajay quipped.

"Chup kaar," she snapped at him. "We have *guests*." Her smile, as bright as a sunbeam, brightened the room. "Would you like some cha? Why don't you sit and have your discussion? I'll have the cooks bring it out for us with some biscuits. Then, when you're done, we'll have a late lunch."

"Thanks, Mumma," Ajay said.

He waited until she left before he motioned for all of them to sit.

"Why don't you talk about the phone call?" he said to Raj. "I think we should start there."

Raj nodded, and then with her hands folded in front of her, she recapped the conversation she'd had with Roshan.

Hem swore and Ajay's father sucked in a deep, audible breath.

"I thought the mole was Sahar," Ajay's father said.

"Apparently not," Ajay said. "She never went to work for WTA. Completely vanished. And, apparently, Sri knew about her disappearance and never told me."

"Did you tell Zail and Bhram?" Hem asked.

"Not yet. I know they need to be brought up to speed."

Ajay's father raised a hand to silence his sons. He shifted to look at Raj. "You didn't have to bring this information to us."

"If you're going to buy my company, you need to know that both I and my business are built on integrity. I also feel . . . responsible. My people discovered Sahar Ali Khan's background. But maybe we were wrong after all. I would like to lend my services in any way I can."

Ajay clasped her knee and squeezed. He realized everyone had seen the gesture and focused on his hand. He immediately pulled away.

As the conversation continued around them, he realized that his father's bright smile was focused on him, despite the chaos their company was in. Deepak Singh was going to tell his wife that Ajay had touched a girl, and it was going to be all over for him. How was he going to address his mother when things were still so new with Raj?

"I think you guys need a red herring," Mina said, her words breaking his focus from the woman at his side.

"A red herring? What do you mean?"

"A distraction. You need a distraction that will take WTA's attention away from the mole and onto something else. Luckily, you have one."

"Still not following, Mina," he said.

"Look, WTA wants information the mole can provide. Robert, Raj's ex, is now WTA's representative. It would be important for him to know the mole, assuming that Robert was the kind of guy to play dirty."

"He is," Raj said without a qualm.

Mina grinned. "If you announce that Bharat is buying your company, Raj, would Robert care?"

"Probably, since our divorce—" She glanced at Ajay's father. "Our divorce isn't final yet. My ex would be concerned about how it would make him look. He'd most definitely confront me about it."

"So not only would he be distracted from finding out Bharat's trade secrets, he'd also possibly let something slip when he speaks with you. Something that we can use."

"And it'll teach Robert a lesson, which I wholeheartedly support," Raj said, her voice hard. "We have to move quickly, though. Ajay, what do you think? Are you ready to make me an offer for my business?"

Isn't that the multimillion-dollar question? he thought. "It's a stretch that all of this will work. We can test your theory by spreading the rumor that we're buying your company."

Mina shook her head. "There might be other people involved. You're going to have to make it a real thing. That's what you want anyway, right?"

Ajay still needed answers about her financials, her company focus and strategy, and her client sales contracts.

Most importantly, he hadn't had an opportunity to talk to Zail. The news would affect him the most, both from a security perspective and from a personal one.

Zail was his baby brother. His feelings had always been the softest. Ajay needed to think about Zail over Raj at this point. Family came first.

"Puttar." His father's voice cut through his thoughts. "You can't make everyone happy," he said softly.

Ajay faced Raj again. The light filtered through the floor-to-ceiling cathedral windows and shone on the deep inky black of her hair. This move would effectively tie their histories together forever. It might still be a business decision for her, but his family's legacy was personal to him.

The corner of her mouth curved, and she raised that perfectly arched brow, the move a direct challenge. She was asking him what he was waiting for, and he wished he could answer her. He wanted approval, trust, and belief that he was meant to lead this company, lead the family business that he'd loved from childhood.

But sometimes that meant taking risks and not receiving the family validation he craved.

Ajay pulled out his phone and called Rafael.

"Rafael, I know it's a Sunday, but I need you to get my head of communications on the line for that meeting in an hour. Tell them to prep our standard release for an acquisition. We're about to purchase a company."

"Yes, sir. Is that all?"

Ajay pulled the phone away from his ear. "Raj, do you want our communications team to draft the release for your office, too?"

The withering look she shot him had Ajay grinning before he told Rafael he was good.

"I'm trying to help," he said when he hung up.

"Stay in your lane, Singh. The company isn't yours yet. You still haven't given me a dollar amount."

"Then I guess we better get to work finishing the financial assessment if we're going to print tomorrow with the news."

Raj whipped out her own phone and stood. "Hey, Tracey? I need you to email me a few files from Legal. Oh, and get Harnette on my calendar for an hour from now, please."

She excused herself as she left the living room. Ajay's mother had reentered and watched as Raj passed her, phone in hand.

"She's perfect for you, my baby," Ajay's mother said. Her round face beamed with joy. "You both know how to order people around on your phones."

"Aunty," Mina said with a grin. "You haven't seen anything yet."

AJAY'S MOTHER INSISTED that, before everyone got to work, they all sit and have a quiet lunch. Raj politely accepted even though she was honest enough with herself to admit that she was terrified Ajay's family wouldn't approve of her.

As they surrounded the large marble table and talked about Bharat and Ajay's family, Raj thought about her mother, and how every time family friends came over for a meal, Raj was required to help in the kitchen and put the food on the table. Her mother would praise her, would tell everyone what a good girl she was and how great a wife she'd one day become. Ajay's mother didn't look like she expected the same from the women her sons were involved with. But, of course, Raj would have to reserve judgment.

She was, after all, a soon-to-be divorcée, and even though she wore that badge with pride as she started the next part of her life, she wasn't ignorant of the fact that people in her own community were going to judge her.

Ajay must've sensed her unease because he kept asking her if she liked the food. Which she did.

It brought memories back and forced her to face the fact that she'd have to make a decision about seeing her mother soon.

LESS THAN AN hour passed over food and conversation before everyone stood from the table, ready to get to work.

"The daal was truly excellent, Aunty," she said to Ajay's mother.

Unfortunately, the woman began tearing up again.

"Oh, I'm—I'm so sorry," Raj added in English before Mina ushered her outside and down the path toward the houses in the distance.

"I don't understand. Was it something I did or said?"

Mina shook her head. "You spoke to her in Punjabi. That matters to her. She'll calm down now that Ajay and Hem are working at the main house and we're not right in front of her face. Ajay gave you the code to his place?"

Raj nodded.

They headed toward the bungalows lined up against

the backdrop of shrubbery and idyllic landscaping. Ajay's place stood in the center, and Raj couldn't think of anything but how adorable it looked with its front porch and potted plants.

"I don't know why Ajay lives in the city when he has this," Raj said.

"I told Hem the same thing. I think the only one who doesn't really stay on the property often is Zail. Come on. Let's get set up and start on this offer. Did your legal team send you anything? It'll be faster if I help."

Raj punched in the code on the front door and stepped inside to the smell of sandalwood and lavender. The honey-colored wood floors gleamed with polish, and the masculine decor was equally elegant and homey.

At first, being in Ajay's private space felt invasive, but they were together. They'd agreed to trust each other. This was a part of that . . . wasn't it?

She walked over to the frames sitting on the mantel under the mounted TV. Ajay and his brothers smiled back at her from the pictures. She didn't know if his mother had decorated for him, or if he'd taken the time to frame those moments himself. Would he ever frame a picture with her in it?

Raj sat down at his beautiful wood dining table as she thought about the short time they'd shared together. The dinner, the Fire Lounge, the date. She'd opened herself to him. She'd trust him, just like he'd asked her to, and he'd told her that he expected more from her.

He better frame pictures of their time together.

And if he was even thinking about being patronizing and dumping her after he bought her company . . . Well, he'd have bigger problems on his hands than a company mole selling trade secrets.

"Do you want something to drink?" Mina asked as she rounded the kitchen island and pulled out water from the fridge. "He's pretty stocked, but if you want chai, I can make that, too."

"No, darling," Raj said, trying to tamp down her self-righteousness. "Sit. I want to get started."

Mina complied. "Can I ask you something first?"

"Of course."

Her best friend twisted her hair on top of her head, and then folded her long legs so she could hug them against her chest. "Between the meeting in Ajay's office where you asked him to make an offer for your company and now, you've slept together."

Raj let out a deep breath. "Yes."

"Is it serious?"

Leave it to Mina to narrow in on the most important thing. Wasn't that what she'd just been contemplating?

"Let's just say," Raj started slowly, "that we're exploring all options."

Mina snorted. "You're so full of shit," she said.

Raj grinned. "I'll let you know when I'm ready to be straightforward."

"You better. I want details."

"Of course," Raj replied. "Remind me to tell you about how he came to get me from the Ice Palace."

Mina's eyes widened. "Why can't you tell me now?"

"Because, darling." She picked up her phone to dial in to the conference line her assistant had set up for her. "We have work to do."

TWO HOURS LATER, Raj knew why Mina was considered one of the best mergers and acquisitions attorneys in the business. She was ruthlessly meticulous about details and made sure that she remained fair as she helped Raj position her company in a way that would get her a premium price for her business. She felt such immense pride in her friend and wished that there were opportunities for them to work together more often.

"Thank you," she said as she shut her laptop. "I think that's all we can do until Ajay gets here."

Mina nodded and stretched her arms above her head. "Hem just texted and said they're done, too, so Ajay should be back soon. Apparently, it took them a while to get Zail under control, which is why their call ran longer than ours. He's not very happy."

"Zail? Why?"

Mina opened her mouth to answer, but then she got a look in her eyes that had her pausing. "How about you ask Ajay? I think it's better he explained their brotherly . . . disagreement."

Raj wanted to press for more information, but the sound of the front door opening had her shifting in her seat.

Ajay stood with a haggard expression on his face at the entrance. "Sorry I'm late," he said. He toed off his shoes, strode over to the dining table, and set his laptop down. "Mina? Hem is next door. Raj and I will finish up in here, and if we have any questions, we'll come find you."

"You sure?"

"Yeah," he said.

Mina began gathering her things. "Getting a framework together for an offer is doable," she said. "It helps that Raj's company is a smaller size, and her records are meticulous. We also have a market analysis for you to review."

She looped the strap of her bag over her shoulder and, with one last wave, walked out. Seconds later they were alone, and the house was blissfully silent. Ajay dropped into the chair that Mina had just vacated. He tilted his head back and let out a deep breath.

"I'm assuming that not everyone is in agreement with the plan," Raj said. "Mina mentioned that it was hard to get Zail under control. She suggested I ask you about that, but I think I can figure it out on my own. Your brother doesn't want you to buy me out."

"Unfortunately," Ajay replied. His eyes remained closed, and the thick cords of his neck were fully exposed, above the open neck of his long-sleeved shirt.

Seeing him like this, relaxed in his home, Raj felt a little tingle in her belly. She was wound up because she couldn't quite seem to understand what was happening between them. He was a little stressed because his brothers weren't being as supportive as he'd probably envisioned. They could probably both use some physical exercise to ease the tension. Technically they weren't in Ajay's parents' home, just on the same property. That had to be acceptable, right? It wasn't as if she was going to seduce him under the same roof.

Raj took a moment to think about what underwear she had on. Yup, definitely seduction material. With a slow, knowing smile, she stood to retrieve a bottle of water for him.

"Now your father's comment at the house makes more sense," Raj said conversationally, as she brought the bottle to his side of the table. "There is no way you'll be able to make everyone happy all the time."

"Don't I know it." He peered up at her as she moved in to lean against the table at his side. She held out the bottle and waited for their fingers to brush before she let go.

Ajay gave her a confused look and drank deep.

Oh, buddy, you have no idea what's about to happen.

Her skin prickled with awareness as she took the bottle and set it aside. "Do you want to know what I do?"

"For what?"

"To combat the loneliness at the top," she said. She slid closer. "I work."

"Mmm-hmm." He brought her to his side so that her hip was pressed against the arm of his chair. Like a choreographed dance, she leaned down at the same time as his hand came up to cup the back of her neck.

He was being very accommodating, she thought, as his fingers kneaded into her soft skin.

"Is that all you do, Rajneet? Work off the stress and expectations?"

Her mouth curved at the sound of his soft words. "No, actually. Let's just say I have someone help me release the tension when I need it the most."

"I see that now, Raj. How does a man audition for this role?"

She nipped at his lip and then licked at the hurt. "No audition necessary for you. Darling."

"I like the sound of that. I like the sound of that." He tried to pull her down for a kiss, but she evaded his clever, clever hands.

"I don't think you understand what seduction means," she said, enjoying the game now as some of the tension from the day was replaced with desire. "You've been making all the moves so far. Touching my hair when we first met and then again in your office when I came to see you. The way your hands wandered when we danced at the wedding. And then that kiss in your apartment. You came to the Fire Lounge, and then took me out on a date."

"Followed by some unforgettable fucking, wouldn't you say? Come here. Let me take care of you."

Before he could grab for her again, she slithered out

of his reach. With her eyes on his, she pulled her sweater over her head, revealing a black satin cup that barely contained her full, plump breasts. "It's my turn to make the first move."

The unmistakable lust on his face ramped up her own, and she had to hold out a hand to stop him even as he vaulted out of the chair to grab for her. "Sit back down, Ajay Singh. There's something I haven't asked you yet. You have a filthy mouth when you're fucking me. Is that just your style, or did you know that I love it?"

"I knew the moment I met you. I'm going to take you in a moment if you— Holy hell."

She took her time now, enjoying his reaction as she slithered out of her pants.

"It's like fucking Diwali, Rajneet." He was breathing heavy as she stood in front of him wearing matching satin lingerie, albeit one of her most comfortable sets. She tugged at the thin black strings high on her hips that held up the small triangle at the apex of her thighs. Ajay's stare went straight to her crotch.

She moaned, feeling herself moisten even more, and yanked out the elastic band that held her hair in its subdued ponytail. She shook out her hair and stood, offering herself to the powerful man in front of her who looked at her body like she was a goddess.

"You're wound up. I'm wound up," Raj said hoarsely. "Let's take a break and relax. Do you remember how you had a taste of me? Maybe you want another one. Your very own happy hour."

She motioned for him to sit again and stepped between his knees before hoisting herself up on the table. She slid the laptops and paper out of the way, then lifted one foot at a time and rested them on either arm of Ajay's chair.

With her eyes on his, she spread her knees, exposing the wet patch between her legs. Raj gasped when Ajay reached down to give himself one quick stroke and adjust his cock through the fabric of his jeans.

"I do enjoy a cock tale," he said. "This happy hour is going to be delicious."

She groaned when he finally gripped her ankles and stroked up her calves to her knees. He pushed her legs farther apart before running his fingers down the insides of her thighs, making her quiver.

"What do you want, darling? Need me to make you feel good?"

Raj cupped his chin with one hand, feeling the softness of his beard as she said the words that had been echoing in her head from the moment she stripped out of her shirt. "Eat me. Make me come."

She'd barely finished speaking before Ajay grabbed her behind the knees and pulled her to the edge of the table. His chair scraped forward, and he ran his bearded cheek down her left thigh before pressing a hard kiss on her plump, satin-covered mound.

Raj moaned and then let out a gasp as he hooked a finger through the crotch of her panties. His knuckle brushed against her aroused clit even as he yanked her underwear up so that the fabric separated her lips and stretched tight between her cheeks, rubbing teasingly against her aroused pussy.

"Lay back," he said, and she immediately obeyed his sharp order, her heart pounding, her body begging for more. He'd been so good for her before, so in tune with her needs, that she craved this again with him.

His breath trailed along the thin, tender skin of her inner thigh, inches above her wet, throbbing core. He rubbed his beard over the same line of skin, raising goose bumps.

"You smell delicious," he said. "Spicy and hot. Did I tell you that last weekend? Do you think I can taste your come on my tongue again?"

She writhed on the table, unable to stop herself, and rolled her hips toward him, begging for more.

"Yes!" she gritted out through clenched teeth. "Dammit, Ajay, am I going to have to give you a road-map tonight?"

Their eyes met over the slope of her stomach, the valley between her breasts.

"You'll wait for your orgasm now, Rajneet," he said.

Her head fell back against the table at the feel of his tongue stroking the length of her pussy. She let out a squeal as Ajay feasted on her clit, plunging his tongue and fingers inside her and over her clit.

"More," she panted as she writhed, begging him to please her. She'd never begged in her life, but it felt so good, so overwhelming. Ajay made oral sex an art and she wanted it all the time now. She tugged down the cups of her bra and began kneading her breasts, pinching her nipples.

"You taste delicious, Raj," Ajay said in Punjabi before he stroked her again with his tongue and then worked her turgid nub between his teeth.

She began shaking hard, panting and swearing at him, urging him to move faster, to eat her harder. Then she gripped the undersides of her knees and pulled her legs to her chest to expose all of her core.

Without missing a beat, he gripped her hips and pulled her tighter against his mouth.

She was delirious. How had the tables turned this fast? How had she gone from seductress to being seduced?

"Are you ready for me?" he asked, his voice hoarse.

"Yes," she whined in a high-pitch voice. She was wound so tight, breathlessly waiting at the precipice of her release. "Please. Please."

He moved faster and harder until she exploded, shaking and writhing from the force of her orgasm. It rolled inside her like waves of fire and pleasure. Raj didn't know how long she lay there shaking, but her legs had gone lax and draped over the edge of the table.

"Soni," he said hoarsely. She lifted her head at the endearment and watched as he pulled his fingers out of her and slipped them into his mouth. He moaned in delight, and if that didn't cause her an orgasm after-quake she didn't know what did. She lifted up on her elbows, waiting for his next move, which thankfully didn't take long.

Ajay unbuckled his belt and unzipped his jeans. With the dimming light of day casting the room into shadows, she saw the need in his eyes as he stroked the thick, long length of his penis.

Lifting one hip, he removed his wallet from his back pocket and pulled out a condom.

He tore it open with his teeth and rolled it over the length of him before he looked back at her expectantly.

Without another word, Raj slid off the table, straddled his lap, and inched forward so that she hovered over him.

Reason began to slip away again, and she unclasped her bra, sliding the straps off her shoulders as she spoke filthy, sexy words.

"Do you want to wreck my pussy again, Ajay?"

He squeezed her butt cheeks. "I think I already have, baby. You don't want another man's cock, do you? You're addicted now. Just like I am."

A tickle of fear scraped the back of her throat because there was a damn good possibility that he was right. Before she could object, he took one tightly budded nipple in his mouth.

And her decision was made.

Raj gripped him in one hand and guided the thick head of his cock into her opening. Their groans twined together even as he began rocking. She tossed her head back, her hair flowing around them, her breasts thick and heavy, bouncing with each thrust.

"You fill me up so good," she said, her words breaking as their pace increased.

"I'm fucking you hard, darling. I'm fucking you until your pussy knows only me."

Her hands raked through his hair and tugged, trying to get purchase, to get hold of him even as he gripped her hips harder and, using sheer force and upper body strength, began lifting her up and slamming her back down on his dick.

She let out a scream and succumbed to his rhythm. Her back arched, and when they were moving too fast, too hard, for her to steady herself, she lifted her arms over her head to hold her hair back.

He swelled impossibly bigger inside her and even as she felt his orgasm rise, her own release tore through her.

Ajay jerked her forward so that her breasts pressed flush against his chest. Unable to do anything but succumb to their passion, Raj drowned under the feel of his brutal kiss, knowing deep in the protected vault of her heart that she'd fallen carelessly past the point of no return.

Chapter Fifteen

Ajay

AJAY WOKE WITH the instinctive awareness that that it was almost four in the morning. He couldn't help but smile, even before he opened his eyes, because he felt Raj in his arms, in his bed. She shifted, as if hearing his thoughts, and her bottom snuggled against his morning wood. It was tempting to touch her, to wake her, as well, but she needed sleep. Today was going to be a long one for everybody. He grabbed his phone from the side table and turned off his alarm.

Raj shifted again, and her adorably sexy sigh of contentment echoed like a quiet whisper in the dark of the room. His vision adjusted to the early-morning shadows, and he propped his head in his hand and looked down at her full, relaxed mouth, the thick fan of lashes forming a crescent shape on her cheeks, and the smooth, naked skin scrubbed free of makeup.

She looked so innocent now, unlike the reserved woman he'd gotten to know. And then, when she set out to seduce him, who would've thought this strong, smart, gorgeous, classy woman would accept his filthy demands and beg for more? The things they'd done together still made him grin.

He waited for a few more minutes, enjoying her warmth, the softness of her skin, and her presence in his bed, before he slid from under the covers, phone in hand. He set out a towel and a new toothbrush for her in his bathroom, then he grabbed a pair of boxers and left the room.

He switched on lights as he moved through the kitchen but paused when he saw the small swatch of black panties hooked over the arm of one of his dining chairs. He took the underwear, walked over to a small side table in his living area, and shoved them inside a drawer.

He'd deal with his feelings about why he wanted to keep them later.

The rest of the kitchen was in decent shape. That surprised him since they'd gone at each other like animals. He knew that he needed time to figure out how he felt about her, but he couldn't stop himself from wanting her and wanting to be with her. He had to practically beg her to stay the night so he could have this morning moment when she was unguarded and curled next to him.

And wasn't their timing so damn complicated? He began to load water and beans into his coffee machine for a freshly ground brew. He thought about chai, but that would have to wait.

Ajay leaned against the counter, head bent as he untangled his night with Raj from the call he'd had with his brothers and his executive team the day before. Zail had reacted to the news just as Ajay'd imagined he would.

"I told you, brother. I told all of you! Sahar didn't do this!"

Luckily people like Tushar supported his decision. "By purchasing Ms. Hothi's company, we automatically have stronger cybersecurity measures. Her service area is a natural extension of ours, and she has a reputation for being one of the best."

Zail disagreed, fighting bitterly with everyone until finally Ajay had to end the call. He still remembered the way his brother Hem had tried to comfort him.

"Brother, you're putting too much pressure on yourself."

"How does it look to our board and our shareholders if my own brother doesn't support me? I'm already failing, and I haven't even gotten the CEO title yet," he'd said.

"You can't compare your situation to Dad's and mine. Dad literally had no one else that challenged his decisions. And when I was in charge of operations, Bharat hadn't gone public yet. The company was still a midsize, privately owned family business. You have to have faith that this is going to work."

The coffee machine beeped and he poured himself a cup. Walking to his windows, he watched the promise of a fall sunrise struggle to come to light.

"I hope you're right, Hem," he murmured to himself. He'd have to have faith and convince Zail that this was for the best.

Now that he was fully in the right mind to work, he looked at the time and decided to take a chance and call his brother. He let out a deep breath and pressed the phone to his ear. It was two thirty in the morning in California. Zail would be up.

The ringing stopped and a gruff grunt was the only answer he received.

"I wanted to check to see how you're doing."

"You mean after you cut off the call yesterday because you didn't like what I had to say?"

"Zail, you wouldn't listen to anyone."

"That's because you have lost your mind and have decided to actually buy the company that started this whole mess in the first place!"

"You heard from the data team yourself. The information was fed to the security consultants we hired."

"That just makes her incompetent."

"No more than we are." Ajay heard the sound of a car door slam. "Are you going somewhere?" he asked.

"Yeah," Zail replied. He had a sharp bite in his voice. "My team has been effectively shut down since last night, so I'm coming back to the East Coast. I'm taking the family jet, so I should be there before noon. Someone needs to convince you and everyone else in that office that you're thinking with your dick and that there hasn't been a single thing of value she's brought to the table."

"I've only wanted what's best for this company," Ajay responded. "And it's fucking pissing me off that you're accusing me of putting my personal feelings in front of a solid business decision. I need you to get yourself together and support this purchase, Zail."

"No." The sound was final and had a hint of bite to it. "And if you go through with this purchase, next month at the board meeting and quarterly shareholders' meeting, I'll fight you."

Ajay felt his stomach pitch, and his coffee sloshed over the rim of its cup and splattered onto the floor. "What do you mean?"

"I mean, bhai, that I'm going to vote against you as CEO and call into question your decision-making capacity. I won't let you screw all of us."

Ajay felt as if his brother had just driven a knife into his back and twisted the handle. The hurt from Zail's accusation was strong enough to bleed. He placed the cup on the nearest table, taking a moment to get his breath back.

"You'd jeopardize the future of Bharat, Dad's dream,

because of your hurt feelings? You're the only one acting this way, Zail. Papa and Hem are on board. So is Bhram."

"And none of them are thinking clearly. Or maybe none of them know about Rajneet Kaur Hothi's background."

"What are you talking about?"

"I spoke to Sri myself. He said you had a little research project that I should know about. He told me everything. Hothi's father's opium operation, their drug-trafficking connections. All of it. How could you be with someone whose family is in the same business that almost killed our uncle?"

Ajay had completely forgotten that he'd asked Sri to look into Raj's story. But that had been before. Before he spent time with her and slept with her.

Before he trusted her.

His blood began to boil. Sri was under strict instructions that the information was for him only. He had no right to share any of that intel with anyone but him. Ajay knew now that it was time for his head of security to go.

He'd have to take care of that later.

"Zail," he said, cutting off his brother. "Fighting me and my CEO nomination is going to create tension with the board, uncertainty with our shareholders, and potentially jeopardize our clients. Think about what you'd be doing."

"You think I give a shit?" Zail yelled back. "This woman cost me *Sahar*."

"I think you're shifting the blame there, brother. You cost yourself Sahar, and now you're not thinking about the repercussions for the rest of us."

"I've had hours to think," Zail replied. "I'll be seeing you real soon, bhai."

Zail hung up the phone, and the rage, the feeling of betrayal, had him hurling his phone across the room.

He'd whirled toward the kitchen, and that's when he saw Raj, dressed in the same clothes she'd worn the day before, standing on the staircase. She didn't have her mask on, the one that hid her so well from everyone, including him.

"I think I'll call myself a car."

"What? Why?"

"Because it's not my place to be here right now, I think."

It took him a moment to realize that she was telling him she was leaving. He was breathless from the one-two blow. His brother had just pulled his support for Ajay's CEO position, and Raj, the reason for Zail's animosity, was going to leave him to deal with it on his own.

He rubbed a hand over his face. "I'm going back into the city in a little bit. Let me get dressed and I'll take you."

She shook her head. "It's out of your way. And it's better if you stay here and I go back alone. I heard some of that conversation. One-sided, of course, but I knew what was happening."

"Zail's temper is getting the best of him right now.

He'll come for a visit and we'll talk it out. That's what family does."

She gave him a wide berth as she went over to the dining table and started gathering her things. That distance only angered him more. He knew that he was spoiling for a fight. He felt it bubbling inside of him.

Let her go. Let her go so that you can breathe. Then talk to Hem.

He didn't need the complication of a woman in his life, even though that woman was better than anyone he'd ever been with before.

She gave him a serene smile. "It's been an enlightening weekend, darling."

He ground his teeth at the endearment.

"So that's it? You're going to leave when something gets a little uncomfortable? I thought you stopped being so afraid of us, Raj."

He saw the flicker in her eyes. The brief flash of guilt that told him more than he wanted to know. "It's a family matter, Ajay. You have a lot of family. I don't want to get in the way . . ."

"Too late."

She looked up from where she was sliding her laptop and files back into her bag. "Excuse me?"

"Too late. Zail found out about your family's poppy farms and their connection to drug trafficking in Punjab."

"What? *How?*"

"I had asked Sri to look into your background. He told Zail."

"You had that son-of-a-bitch do recon on me? Who else is he going to tell? I told you that he's a problem!"

"Yeah, well, he's not my only one. Zail is pulling his support for my CEO nomination, which will cost me the seat because he thinks I should not acquire your company and I definitely shouldn't be involved with you. I think that means you're very involved. Instead of standing your ground, defending yourself by my side, you're leaving."

"It's just business, Ajay."

"It's not just *business* to me. It's family. It's my goddamn life. It's our life."

Raj swung her bag over one shoulder and gave him that same infuriatingly serene look. "I didn't realize when we started sleeping together that my obligations included making your brothers happy, too. Was that in the fine print?"

"No one is asking you to make my brothers happy," Ajay said, crossing his arms over his chest. "But I did ask for your support."

"And what am I supposed to do to support you? Talk to Zail and say, *Listen to your brother. I'm actually a nice person.* Yes, that's going to work really well."

"Well that's sure as hell better than escaping and leaving me holding the bag."

Her fingers clenched the strap of her bag. "I understand that you're mad at your brother. I don't appreciate that you're taking it out on me."

And because that was exactly what he'd been doing, he felt the rage grow bigger inside of him. Before he could stop himself, he moved in until they were inches apart. "Tell me how you feel about me. Is this just business, too?"

"I thought that we already talked about this."

"No, we agreed to some terms, used a few labels, but you never shared how you felt. It's been a week, Raj, but we've been dancing around each other since the Gen One gala. Don't tell me you haven't figured it out yet."

She stepped back. "Like I said. We talked about this. I'm referring to how I will only give you what I'm ready to give, and calling me a coward or trying to put me in my place will not work. Call me when you're done throwing your tantrum, Ajay."

There was that flicker of doubt in her eyes, and he gripped it with slippery, desperate fingers. This was going to hurt them both, but it was the only way.

"I won't."

"Excuse me?"

He moved away from her now, resuming his post near the windows. His brothers' smiling faces judged him from their frames on his mantel, and he had to force himself to remain focused.

"I won't call you, Raj. I knew you were going to do this. I knew that after you saw how great we were together you'd use any excuse to backpedal. But you're right about one thing. It's your decision. When you're ready to tell the truth, then you can call me. Until then, I'll only speak to your attorneys. That's how you wanted it in the first place, right?"

"Why are you doing this?" she asked, her voice cracking. The sound was deafening to his ears. "I don't know what you want from me, Ajay."

"I've already told you." He held his ground, refusing to go to her. "I want you here. I want you with me. I want you to accept that there is something between us, and it's fucking scary but it's worth it."

"I . . . can't. I have to do what's best for me."

"With no care in the world for how it affects other people, right?"

He saw the shock on her face and the hurt. "I knew we'd be done someday, but I never thought it would be so soon," she whispered. "At your request, we'll leave this to the lawyers."

Ajay heard the clear snick of the door closing behind her.

It took every ounce of willpower he possessed not to race after her, to give her whatever she wanted, but he couldn't. She was the one who'd taught him to never settle for less than what he deserved.

He crossed the room and picked up his phone from where he'd thrown it. The screen had a crack in it. The device still worked, though. He'd just hold on to it and carry it around wherever he was, like tucking it under his pillow when he slept, or putting it on the vanity when he was showering so he could hear it.

If Raj called him and told him how she felt, asked him if they could try again, he'd do everything in his power to prove that she deserved happiness, too, and he was eager to give it to her. But until then, he'd have to focus on his first love.

His father's company.

The only problem was that work was starting to let him down, too. Hopefully if he put in the effort, things would go back to normal.

That way, Ajay could figure out a way to stop hurting.

Chapter Sixteen

Rajneet

RAJ NEVER CRIED over men, but Ajay had made her weep. Their argument circled her mind as her car carried her along the early-morning New Jersey streets.

She'd felt uneasy from the moment she'd woken up alone in that bed. She'd never experienced the morning-after scene. She couldn't chance it. After she married, it had been imperative for her to keep her hookups short and sweet. No small talk, no dinner dates, no expectations.

But she'd fallen asleep at Ajay's house and in his arms. When she'd woken in an empty bed to the sound of his raised voice coming from the living room, she knew that she had to get out of there, go home, and build some space between herself, Ajay, and Ajay's family.

She pinched the bridge of her nose as the ugly memory of his one-sided conversation echoed in her head. And then, when he'd looked at her, she'd seen pain in his eyes. However, comforting him about the state of his feelings for her were outside the boundaries she'd set for herself and for their relationship.

And then he'd delivered a blow that had rocked her back on her feet. *With no care in the world for how it affects other people, right?*

Her parents had accused her of the same thing when she decided to stay in the States. Her brother had made the same accusation. Even Robert occasionally used to tell her that she would make decisions and screw the consequences.

Did people really think she was that heartless? That selfish?

Ajay had no right to push her, to demand anything from her. More importantly, if he didn't get what he wanted, he was supposed to accept it as Raj's right to choose.

Sure, he'd gotten angry, but she was an intelligent woman who was smart enough to admit that he'd been right about one small detail.

She was a coward when it came to her feelings.

The truth was that she felt safe when she told him her secrets, and it infuriated her that Zail would hurt him the way he did. Ajay took care of her needs, her wants, and given time, he would've most likely supported her dreams, too.

From all the things she'd seen and heard in the media, in articles, and from girlfriends, relationships were supposed to be reciprocal. All he'd wanted was the same thing in return and she'd failed miserably.

She just didn't know how to be there for him in the ways he wanted. So maybe it was a good thing that he'd told her that he wasn't going to call. If she was destined to fail, then there was no use starting in the first place.

Her phone blinked with a new message and she scrambled for it. Her heart sank when she saw that it was another work email. Brushing a tear from her cheek, she leaned forward so that she could speak to the driver. "Excuse me, sir? Can I send you another address? We need to make a quick stop."

"Sure," he said. "Do you know where in Manhattan it is? I was going to take the George Washington into the city."

"You still can," she replied. "But you'll have to take the West Side Highway from there. We're going to Midtown. I need to stop at an animal shelter to see my dog."

BY MONDAY MORNING, she'd gone through the seven stages of grief. True to his word, all questions were forwarded through Legal. He hadn't even had the decency to send her the formal offer letter as interim CEO. He'd had his chief financial officer and Tushar do the honors.

That was okay. She was a boss bitch, and even though

he'd made her happier than she'd been since she started RKH Collective, she didn't need him to survive.

At eight a.m. on the dot, she was walking into her building, freshly showered and dressed in her favorite black dress with a creamy white pinstripe blazer draped over her shoulders. The outfit made her feel powerful, confident, and in control. It was the power suit she needed to forget about the fact that she hadn't heard from Ajay.

Honestly, it probably wouldn't have been enough on its own, but she'd managed to squeeze in a few minutes of cuddling with her sleepy puppy the day before on her way home from Ajay's bungalow. Khunda had been so drowsy, warm, and soft against Raj, and that implicit trust had calmed her erratic thoughts, setting the tone for the rest of her day. Being armed with that feeling, as well as the news that she'd be able to take Khunda home as early as the next weekend, did more for her than she could've imagined.

Who needed men when she had the most adorable dog?

She pushed through the front doors and smiled at Tracey, who stood from her desk. "Morning! Any chance you can grab me some breakfast?"

"No problem. Avocado toast, poached egg, cinnamon latte, hold the foam?"

"You're a goddess. Please also get yourself something. Maybe bagels for everyone. It's going to be a hard day today. Any messages?"

Tracey followed her into her office.

"Your brother called," she said. "Twice."

"Ignore him."

"Done. You also have messages from most of your executive leadership. They want to meet with you since you sent the internal memo about the buyout."

Raj had prepared for that. She picked up her phone and texted Tracey the list she'd typed up on her drive in that morning. "I need in-person meetings with that list of people and in that order. Twenty minutes each. We'll arrange for longer sit-downs later in the week once we go public. Tracey, what's the mood in the office?"

"It's Monday morning and we're the first ones here, but I'd assume it'll be nervous." Tracey shrugged. "I am, too. What if we all lose our jobs?"

"You won't," Raj said. "Especially you. Wherever I go, I'll take you with me."

Her assistant grinned. "Well, of course. What would you do without me?"

"We won't have to find out."

Raj had thought about the best way to talk to her company and address the buyout with her employees. They'd been the bones that held her body of work together. They were her most valuable asset, and she wanted to make sure they all knew why she was doing this.

"Hey, Tracey? Before you go, can you connect with Harnette and her team? Ask them to set up a town hall today for three p.m."

"Today?" Tracey's eyeballs practically fell out of her head. "You want her team to set up a town hall for the entire company by *three*?"

Raj nodded. "It's best to rip it off. Like a bandage. I want to talk about my memo, and then the buyout strategy going forward. We'll even open up for questions."

"Absolutely. Anything else you need, boss?"

Yes, she wanted to say. She wanted Ajay, wanted to make sure he was okay. She wanted to stop being so afraid of giving up more of herself, and she wanted to stop being so angry that Ajay knew that about her. More importantly, she wanted to ask Tracey what she was supposed to do to fix things. Those were all *her* problems, though.

Instead, she smiled up at her assistant and opened her laptop. "If you could get Kia on the line from Gen One. I think I'm ready to accept the nomination."

"Wow, sure. I'm on it."

Raj had barely started sifting through her emails when she heard commotion outside the glass walls of her office. With mild surprise, she watched Robert storm past Tracey's desk toward her. She shook her head at her assistant, who'd already picked up her cell in a wary move that said she was about to call Security.

"Raj," Robert barked as he burst in. The glass door rattled as he slammed it shut. "What the hell do you think you're doing?"

She crossed her legs and leaned back in her chair. "You'll have to be a little bit more specific, Robert."

"Selling to *Bharat*? Are you out of your mind?" His face was molten red with fury, which obviously clashed with the color of his pale beige suit.

"Why would I be out of my mind?" She'd known that her ex wouldn't have the ability to stay away from her, that the minute he heard about the offer, he would come running. What Raj hadn't anticipated was that he'd be knocking on her door an hour after an internal memo went out.

She raised a brow and tilted her chin up in that way she knew Robert hated. "I can't imagine who would have the balls to tell you the news."

"I used to work here. Of course someone is going to tell me your harebrained idea. Do you know how this makes me look?"

She picked up her phone to look at the time. "Am I supposed to care?"

"My wife is selling the company we started together to a company that WTA is targeting for a takeover. A company that is my account at the firm!"

"Let's get a few things straight," she said as she stood and planted her hands on the glass desk. "*I* started RKH Collective. You had nothing to do with it, you sniveling piece of shit. And second, I am no longer your wife in any sense of the word. I am your ex and your reputation is no longer my concern. Do not barge into my office like this ever again, otherwise I will have you thrown out on your ass, understood? I bet WTA would love to see that."

"You *bitch*."

"I've been called worse."

He lumbered around the office like a wounded bear. "What happened to our years of friendship? What happened to the partnership we had and shared?"

"I asked you the same things when you stole information from me for your own advantage. What was it you told me? That you thought I would do the same thing." She looked at her nails and then buffed them against her shoulder. Whoever had said revenge wasn't satisfying obviously hadn't done it right. "It's a premium offer, and obviously a great business move for Bharat."

Robert's skin color deepened until it was almost purple. "I could get fired for this. My boss thinks that I screwed up, that I'm playing both sides now, and that's because of you."

"Oh? Well, that's your problem."

He straightened and adjusted his tie. "No. It's going to be your problem."

His bitterness had Raj looking up. There was that sharp edginess in his expression, the one that told her he was about to cheat to get his way. Raj adjusted her blazer over her shoulders like a cape.

"Are you threatening me?"

"Of course not. That's illegal." He straightened the knot of his tie. "But if you think my reputation isn't important to you, then you obviously haven't thought about what this could look like to the board at the Gen One. How do you plan on becoming the head of the foundation if your personal life is in chaos? Divorcing one man while obviously sleeping with another?"

"I plan on leading the same way I've always led my business. If they don't like it, they can go to hell," Raj said calmly, even as her heart raced at the thought of not getting the foundation position. She'd worked through a potential backup plan, just in case she didn't secure her seat, but that plan had included Ajay by her side.

By her side.

Dammit, she was starting to understand what his expectations were.

"Robert," she said with a dismissive wave of her hand. "With the company sale, I'll be flush and have some time to reassess my priorities. You know, I haven't been to Bali yet."

"This is a joke to you?" His voice was back to a reasonable volume. "Well, how about this one? WTA is still a major shareholder of Bharat. My company has every right to propose that Bharat stop the acquisition."

She froze, but kept her calm, cool expression firmly in place. "And how do you plan on doing that?"

"By filing an injunction."

"On what grounds?"

"Bharat can't buy you out if you're in the middle of litigation."

She felt a prickle at the back of her neck. There was something she'd missed, something she hadn't planned on happening that Robert obviously had. She crossed her arms over her chest. "I'm not in the middle of litigation."

"Oh? What do you think your divorce is?"

"We're settling," she bit out.

"Not anymore." His grin was ugly now, and all of the good memories she'd had of him over the years, the late-night TV shows, the heated arguments over business, the friendly meals that one would have with a roommate, were tainted forever.

"You'd seriously stop our divorce for WTA? For a company that probably thinks of you as disposable?"

"Nice try, darling," he said. "You'll be hearing from my lawyer. Looks like the divorce is going to take longer than you thought."

With that parting shot, he turned on his heel and left the same way he'd come. Raj waited, thinking through the best way to handle the situation. It took her less than a minute to plan out her strategy.

Her first call was to her head of IT and her security department. "I need you to scan every corporate email account and cell phone to see who has been in contact with Robert over the last month. Start with the legal department."

"What are we looking for?" her employee asked on the other end of the line.

"Anything that shares our company information with him."

"And if we find something?"

"Send it to Tracey. I'd like to fire them personally."

After a few more instructions, she put in a call to her divorce attorney, who assured her that Robert's only course of action was to delay the inevitable.

Tracey walked in just as she finished up and left a paper takeout bag. "You have ten minutes to eat before your first meeting," she said.

"Thanks, Tracey."

That also meant she had ten minutes to call Bharat about Robert's threat. Ajay needed to know about her morning visit from her ex-husband. She didn't want him to be blindsided.

Even though she wanted to talk to him, to text him, to connect with Ajay personally, she honored his wishes and put in a call to Tushar. Ajay's head of Legal would just have to relay the news. She had work to do.

Chapter Seventeen

Ajay

"HAVE YOU LISTENED to a word I've said?" Bhram called out in Punjabi. "I've been trying to talk to you about this for over a week."

His cousin's voice broke through the clouded mess of Ajay's thoughts. He'd been staring out at the crystalline New York skyline. Chrome, glass, and steel buildings glinted against a robin's egg blue backdrop. He loved his view. Ever since Bharat had built out office space in the Park Avenue location, he'd come stand in his father's office, now his, and just watch the city. It was even better than the sparkling cityscape from his penthouse.

He faced his cousin, who looked way too alert for

taking a red-eye from London. "Sorry, Bhram, run that by me one more time."

"You don't care two tits about our UK office expansion." His cousin's expression softened. "Have you heard from her?"

Ajay shook his head. "Since the news broke, we've both been busy."

"I'm sure, but brother, either you go to her, you talk to her and clean up the mess between yourselves, or you let her go. You have to get your head in the game, and your personal life is distracting you from what's always been the most important thing in your life." He held up his tablet with the opinion section of the *Financial Times* on display. "These are serious allegations that are getting visibility. They can ruin your chances of securing the CEO seat."

Ajay took the tablet and scanned the text. The article was ugly, just like the three that had come before it since the news broke on Friday.

Bharat, Inc., is attempting to bolster its market value and its reputation by acquiring a cybersecurity and physical security services company. Although, on its face, the acquisition appears to be a sound decision to expand the Bharat portfolio, the company in question is owned by Rajneet Kaur Hothi.

This means one of two things. The first is that WTA succeeded in establishing itself as the technology giant pulling strings on Bharat's next move (see yesterday's article on the relationship between Rajneet Kaur Hothi and WTA). The second, which is more of a commentary on business engagement in a globalized economy, is that South Asian entrepreneurs are banding together to fight the lack of diversity and inclusion in the business world.

One truth remains: the heir apparent of Bharat, Ajay Singh, has not made a public statement regarding the company's position, which doesn't give investors confidence in the man touted as the next CEO of Bharat.

Ajay dropped the tablet back on the dining table. "Wouldn't they love to know that my own brother is the reason why I'm not at a press conference right this moment? That Zail is holed up at Bharat Mahal waiting for me to say something so that he can make a move against me and against Raj? Both my brother and father are convinced this is a lesson that I have to learn on my own as a leader. Easy for them to say. They never had to deal with something like this before."

Bhram shrugged. "I'm still stuck on the racist bullshit about South Asians banding together to take over the world. These colonizers, man. Always feeling threatened."

"You're not helping, cousin."

Bhram stood and buttoned his suit jacket. "I think

you need to go to Bharat Mahal and stay with your family until you can talk this out and come up with a solution. I'm happy to watch things here while you're busy. I'm staying . . . nearby."

"No, you need to head back to London. Even if you have to go for a weekend and then come back for next week's meeting. I don't trust our uncle alone with the caretakers. He hasn't been in recovery long enough."

"Don't worry about Gopal," Bhram said. "The people in charge are very qualified. You have enough on your shoulders to think about. Focus on the acquisition and leave the rest to the competent people in the company."

"Thanks, Bhram."

Rafael knocked on the doorframe. His gaze slid over to Bhram, held for a moment, then returned to Ajay. "Sri is here to see you."

As if his day couldn't get any worse. He'd been avoiding his head of security until he could compile the information he needed before terminating Sri's employment.

"Does he know I only have five minutes before my next call?"

"I told him."

"Good. Send him in."

When Rafael didn't budge and continued to stare at Bhram, Ajay stuck two fingers in his mouth and let out a piercing whistle, just like Mina had taught him.

Both his cousin and assistant jumped.

"Rafael, sooner rather than later."

"Right. Okay. Bhram, I can show you out."

Bhram was out of his chair like a shot, following on Rafael's heels. Ajay rolled his eyes. Watching those two was like watching a telenovela crossed with an Indian soap.

Sri appeared moments later, wearing his customary black sweatshirt and Chucks. He was the oldest member of Raj's security team, the most senior member, and he still looked like he was trying to fit in at a Silicon Valley tech mixer.

"How can I help you, Sri?" he said.

"Uh, sir, I wanted to ask if there was a problem."

Ajay motioned to one of the chairs. Sri shook his head. "What do you mean?"

"Sir, my team and I have been working to locate Sahar Ali Khan for a while now. Same with intel on WTA and, most recently, Rajneet Kaur Hothi. We've been working hard—"

"With zero results."

Sri glanced to the side, failing to look him in the eye. "Be that as it may, in my opinion as your security lead, it's important to continue looking."

This son of a bitch, Ajay thought. He'd trusted him. He'd defended him.

"I agree with you, Sri, but this isn't supposed to be a difficult project. I haven't gotten any information from you that shows me you're making headway. That's why I asked Legal to look into your team."

This time, Sri's cheeks went ashen. "Sir . . ."

"Nothing to worry about. Just making sure we don't have another data leak. You understand."

"Sir, we were blocked out of the system last night. If I could get access and download some of the files I need to work on, then I won't be so unproductive."

"No need," Ajay said with a wave of his hand. "You'll get paid regardless."

"But this is my job." For the first time in the years they'd worked together, Sri's voice rose in volume. "If you don't trust me to do it, then I shouldn't be here."

"I don't trust anyone but my family," Ajay said. *And Rajneet.*

Sri looked like he wanted to argue, to press the matter. Ajay was ready for him. Sri had to be dirty after all of this. And if he was, Ajay would nail Sri's ass to the wall. He just needed to find out what Sri's motive was in all of this.

Rafael poked his head through the door again before Sri could get a word out.

"You have a call."

"Take a message. I have a staff meeting in minutes."

"I know. You'll want to take this one."

Ajay glanced at Sri, then back at Rafael. "Fine. Sri, you can go."

"Uh, yes sir. If we could maybe talk soon—"

"Next week," Ajay said as he grabbed the receiver.

He waited until Sri and Rafael both had exited his office before he spoke into the mouthpiece. "This is Ajay."

"It's Raj." Raj's throaty voice gripped him like a vise. He took a shallow breath.

His blood ran hot and cold. The back of his neck prickled. How long had it been? Eight days? Ten? He was obsessed and had just come to terms with the fact that he was probably going to have to go back to her, to grovel and apologize because he wanted her in his life.

"Do you need something?"

"I apologize for disrupting you at work. I know you're mad— I need your help. My housekeeper isn't home, I couldn't get in touch with Mina, and I didn't want to bother my assistant. I gave her today off. I don't know who else to call."

He could hear the watery panic in her voice, and because he'd never known her to panic before, his instincts went on red alert. "Where are you?"

"I'm at my place. Can you . . . Ajay, can you come?"

"I'm leaving now."

"O-Okay."

The sniffle, that delicate sound of tears in her voice, had him panicking, too. Was she hurt? Had something happened to her? He had so many questions.

"I'll be there soon," he said softly, and hung up the call. Ajay buttoned his coat, grabbed his cell, and bolted out the door.

"Cancel my obligations for the rest of the day," he said to Rafael as he passed by his desk. "I'll take the staff meeting in the cab."

"Sir, you have two with board members that cannot be rescheduled or canceled."

"Have Dad or Bhram take them."

He exited his office and walked as fast as he could to the elevator banks without calling attention to himself. Should he call 911? What if she was seriously injured? Could it have been her ex-husband? That bastard might have come back at her for revenge.

Ajay pushed through the steel-and-glass front doors and onto the sidewalk. His hand went up and a cab slowed just as he approached the curb.

Without waiting for it to come to a complete stop, he yanked open the door, slid onto the torn leather seat, and barked directions at the driver.

He'd see Raj in nineteen minutes, and somehow, he had to work before he got there.

Chapter Eighteen

Rajneet

RAJ WASN'T GOING to call him. Instead, she was going to pretend that she never had a brief, explosive, incredible week with a man who understood her, and focus on the next phase of her life like she'd planned when she first filed for divorce.

But when Khunda disappeared, Ajay was the only person she wanted to call for help. She watched for him out the front bay window, counting down the minutes, while periodically calling her dog's name. When a cab stopped in front of her house, she yanked open the front door, her throat tightening as Ajay ran up her steps in a few short leaps.

"What is it? What happened? Are you hurt?"

She shook her head, closing the door behind him. Her accent was thicker than it had been in a while as she burst out, "I'm so sorry. I know you're upset with me. I didn't want you to see me like this." She motioned to her hair that was piled on top of her head in disarray, her leggings, and her thin off-the-shoulder sweater.

"Soni, what happened?" he said, softer this time.

The nickname was the last push over the edge. She let out a sob and sank into his arms. He wrapped her close, filling the emptiness that had haunted her all week. His beard rubbed against her temple, and he stroked her back as she let go of some of her tension and stress and some of her tears.

She didn't have anyone else who wouldn't judge her for panicking over a dog. It took her a few more moments before she could pull back and stand on her own. He brushed a tear off the curve of her cheek with his thumb, stroking the grayish bruises under her eyes that she hadn't had the heart to conceal. "Want to tell me what's wrong?"

"It's my dog."

"Your dog?" His eyebrows shot up to his hairline. "Khunda? You were able to pick her up already."

"It was time," she said, sniffing. "They said Saturday, but this week has been . . . hard, so I pushed Jill and asked if I could get her today."

The excitement she'd felt, the pure joy of finally having a dog, knowing she would soon have Khunda, had brightened up her whole week. She'd been able to redirect her confusion and grief about Ajay toward buying toys, a bed, water and food dishes, and securing private dog training classes.

Raj motioned for Ajay to follow her into her sitting room with its cream and mirrored furniture.

"I brought her in here," Raj said, pointing to the plush bed she'd purchased and arranged next to the fireplace. "She seemed fine, but when I tried to leave, she started crying. I needed to use the bathroom, so I took her upstairs to my en suite with me and left her right outside the door. She's less than three pounds, Ajay. When I came out Khunda was gone. I can't find her anywhere. I don't know what to do."

"Okay," he said slowly. "We'll find her."

The way that he'd paused had her heart sinking. He'd given her distance now and repeatedly tugged on the sleeves of his suit jacket.

"Oh. You must think I'm . . . I panicked. You came all this way."

She'd never felt quite this embarrassed before, as she turned toward the hallway again. He was looking at her like she had an alien head growing out of her neck. What had she been thinking? This wasn't the type of relationship they'd agreed upon. She was being silly.

"I am so incredibly sorry for wasting your time like this. I-I don't know what to do, but I can figure it out. Let me at least pay for the cab back—"

"Raj, you're going to piss me off."

Her shoulders snapped back. "I beg your pardon?"

"I think you heard me the first time." He scrubbed his hands over his face. "Look, Khunda isn't going to go anywhere. She's going to be fine. Why don't we look for her, then we can talk?"

Raj nodded. "I really am—"

"Raj, I'm glad you called me. I'm *relieved* that I was the person you came to. But we're going to have take some time to talk about this, and you're distracted. Come on. Show me where you put her."

"Okay. Okay, I can do that." She led the way back to the front of the house and up the spiral staircase to the second floor. Her bedroom was to the left through a set of French doors. Ajay had seen it the night after their date; he'd come home with her and spent a few hours in her bed. Fortunately, Kaka had come and cleaned it, considering the mess Raj had made during the week.

"Where did you leave her?"

She pointed to the bathroom and to the floor right next to the door. "She was right here."

"And she doesn't bark or anything when you call her name?"

"No, neither the Punjabi pronunciation nor the Americanized version they'd given her."

Ajay got on his hands and knees in his hundred-thousand-dollar suit and peered under her bed. "I'm assuming you checked under here?"

"Yes, all over the house, including the basement apartment. Ajay, you're going to crease your suit."

"I'll get it ironed again. And I wouldn't waste your time with looking anywhere other than the top floor."

"Why do you say that?"

"Because she's too small for the stairs."

She paused at the thought. Ajay was right. There was no way Khunda could've made it down the stairs with her size. And did she even know how to climb them in the first place? Raj would have to get safety gates to make sure there were no accidents.

Ajay stood and crossed the room into her dressing studio. He flipped on the lights. The recessed lighting filled the space with a soft sunlit glow. Everything looked exactly as she had left it that morning. Her jewelry island stood in the center of the room with a sparkling marble countertop. Her makeup vanity with lighted mirror was organized, and her wall-to-wall cabinets, featuring a glass case filled with her vintage handbags, were in order.

"This is like a shrine to designer clothes," he said. "Is everything color coded?"

She glanced in the direction he'd pointed. Her wall of heeled shoes was color blocked from top to bottom. "How else am I supposed to get dressed fast and efficiently in the morning?"

He grinned at her, the first smile that she'd seen in so long. His eyes twinkled with a hint of wickedness. "Only you, Raj."

A faint rustling sound came from one of the baskets tucked in the back corner of the closet.

"Oh my god."

Ajay got on his hands and knees and crawled toward it. He gently pulled her linens hamper out. Khunda lay on her side, paws stretched out, eyes shut. She yawned and stretched.

"Khunda!" Raj scrambled to Ajay's side and gently scooped her puppy up. She'd never been so relieved in her life. Khunda's tiny tongue peeked out and licked at her chin. "You had me so worried," she said in Punjabi.

"When she didn't see you, she probably got scared and wanted to find your scent. That's my guess anyway. Your sheets were probably the next best thing for her."

Raj stroked a finger over Khunda's forehead. "Thank you," she whispered. "For coming all the way out here to help me find her."

"You're welcome."

He crossed his legs and settled on the rug next to her. That suited her just fine as she didn't want to move, either. She rocked her puppy, who lay so sweet and trusting in her arms. It took only a minute or two before Khunda's big brown eyes drooped with fatigue and she was fast asleep again.

Ajay was making a move to stand and go when Raj spoke.

"I know that this is not the most comfortable spot to have that conversation, but if you're up for it, I'd like to talk."

"You would?" he said.

Raj nodded.

He took off his coat and set it on the rug next to him. "Okay," he said.

"Ajay," she started. Swallowing her pride was like choking on a fistful of nails. "I know you think I'm a coward, for good reasons, but I'm intelligent enough to know when a good deal is going to slip through my fingers because I'm holding myself back."

"Are you going to tell me what was going through your mind last weekend? What happened?"

She rocked Khunda, comforted by the sound of tiny puppy snores. "Last weekend was sort of . . . Well, I reacted the same way I reacted today."

"You reacted like you lost your dog?" he said.

She smiled at his skepticism. "Today wasn't supposed to be like this. I did my research, and I have the time and the resources to successfully take care of one three-pound dog. Less than twenty-four hours later, I'm panicking. It's not as easy as I thought it would be."

"Love," Ajay said, "no matter what kind, is never easy."

The word frightened her. She didn't think they were ready for it yet. It was too new, too powerful to say when they had so many battles ahead of them. Her company, his family, everything.

"You and I weren't supposed to be like this, either. We were attracted to each other. We were going to have good sex, and then I would move on with my life and you'd move on with yours. But it didn't turn out that way."

Ajay shook his head.

"Did I ever tell you that Robert used to call me ice princess as a joke? He'd laugh about it because I'd have everything under control, but when something like this happened, he'd say that I'd thawed and become human. I think it scared him. I'm normally capable of doing anything and everything I want."

"I won't argue with you there, but Raj, tears don't make you any less royal."

Only Ajay would compare her to royalty when she was bedraggled and exhausted. "When I didn't know what to do, I had to learn on my own and cope on my own. But losing a dog is so much different than any business-related loss I've faced."

He reached out and scratched Khunda's tiny head. "Happy to search for puppies in laundry baskets anytime you need."

"Ajay," she said, letting out a deep breath. "What I'm trying to tell you is that I want to be with you, but I don't know how and that really is . . . frightening. I'm irritated that you were right about why I ran, but I'm not irritated enough to stop caring for what we could have together. If that's what you still want, too."

His mouth gaped, then he stroked a hand over his beard. "So, what you're saying is that the panic you just felt, the panic associated with not knowing what to do with Khunda, is the same panic you feel around me? But you're willing to overlook it, even though it irritates you that I was right?"

"Well . . . yes. That's an accurate summation."

"Raj, I don't have a lot of experience with serious relationships, either. My connections with women have been mutually beneficial and short. This is all new to me, too." He scooted forward and cupped her face, his voice softening to a gruff whisper. "But I know you're worth it. The question is, am I going to have to fight with you every step of the way or are you going to be willing to adapt?"

She leaned into his touch. "You're going to have to be patient with me. You can't expect me to keep up and accept everything you want from me. And I'm admitting that I was wrong here, but there is a very good possibility that you'll be wrong about something, too, darling."

He grinned at her. "That's fair. I'm sorry I put you in that position last weekend."

She'd replayed that scene so many times and thought about how she would react so differently if she got the chance. "I'm sorry for not being there on the weekend when you spoke to your family about the buyout."

"That's okay. I understand why you didn't want to be in that position. Zail will . . . Well, that's a story for dinner maybe. Frankly, talking about it is miserable, and I've had enough of that without you in my bed this week."

The knot that had formed in her stomach on Sunday began to loosen. "The feeling is mutual," she said.

He leaned forward and kissed her forehead, then sighed, strong and deep. "Raj, *be with me*. Stay with me. Stand by my side while I stand by yours. We'll get through anything that comes at us. As long as we're partners instead of adversaries."

"Yes. Yes, I agree. Thank you for not giving up on negotiations, especially when the other party was falling apart and the deal looked raw."

"The deal didn't look raw."

"That's sweet of you to pretend."

Ajay laughed. "Darling, I know a good deal when I see it. We'll figure out the rest of the bumps in the road as we get to them. For now, I'm glad you're happy with Khunda. I'm glad that you're here and I can hold you again. Now maybe we can celebrate."

"Celebrate? Celebrate what?"

"You're selling your company, we're together, and I have it on good authority that Bharat and a few other corporate members of Gen One are supporting your nomination for CEO."

"I still have a few hurdles to jump over. My ex-husband being one of them. He's determined to put roadblocks now that he knows about the sale."

Ajay's head jerked up, his gaze narrowing. "Is there anything I should know about? Anything I can do?"

"No. I can handle Robert. I am just biding my time. And you're right. We should celebrate. What do you propose? Dinner?"

Ajay nodded. "Tomorrow night. Spend some time with Khunda tonight, then bring her over to my penthouse around six."

"I believe we can arrange that."

"Good." He reached out and cupped her face, bringing it to his for a soft, sweet kiss. "I missed you. A little bit, because, you know. We're new and all."

"Missed you, too," she said as her lips curved into a slow smile. "A little bit."

He leaned forward again, but this time his mouth was covered by a small slobbering tongue. He looked down at the bright eyes of a dog.

"What? Khunda!" Raj giggled when Ajay picked up the wiggling puppy and dropped her ceremoniously back into the dirty clothes hamper.

"Stay put, pipsqueak," he said. "I have to kiss your momma and make up for lost time."

Chapter Nineteen

Rajneet

THE NEXT EVENING Raj leaned closer to her mirror to make sure that she'd successfully covered the shadows under her eyes. Her attorney's voice blared from the speakerphone on the vanity counter.

"Your date hasn't changed, but that doesn't mean he's going to stop trying to delay your divorce, Raj. You have to be prepared for that."

"I've never been the type of person to sit back and wait. That's why I'm working on a backup plan to keep Robert in his place."

"Do I want to know what that is?"

"No, but I'll keep you posted if I have to put it into effect. Thank you for the update."

"No problem."

The line went dead, and Raj examined her appearance. No one would be able to tell that she'd panicked the day before. She looked at Khunda, who had fallen asleep on the bed Raj had bought for her dressing room.

"Robert doesn't know me as well as I thought he did. And this time, I'm not going to underestimate him."

Khunda lifted her head and blinked sleepily at her.

"And you! You had me so worked up yesterday that I practically told Ajay that I was falling in love with him. A general never shares her intentions before the opposition."

Khunda yawned and licked her paw.

"You're right. Ajay had told me that I needed to think of us as partners, not adversaries. Well, he knows his partner's weakness now."

Raj picked Khunda up and gave her a little cuddle.

"You like Ajay, don't you," Raj said in Punjabi as she carried her tired little Chihuahua out of the dressing room. "Hopefully you sleep nice at his house and only wake up once in the middle of the night. You were such a good girl, using your pee pads and sleeping near me. I'm so proud of you."

Raj put on Khunda's light fall jacket and attached a harness. Twelve years ago, she would've never thought she'd be the type of person to talk to dogs, but here she was, having a full conversation with her new housemate, and doing it with a bounce in her step.

When was the last time she'd felt this satisfied? It

had to be before she filed for divorce, before Robert quit working for her, and before he'd asked her to change the nature of their relationship.

Sure, part of her joy was because of her connection to Ajay. And now that she'd made the decision to spend more time with him, no one, especially not her ex-husband, was going to stop her. She deserved to be happy.

She zipped up her vest over a cowl-neck sweater and put on her walking heels while Khunda chased her tail. Raj then carefully strapped Khunda into her pet stroller. The partial awning was tied back so Khunda could enjoy the view, and her overnight bag, along with Raj's, was already tucked in the storage basket underneath.

Kaka helped carry the stroller down the front steps.

"Where are you going?" he asked. "I just got home from my trip and you are running around already."

"I've been busy! Why don't you go home?" she said to him in Punjabi.

He blinked owlishly at her through his wide-rimmed spectacles. "Then what would you do for dinner? I'm making subzi with roti. Eggplant."

"As delicious as that sounds," she said as she adjusted the strap of the purse that she'd grabbed, "I am going out. I'll eat it for breakfast. Or you take it with you. I'll see you tomorrow."

Kaka gave her a narrow look and then said, "Call me if you need me to pick you up."

He patted Khunda's head and went back into the house.

Checking the harness one more time, she took a deep breath of fall air and walked to the corner of her block. She planned on strolling all the way from her brownstone down to Ajay's penthouse. It was almost three miles, but the weather was beautiful and Khunda could use some social engagement.

She'd made it five blocks before a familiar figure stepped into line beside her. She schooled her face to hide any surprise.

"You're still here," she said to her brother.

Guru nodded. "I knocked on your door. I almost gave Kaka a heart attack. The old man practically cried with happiness when he saw me. He almost bolted after you but I told him I'd catch up and surprise you myself. I can't believe he's still with you."

"Of course. He always loved me the most," she said with a smirk. She knew that it irritated Guru to hear her say so. "What can I do for you?"

He shoved his hands into his jeans pockets as he matched his stride to hers. "I told you that I'd wait until you make up your mind. I didn't expect to be sitting around while you went out and purchased a rodent. Do you know how ridiculous you look pushing it in a child's stroller?"

"Khunda can't walk that far. She gets tired. And your attitude is not the best way to convince me to do something."

"Right," he said.

"Is there a reason why you're following me?"

"I'm taking a break from work and decided to spend time with my sister. I have to admit, you've developed a fascinating life for yourself."

"Thank you."

"And now you're selling that life and starting over. Again."

The news of the buyout had gone viral, so it wasn't a surprise that Guru had picked up on it, too. "That's not your business."

"I'd like to know, though. I've always been curious. Why RKH Collective?"

"Small talk, Guru? Really?" She maneuvered around a group of tourists, irritated when Guru kept up. He'd dressed casually to blend in today. However, Raj could tell that his jeans were brand-new, along with his button-down and leather jacket.

"We're here, and no matter what happened in the past, I still wondered about you," Guru said. "You look like you're headed toward a particular destination. Until we get there, why don't you tell me about your company."

She let out a sigh. "Why? So you can try to guilt me into helping you?"

"Seems like that would be a waste of time since you're selling it," he said in Punjabi. "Come on, gudiya. Tell me why you wanted to start this business instead of coming home and helping the family business."

"Besides the fact that I would've been forced to be a good stay-at-home, barefoot-and-pregnant type, and you'd never have taken me seriously?"

He hunched his shoulders. "There is nothing wrong with that."

"As long as the woman has a choice. That wasn't my choice. RKH is a success without you. I started in workforce solutions and worked my way up to high-end cybersecurity services with zero help from the family."

"That doesn't surprise me," he said with a snort. "You were always good at snooping. By thirteen, everyone knew that you were the person to go to for the latest information on everyone in Punjab."

Raj held back a smile. "I've channeled my strengths toward profitable opportunities."

"How did you get the capital to start?"

"Robert came into the first leg of his trust and provided the capital. I paid back his loan within eighteen months of opening my doors."

Guru stroked a hand down the length of his beard. "Talk about a roaring success. I assumed you kept him on payroll as a formality since he was funding your little business."

"Absolutely not," she said. *Stupid man with your sexist binary gender role assumptions.*

"Robert went to law school, worked for a top-ten firm for a few years, and then came to lead my legal team."

"And he's the only one who knows about your past. About where you come from."

Raj moved to the side of the sidewalk and looked up at Guru's handsome face, his gray pagadi that matched his shoes.

"Why are you doing this?"

"Can't a brother get to know his sister after she's all grown-up?"

She wasn't falling for it. Raj had been alone too long to easily trust the words that came out of people's mouths. "I have a lot of important projects I'm currently involved with, Guru. When I have time for you, for the family that made it so very clear that I was no longer family, then I'll let you know."

Guru nodded, then reached down and scratched a finger over Khunda's head. "We're all proud of you, you know."

She raised a brow.

"Papa is the least vocal about it because he's always been as stubborn as you. About a year after my last visit to the States to see you, Mumma started asking me to keep tabs on you. To make sure you were safe. I thought that we knew everything we needed to about your life, but it looks like we were wrong. I was wrong. You're so accomplished, Raj, but you haven't changed."

She tilted her chin up and squared her shoulders. "You don't know me at all, Guru."

He leaned in close so they were eye to eye. "You'll never truly be free until all your secrets are out of your closet, Raj. You're going to continue to close yourself off from friends, from *the Singhs*, as long as your past remains in your past."

"If I see you stalking me one more time, Guru, I'll have you arrested. Are we clear?"

He stepped back, his mouth set in hard lines. "Crystal, gudiya. Crystal clear. Just don't say I didn't warn you. Enjoy your walk."

He turned in the direction they'd come from. Raj watched until he disappeared into the light flow of Sunday evening pedestrian traffic. When Khunda whined, she started moving again.

"Yes, my love," she said. "I'm looking forward to the rest of our evening, too."

She walked out of her way, doubling back once to make sure that she wasn't being followed. The whole excursion took forty-five minutes and gave her time to think about what her brother had told her and the way he'd left.

Two blocks before she reached Ajay's building, she took Khunda out of her stroller so she could practice walking on a leash and do her business. Standing in the dimming light, she wondered if avoiding her past was the best idea. Would she regret not going to see her mother? Would her mother be lucid enough to even recognize her?

Khunda squeezed her little body between Raj's feet and sat, indicating that she'd done her business and was officially tired again. Raj strapped her back in and walked to the end of the block where Ajay's brightly lit building stood, creating a pillar that shot straight into the sky.

A man in uniform held open the door for her. "Welcome. Are you visiting today?"

She nodded. "Rajneet Kaur Hothi for Ajay Singh."

He led her over to the large mahogany concierge desk where an armed security guard scanned a computer. "Yes, Ms. Hothi, you're to have your fingerprints scanned so you can have open access to Mr. Singh's floors."

"Thank you, but I don't—"

"Please place your thumb over the scanner," he said.

To save time, she stopped arguing and followed the instructions. She smiled when the doorman petted Khunda and asked if her puppy could have a treat.

"I don't know what kind of treats she likes yet," she said. "I've tried a couple brands, but nothing really gets her excited."

The doorman pulled out a tiny triangle from his pocket, and to Raj's surprise, Khunda sat back and put her paws up to beg. She took the offered treat and finished it in a few greedy bites before settling down again.

"That's amazing," Raj said. "What were those?"

The doorman smiled. "Peanut butter dog treats. Don't go for the fancy or the fruity kind. Basic peanut butter will always work."

"Thank you," Raj said. She smiled at Khunda. "I'll be investing in a few boxes."

"Ma'am?" the concierge said. "You're all set."

"Elevator to the far right, correct?"

"Yes. The desk will no longer need to key you in. You'll then be able to access all of Mr. Singh's floors. Have a good night."

She thanked them and pushed Khunda into the elevator. The key panel lit up, and she was soon taking a slow, gliding trip up to Ajay's floor.

His front door was ajar, and she heard the music first. Khunda's tail began wagging and she sat up, peering around.

"Yes, I'm excited, too," Raj whispered as they walked into the penthouse. Ajay stood in bare feet, wearing a button-down and jeans. His sleeves were rolled up to his elbows, and he had a kitchen towel draped over one shoulder.

"Hello there . . . Holy hell, you got your dog a stroller."

"Don't start," she said. "Did you just give me the figurative keys to your penthouse? I had to submit my biometrics downstairs."

"My house is your house," he said in Punjabi before leaning in to kiss her. She felt a zing when he pressed in deep, holding the back of her neck so she'd sink into the brief kiss.

He licked his bottom lip, and she watched the quick movement, already looking forward to another taste.

"Hi," he said gruffly. "Come in. I'm cooking again. We can get Khunda set up and out of that godforsaken contraption before we get you a glass of wine."

"That sounds . . . great," she said. She took Khunda out of the stroller and set her on the ground so she could run around and sniff. Raj would have to get the pee pad set up in case of emergencies, but she wanted to take a moment to enjoy the space.

The first time she'd been in Ajay's penthouse, she'd been dazzled and hard-pressed not to show it. The windows gave her one of the most magnificent views of the New York skyline she'd ever seen. He had a beautiful fireplace surrounded by plush leather sofas. His kitchen was twice the size of hers, even though her brownstone had more square footage.

The design was comfortable and homey but had his masculine stamp on each and every detail. Unlike her, he'd most likely picked out his own furnishings. She hated her decor. She'd have to add it to the list of things she wanted to change.

Khunda yelped and scurried behind the couch. Raj rushed after her, freezing in place when she saw that Khunda was trying to get inside a small dog pen wedged against the windows. A carpet was fitted inside along with a feathered dog bed, water bowl, food bowl, a couple of toys, a pee pad, and a long dental chew. "Is that all for Khunda?" she said.

Ajay had returned to the kitchen where he was pouring two glasses of wine. "Yes, I had Rafael set it up earlier today. I wanted to make sure you were comfortable, and that probably wouldn't happen if your dog wasn't comfortable, too. Why don't you put her in there? See how she likes it."

"I have a feeling she will," Raj said after swallowing the lump in her throat. She gave Khunda a minute to inspect it before she put her inside. The Chihuahua immediately began sniffing the carpet, then the pee pad, and finally she lapped at the water in the small bowl. Raj expected her to want to come out, but she plopped down and began gnawing on the dental chew.

"Looks like the pen is a success," Ajay said, and passed Raj a glass filled with a bright yellow wine. "This is a new blend from our Saffron Fields vineyard. Let me know what you think."

She smelled her wine, then swirled the liquid before taking a taste. It was rich, crisp, and deliciously fruity. "This is perfect."

He ran a hand up and down her back. "I'm glad. Want to come keep me company in the kitchen? Tell me about your day."

Raj looked down at the beautiful dog pen and her happy puppy, then at the wine in her hand. She squeezed her eyes shut, hoping that she was making the right decision.

"Raj?"

"I spoke with my brother, Guru. He's still in town."

Ajay's eyebrows V'd. "What did he want?"

"I'm not exactly sure. That's what I'm trying to figure out. There has to be something more than his interest in wanting me to go back to see my mother."

"Do you think it has something to do with money? Or your business?" Ajay pushed a tray of samosas forward along with a small dish of green chutney. "Don't get too excited. My mother made these."

"And here I thought you'd slaved away, stuffing sa-mosas for me," she said, plucking one off the end of the tray. "But to answer your question, I have no idea. I was thinking that maybe you'd help me to problem solve."

Ajay grabbed her free hand and pressed a smacking kiss on her knuckles. "That is one of the sexiest things you've said to me recently."

"Well, there's more where that came from. I can go into workforce analytics, but that might be too hot."

Ajay groaned. "Let's save the human resources conversation for dessert. I may not be able to contain myself, and I'll have to bend you over the table."

Her pulse jumped. And wasn't that exactly what she wanted him to do right that second? "Why not now?"

"Raj, you should know that there are only two things that have a chance at rivaling sex. Good whiskey and—"

"Good food," she completed. "Fine. I'll behave and wait. But Ajay? That's not going to last very long."

"I sure as hell hope not."

Chapter Twenty

Ajay

RAJ WAS ADAMANT that her former employee, Roshan Patel, was trustworthy and could help uncover the additional security breaches at Bharat. Fifteen minutes into their meeting, Ajay knew that Raj had been right again.

"And this is all the information on Sri's access history that you were able to get?" Ajay said to the video chat screen that he'd pulled up on his monitor.

"Yes," Roshan said, his voice crystal clear through Ajay's speakers. "I also sent you the information that he'd saved on Raj's family. I've known her for years as my boss, and I have to say, it's a pretty colorful file. Her family most definitely has a connection to an opium operation, but it looks like there is zero connection with your family in Punjab."

"Roshan—"

"Don't worry," he said, holding up his hands. "I won't tell a soul, including my grandmother. Not only for the sake of my job, but because I owe Raj. She's good people."

"That she is."

"Anyway, if you need anything else let me know. I'm assuming that I'm reporting to you for the time being and Sri isn't supposed to know that?"

"Yes. And if he gives you a problem, let me know and I'll talk to him."

"You got it, boss."

Roshan waved, and Ajay closed the window.

"Ajay."

He looked over his monitor to see Rafael standing in the doorway.

"I didn't even see you come in. What's up?"

Instead of sporting the cool, collected demeanor that was Rafael's trademark, he kept clenching and un-clenching his fists at his sides. His face was painted with worry. "You have visitors. In the conference room."

Ajay stood, dread sitting heavy in his stomach. "Who is it?"

"It's your brother Zail and one of the board members. Your uncle Frankie."

"Uncle Frankie? What the hell is he doing here?"

"It looks like your brother has gone to Uncle Frankie

with some concerns. They're here to talk about it. Hem and Bhram are on their way, as well. They were meeting for lunch nearby, so they shouldn't be long. If you want to wait until they arrive . . ."

"No," Ajay said. "I'll go talk to Frankie and Zail now. Thanks, Rafael."

"Ajay," Rafael said after hesitating in the doorway. "Zail looks like he's spoiling for a fight. He's taking his frustration out on Raj and you. Wait for Hem and Zail."

"No, I'm not going to do that." Ajay straightened the cuff of his shirt so it covered his kara and crossed his office. "This has gone on too long. It's about time people gave me the fucking respect I deserve."

He took his time getting to their largest conference room. The pace gave him an opportunity to leash his temper.

Upon entering the room, he saw Frankie at the head of the table where his father was normally seated. Zail stood at the window in jeans and a suit jacket. Damn programmer couldn't even put the whole suit on.

"I've been pulled away from my very busy schedule because I hear we have an issue," he said to his visitors. "Uncle Frankie? I do believe you're in my seat?"

Zail didn't turn to look at him when he said, "Not yet, bhai."

Ajay raised an eyebrow, and then motioned to his father's friend. "I'm sorry you had to come all the way down here."

"I'm not," Frankie replied. He steepled his wrinkled

fingers. "First, it's quite unusual to hear about an acquisition of a company through an email, Ajay. The board needs to vote on major decisions like that."

"You should know that an acquisition of this size doesn't need board approval. Since the family is still the majority shareholder, we have the authority to make the decision. Out of respect, we'll be presenting the acquisition for final review at next month's meeting, but we'll continue to pursue it."

Ajay stood across the table from his brother, waiting for Zail to acknowledge that what he was doing could hurt their family.

Could hurt him.

"Puttar," Frankie said, pursing his lips. "The next board meeting is critical. Your father was supposed to announce his retirement. It's time. His health has expedited the decision." Frankie took his time pushing to his feet. He adjusted his glasses, the same ones he'd been wearing for years. "I'm sorry, Ajay, but your brother has filled me in on his concerns about Ms. Hothi's integrity—"

"There are no concerns—"

"There is also, of course, pending litigation that is troublesome."

"You mean a divorce? How is a divorce troublesome? Or is that your bias, old man?"

Frankie made a *settle down* motion with both hands, which spiked Ajay's temper even further. "You're young and don't have a lot of experience. Sometimes a pretty girl can get us a little caught up, right? Zail made the right decision coming to me. It's obvious you're not ready to lead Bharat. We can start looking for another CEO now, and in another ten years you can make your case to be CEO at that time."

Zail whirled. "What the hell? That wasn't what we discussed, Uncle Frankie."

"What did you think was going to happen when you asked me to help in blocking the acquisition? This is proof that you boys need to grow up. I have a few great connections that would be more than qualified as CEO—"

"I need you to get out," Ajay said.

Frankie goggled at him. "*Excuse* me?"

"I believe your hearing is still good."

"Your father did not raise you to be like this, Ajay!"

"How he raised me is none of your concern. You are not welcome on Bharat's premises without my express authorization. When the board meeting and shareholders meetings occur, you'll be escorted in and escorted out. Do I make myself clear?"

"How *dare you*—"

"This meeting is over." He opened the conference room door and spoke to the first employee who made eye contact. "Please get Rafael for me. Now. We need him to escort one of our board members out."

Uncle Frankie scrambled forward, pushing Ajay out of his way. "Bharat is a symbol in the community, vital for our success. You're a spoiled child who is running this company into the ground. On my word, I'm going to do everything in my power to make sure you don't take your father's position!"

He left, slamming the conference doors behind him.

Ajay turned on his brother. "Are you happy? Do you see what you've just done by bringing in Frankie, of all people?"

Zail rounded the conference table, his eyes bloodshot. "I had no *choice*. We've only had problems since you became COO. I won't let you make our situation worse."

The verbal blow was a staggering one. "Are you seriously blaming me for the attempted takeover? I never thought in a million years my brother would screw with our legacy, our family, because he's angry over a woman."

"It's not just a woman!" Zail planted his hands on Ajay's shoulders and shoved him two steps back. "Sahar is the key to us ever finishing this software."

Ajay shoved him back. "You're the head of the department, and it's your responsibility to figure out how to fill her gap. If you can't, then maybe someone should take over for you, too, because you're just as much at fault."

"I'm not the one who is sleeping with the enemy. And that makes me wonder how soon you'll drive the company into the ground, because you just don't have what it takes."

The leash on Ajay's anger snapped and he shoved

Zail into the table. "Newsflash, dickhead. Sahar still hasn't been cleared yet, so if you think I'm sleeping with the enemy, then so the fuck are *you*."

Zail roared and tackled Ajay, and they both slammed against the wall. Conference chairs shot in every direction, while the awards on the walls rattled from the sheer force of impact.

His brother was built like a brick wall, Ajay thought as he took a punch to the gut. The pain was momentarily blinding, but he had adrenaline pumping through his body.

He did not have to defend himself to anyone, especially the little kid who used to look up to him and was now trying to undermine him in every way possible.

Ajay pulled his fist back and plowed it into his brother's face. Zail's head snapped back, then he retaliated by getting in a quick jab. Ajay tasted the blood, even as he shoved Zail against the windows. They rattled as the two men rolled on the floor.

Then someone looped an arm around Ajay's neck and yanked him back. Zail was pulled out of his hold at the same time.

"Knock it off!" Hem snapped.

"Everyone can hear you two at it," Bhram said sharply. "You're both being bloody idiots right now. We're not twelve anymore, dammit. You can't punch each other to solve your issues."

Ajay shrugged off his cousin's hold and backed up. He wiped at the trickle of blood at the corner of his mouth, just as Zail stumbled away from Hem, cradling his cheekbone.

The quiet was as sharp as the sound of a gunshot. Zail didn't bother waiting to talk about what happened. He rounded the conference table, giving Ajay plenty of room, and stormed out.

"What happened?" Hem asked as the door slammed.

Ajay waited until he caught his breath. "Zail brought in Uncle Frankie to pressure me into stopping the acquisition. With the board, and his vote, I think Zail expected me to give up Raj's company so I could be CEO. It didn't happen that way. Frankie started talking about how I wasn't fit for CEO regardless of the acquisition and that he's going to try to bring someone else in for the job."

"Bullshit," Hem and Bhram said at the same time.

"Exactly."

"You have to resolve this soon, Ajay," Hem said. "Otherwise it's going to get uglier than it already is."

"Don't I know it." He wanted to go home, to go to Raj's house. But after the scene he'd just caused, he'd only make things worse by leaving. He had an office to run and people who depended on him. He'd do what he had to so that Bharat continued to rise.

"I'll see you two later," he said. He straightened his sleeves and ran his fingers through his hair. "I have meetings." He turned on his heel and strode back to his office.

AJAY BURIED HIMSELF in work, but nothing he did took the edge off. His cousin and brother gave him a wide berth, and Rafael kept people away. He made one appearance in the break room on his floor to get himself some coffee, but he left when someone asked him if he needed ice for his bruised lip.

When he received an email request from Frankie and a few of the other board members to move up the end-of-year meeting, he shut down his computer and texted Raj.

AJAY: Where are you?

RAJ: Just got home with Khunda. Why?

AJAY: Your schedule clear tonight?

RAJ: I've just cleared it. See you soon.

When Ajay arrived at Raj's brownstone, he got out of the car, well aware that he needed to purge his anger somehow before he could have a civilized discussion and evening.

He knocked, and when the woman who occupied so much of his thoughts opened her door, his anger morphed into bright, hot lust. Light filtered into the foyer and glinted along the edges of her hair. Her mouth was painted petal pink, and her feet were bare.

"Rafael called," she said in greeting. "I heard you had a day."

"Where is Khunda?"

"With Kaka. He took my baby for the night so you can have my full attention."

"Good," Ajay said. Then leaned down and scooped her up.

Raj looped her arms around his neck and raised a brow in that elegant, beautiful, regal way of hers. "Well, that's one way to deal with work tension."

He kicked her door closed behind him and waited for her to lock it before carrying her upstairs. Her short, manicured nails lightly scraped through his hair and across his scalp, igniting his nerve endings.

He entered her bedroom, kicked off his shoes, and laid her down on the bed. "You know what I realized?"

"Nope," she said as she leaned back on her elbows. "Tell me."

"That we haven't gone slow, and I haven't given you the attention that you deserve." He removed his coat, his tie, his cufflinks, and then began unbuttoning his shirt.

She reached for the button of her jeans, but he shot her a glare that had her freezing. "That's for me to do," he said.

He stood in boxers, enjoying the way her eyes raked over his chest. After giving her another moment to appreciate him, he gripped her by the hips and scooted her farther up on the bed. The way that she spread her hair out and lay there waiting had Ajay instantly hard.

He picked up one foot at time, delighting in the peach nail polish on her toes, and kissed her ankles. "You have so many secret spots. Remember what I said?"

"That my secrets are safe with you," she said with a sigh.

"That's right."

He stroked up her legs and moved so that he was able to kneel at her side and unbutton her waistband. Her breath hitched and he took a moment to kiss the slope of her stomach, nuzzling her there. Then, when he wanted more, he pulled her pants down, touching, licking, nipping, and kissing his way over every exposed inch.

Ajay purposely bypassed her beautiful plump pussy and smiled at Raj's sound of distress.

"What's that?"

"Too. Slow."

"No, I don't think so. I know my woman prefers fast, hard sex. I know she likes to order me to do things using her dirty words. But sometimes she needs to be worshipped like a goddess, too. It's only right."

He freed her legs, pushing her pants off the edge of the bed, then stroked up and under her thin cashmere sweater. She was wearing strings and skin. Her bra was barely there, and Ajay went a little delirious with the sensation. He fixed his mouth to hers, then reached up to squeeze her chin when she tried to rush him. He didn't want to be rushed. He wanted every moment of this to be etched in his mind.

"Behave," he whispered, and then pushed her sweater up and over her head. His assumption had been right. She was wearing small, sheer triangles that barely covered her dark brown nipples. The cups were secured by satin strips that were more for form than function.

"Did you wear this today hoping you'd get fucked?"

"Yes," she sighed, writhing against him.

"Have you worn these before to seduce a man?"

Her eyes narrowed, and she tried to pull her arms free from her sweater, but he held her wrists captive with the fabric.

"I asked you a question," he said as his free hand slipped under the band of her matching panties and gave her one long, wet stroke.

"N-No," she choked. "They're new."

"A first for us." He bit her nipple through her transparent bra and sucked even as she writhed under him. "Tell me," he said as he continued to stroke and suck her between his words. "Have you ever made love?"

"Have you?" she snapped back.

"No. But I plan on it. Your turn."

She let out a frustrated growl and pulled her hands free. In seconds she'd rolled over him and straddled his waist. "No. Happy?"

"Yes." He sat up, unhooking her bra, and pressed a kiss between the curves of her breasts. "That means that we're experiencing another first together."

He flipped her over so that she was under him and saw the delighted glint in her expression. Raj liked those small displays of dominance, apparently.

And then he couldn't think at all. Their mouths met, and his brain stuttered to a halt. His hands were full of Raj. Their fingers linked and they pressed together, chest to breast. They moved, stroking and sucking at each other until Ajay couldn't think of anything else but being inside her, being a part of her.

With their lips still fused, he curled his fingers inside her soft pussy, rubbing the swollen nub of her clit as he felt her first trembling orgasm crest like a gasp and a sigh. She said his name, and the sound was like an embrace around his heart. With pleasure racing through him, he grabbed the condom from the bedside table she pointed to, put it on, then rolled on top of her again.

"Raj." He settled between her legs, positioning himself. Time suspended as she wrapped her legs around his waist. With their eyes locked on each other, he entered her in one firm thrust.

"Ajay!"

"I'm making love to you," he said in Punjabi, his voice hoarse, as he struggled to focus, to tell her this one thing that was so important. "I'm making love to only you. This is our first. Do you feel it? Do you feel me all the way inside you?"

"Tuhada piyar mera ata hona vala hai."

Your love will be my end.

"No," he said, struggling to speak now. "No, it's our beginning."

He began moving inside her now, keeping his thrusts slow and even. Raj pushed against him, demanding more, but he wouldn't give it to her. He couldn't. He wanted them to memorize every kiss, every lick, every pump of hips.

He felt his balls tighten even as she quivered with her rising orgasm.

And then she came, rolling her head back against the bed, reaching down to grip his hips and pull him flush against hers. He followed seconds later, roaring her name and feeling blinded by the joy between them.

When his brain started to clear, he took stock of what had happened. He knew he wouldn't remember how long they lay together, or who helped who clean up the remnants of their lovemaking. What he would remember forever was resting his head against her breast and feeling her fingers run through his hair.

"Do you want to talk about it?" she asked into the silence.

He closed his eyes and sighed. "Yeah," he replied. "Yeah, I do."

Chapter Twenty-One

Rajneet

RAJ DIDN'T KNOW if practical advice or continuous sex would be enough to soothe the hurt in Ajay's eyes, but hopefully her listening would.

And food. After all, food worked for her.

She poured two cups of masala ginger chai and set them on the dining table. The smell of frying bature and simmering chole filled the house. Khunda chewed on a small hank of rope in her plush, custom-designed chesterfield dog bed. The scene was unusually domestic, but it felt comfortable to Raj. It felt right.

"What are you thinking?" she asked as she stood next to Ajay's chair, stroking his back.

He pulled her close, wrapping one arm around her

hips even as he continued to read through emails on his phone.

"I should've asked Rafael to drop off my laptop and work clothes with my overnight bag yesterday," he mused. "I could've gone straight to the office from here."

"Well, hopefully when Khunda and I move, we'll be close enough that it won't be too difficult to get clothes anymore."

His head jerked up. "What do you mean?"

"I'm going to sell the brownstone," she said. She'd slowly come to the decision over the last few weeks. "It's a part of my old life, and honestly, it makes me nervous that Khunda is so small and could get lost in all the space."

"Where do you think you're going to move?"

"I'm not sure yet. I'll have to do a real estate analysis and determine which neighborhood is the best investment." Raj's plan was to find a location closer to her office, wherever that office would be. As for her proximity to Ajay . . . well, she wasn't going to deny the fact that he was a consideration, too.

Ajay pulled her firmly between his knees. "Raj?"

"Yes?"

"Would you consider moving into the penthouse with me?"

Yes, she wanted to say. *Yes to everything*. But she hadn't gotten to where she was in life by acting impulsively. No matter what she was feeling for him, she had to still be careful.

If she was careful with her heart, then she was being careful of her life and those she loved.

"I don't think that's the best idea under the current circumstances. Our business agreement, and your brother—"

"My brother is going to have to deal with our relationship."

She ran her thumb over the days-old faded bruise at the corner of his mouth and cupped his face.

"How about we wait for the acquisition to end," she said. "By then my divorce will be over, and hopefully, I'll have a start date at the foundation. If that's where I want to be. I honestly haven't decided yet. Let's keep the pretense of discretion going for a little bit longer."

"Okay, but the offer is open. I want more firsts with you, Raj."

"Me, too."

"Garam, garam chole bature," Kaka called out from the kitchen. "Fresh and hot!" He carried dishes heaped with food to the table, along with utensils and bowls.

"Kaka, I've never seen you this happy."

Kaka's smile was bright and toothy. "That's because you're finally seeing a nice *Punjabi* boy who can take care of you. Enough with these gora men. Now eat. Ajay, you need food." He left the room with a bounce in his step.

"I can't believe Kaka just said that," Raj said. She sat down in front of one of the plates.

"I'm not ashamed to admit that I'm glad I have his

approval. He's the closest thing to a father figure you have here."

"That he is." She propped her chin on a fist. "You know, I have to wonder—how is it that you aren't married and settled yet?"

His slow, boyish grin had butterflies fluttering in her stomach. "Because I've been waiting for you?"

"I won't even bless you with a response to that."

He shoved chole and yeasted puffed bread into his mouth. Raj raised a brow, then took a sip of her chai as she waited.

"You're not going to drop this," he said after swallowing.

"No way, Singh."

He wiped his fingers, twisting the napkin between them as he spoke. "I dated on and off in college and grad school. When I worked at Bharat, too. But since Hem left Bharat and I've assumed more responsibility, my relationships have been more like brief connections instead."

Raj kicked him lightly under the table. "You're giving me the summary when I want the whole memo."

"It's not that exciting, Raj," he said. He dropped his napkin and reached for her hand. "Truthfully, I expected to have an arranged marriage, so getting serious with someone was just never in the cards for me. I love the relationship my parents have. There was so much love in our house growing up. I wanted that, too."

"That's admirable," she said, and took another sip of

chai. She thought of the pictures sitting on his mantel at the bungalow in New Jersey. She couldn't imagine wedding photos of Ajay and some other woman squeezed between his brothers and his parents.

Nope, that wasn't going to happen. Not if she had anything to say about it.

She knew that she was being possessive, just like she'd experienced right after Ajay had committed to buying her out. This time she was serious, though.

Her poor, poor man had no idea what was coming.

"My parents wanted an arranged marriage for me when I returned from school, too. I had other plans for myself."

"I can see that."

"All I'm saying is that sometimes things happen for a reason."

"What's the reason for us happening?" Ajay asked.

Raj leaned over and pressed a kiss to his jaw. "Maybe we'll have to keep going until we find out."

"That's an excellent idea," he murmured against her mouth.

Raj leaned into the kiss and was enjoying the smooth feel of his lips and the way they tasted her when they were interrupted by a vibrating phone.

Ajay pulled away and looked at his cell. "It's Hem. And since it's not even seven a.m. yet, he must need something. Okay to get it?"

"Sure," she said.

"Bhai," Ajay said as he picked up. "What's up?"

Raj watched as Ajay's face morphed into shock, then fury. "What the hell are you talking about? I'm sitting with her right now. Let me put you on speakerphone."

Hem's voice came through the speaker a moment later. "Okay. Hey, Raj."

"Hem. What's going on?" Her senses were on high alert because of the stress in his voice. "What happened?"

"I'm so sorry to be the one to break this to you, but it looks like an exposé was just published about your life and RKH Collective."

"An *exposé*?"

"First thing this morning. It appeared in the *Financial Times*, and it's already gotten a ton of views. Ajay, you may want to see what you can do to stop this train."

Raj's heart pounded as hard and fast as a freight train. "Can you forward us the article? We need to see what we're dealing with."

"Sure. Texting it to Ajay's number now."

"Thanks, Hem," Ajay said and hung up.

They waited for the link to come in, then Raj took the phone with steady hands and began to read.

Married for a green card . . .
Cheated on her spouse with hookups at the Ice Palace . . .
Uses information to bribe . . .
Daughter of a drug dealer . . .
Cutthroat . . . ruthless . . . cold-hearted . . .
Sleeping her way to a sale with Bharat . . .
Illicit affair . . .

Raj vaulted out of her chair. Her pulse raced as the words went around and around in her head like a carousel.

There were the ugly truths of her life written for everyone to read, for everyone to judge her. Her whole office would know her life and would now think that she was a corrupt sycophant willing to do anything to make money.

Ajay jabbed a number on the phone she'd dropped. "Rafael? I need you to do damage control right now." He barked into the phone, his words clipped and full of malice. "Communications needs to put out a statement. Put together a task force. I want this shut down. No, I don't care about timing, Rafe. This story dies."

He tossed the phone aside and reached for her, but she held up a hand to stop him.

"I am so sorry, baby," he whispered. His hands fisted at his sides. "I'm so sorry I brought you into this mess. This is probably Sri's leak. I'll get him, though. I should've listened to you from the beginning."

"This has Robert written all over it," she said, surprising herself at how calm she sounded. She closed her eyes and pressed her fingertips against her lids. "I need to stop this before it gets traction."

"This is going to get some press. It's better if you stay out of sight until you have a game plan, and wait until I can confirm how much of this came from Bharat. You might want to get—"

"Legal and Communications on the line. Yes, I know. And you should probably call—"

"Tushar and my father. Yup. I'm on it."

This time when he reached for her, she let him wrap her in his arms. "I'm so sorry. I know how much your privacy and your secrets mean to you. We'll figure this out."

"I can't believe he'd do this to me," she whispered. Tears clogged her throat, and a vague part of her brain was horrified that it was the second time in two weeks that she'd cracked in front of this man. It was the most she'd cried in years.

Squeezing Ajay, knowing that he was giving her strength, she pulled back, wiping at her cheek. "I'm going to have to work from home."

She'd sacrificed so much and worked too hard for her life to watch it crumble like a house of cards. She'd lock up her shame, her fear of rejection, and her sadness later. Right now, she had to focus on damage control.

"Raj?" Kaka entered the room a moment later. He looked baffled. "There are a few people outside the front door."

"Shit," she hissed. "Ajay, get your stuff and get out of here. You can leave through the basement apartment exit, which is farther down the left side of the building. Robert probably gave up my location, too."

"I'm not going to leave you here for the vultures to start congregating."

"I can take care of them."

"I know you can, but you don't have to." He turned to Kaka. "Can you pack Khunda's things for a week?

Raj, go upstairs, get ready, and call a car. We'll get your attorney on the line to help clear the sidewalk in front of your house, too. Then go to my penthouse. You can work from there."

Raj saw the reason in Ajay's logic. She would be trapped like a sitting duck at the brownstone.

With a quick gesture at Kaka, Ajay scooped up Khunda and passed the dog over. "What else can I do to help you get your things?"

"Nothing," she said. "You need to get out of here. I'll go to your penthouse, but it's already looking bad for us with the way this article has positioned our relationship."

"Ask me how much I care about what other people think."

"Sometimes you have to so that you can protect the people you love."

He cupped her face and leaned his forehead against hers. She breathed in his clean, masculine scent and let out a breath.

"There is nothing," he said softly, "that could make me ashamed of being with you. I know your secrets like you know mine. And remember what I said?"

She nodded, her heart clenching with fresh, new love. "We're partners."

"That's right. We're partners, Raj. We'll handle this."

"Together," she said.

His phone buzzed again, and this time he didn't hesitate in answering it. "Rafael."

Raj watched his face morph from determination to surprise and then to anger. "Fine. Set up the meeting for two o'clock today. I'll be in the office soon."

He hung up and reached for her again. "The board has called an emergency meeting. Those who can't make it have assigned Frankie as their proxy."

"They're going to try to block your father from naming you the next CEO of Bharat because of this," she said, already knowing the outcome of the call. "I am so, so sorry." This was all her fault. Her secrets were hurting him.

"Raj, don't even think about blaming yourself," he said. "Come on. We don't have time. We need to get ahead of this."

She nodded and followed him upstairs. Her anger mounted like a horse trapped in a pen, ready to race.

Whoever had decided to mess with her life, whether it was Robert, Sri, or some other idiot, they were going to find out exactly how she dealt with her enemies. How dare someone use her secrets against her? How dare they try to hurt Ajay?

As a plan began to form in her mind, she knew that she was about to play the biggest game she'd played in business and in her life. She just hoped that Ajay's promise for partnership would stay steadfast when it was all over.

Fifteen minutes later, Ajay slipped out the basement apartment exit, and Raj put in a call to Harnette.

"I need to know what your email inbox looks like."

Harnette let out a whoosh of air. "Let's just say that the sales team is getting a few calls from our clients, and that's the good news."

Raj's heart clenched, and she hated herself for it. She lived her life according to her own terms, and no one had the right to judge her.

"I need you to set up a press conference."

There was silence on the other end of the line.

"Harnette?"

"Raj, you don't even agree to interviews. You're going to do a press conference?"

She looked at the half-empty bag packed and sitting on her bed. "Yes," she said. "Today. This evening."

"Okay, then. I trust you, boss. I'll make it happen."

Chapter Twenty-Two

Ajay

AJAY THOUGHT ABOUT kindergarten as he rode into the office. It was his earliest memory of knowing what he wanted to be when he grew up. His teacher had asked him to do a project where he dressed up and spoke to the class about his dreams.

He'd worn a suit and said he planned on leading a business like his father.

As he grew older, he knew his class project had just been a pipe dream. His brother was being groomed for the position. Besides, he couldn't code like Zail or negotiate like Hem. All he had was determination and passion.

Now, as Ajay stepped out of his car and strode directly into his office building, he knew he needed to stop dreaming, to stop thinking that he couldn't do the job that he'd always aspired to. He came from a long line of warriors, and he had to fight for what he wanted.

Rafael met him at the front entrance of the office, tablet in hand. "I cleared your schedule from now until the two o'clock meeting except for one commitment. The land developers out in Napa Valley need an answer today, so I left them on your calendar. Hopefully that's a quick one."

"Thanks," Ajay said. He strode directly to his desk, dropped his bag, and booted up his computer. "I need to know the minute any family member walks into this office. Bhram. Hem. My mother. Mina. Zail. Literally anyone."

"Done," Rafael said. "Do you need me to stall?"

"No," Ajay said. "But don't let them come back here. Send them to the conference room. I have to do some research, follow up on a hunch about our leak." He sat down in his high-backed leather chair and looked at the one friend who had always been by his side. Rafael had started as a consultant, worked his way up the ranks to executive assistant supporting his father, and now he was supporting Ajay. He was driven, smart, loyal, and a friend.

"Rafael, can you close the door?"

Without a word, Rafael did as Ajay asked. "What's going on?"

"I was just thinking how long we've known each other."

A hint of a smile curved at the corner of Rafael's normally stoic face. "Long enough for us to have a few drinking stories together."

"That is unfortunately the truth." Ajay leaned back in his chair and straightened his tie, trying to think of the right words, the right thing to say. "If you were in my position, and you had an article written about your partner, what would you do?"

Rafael let out a breath. "Probably ask you for advice, I suppose."

"No, seriously."

"I am," Rafael said. He sat down in one of the companion chairs across from the desk, tossed his tablet aside, and leaned back in his seat. "Ajay, you've always been the most levelheaded out of all three of your brothers, recent fistfight aside. You are a strategist, your memory is practically eidetic, and you make clients and competitors nervous because your brain can figure out the odds faster than most geniuses in the tech industry. If anyone has advice on how to clean up a shit show and do it right, it would be you."

Ajay wanted to believe Rafael. He needed to believe it. But sometimes having faith in himself was his biggest challenge.

Which was why he needed to surround himself with the best talent, to make sure that he was always focused on the possibilities and not the doubts that circled his mind like vultures.

"I need to ask you something."

Rafael readied his tablet again. "Okay."

"Will you be my chief of staff starting in January when I take over the CEO position?"

Rafael's jaw dropped. Ajay had never seen him so surprised before, and the reaction made him grin.

"Is this because I just gave you a compliment?"

"No, although that was a nice touch. You're the best assistant I've ever had, but I'm going to need to lean on you more. We're three months from the end of the year. Work with the head of HR and ask them to source résumés for a team. You build out that team for yourself, Set it up according to your specifications. Work with our experts in-house if you need help. Then find me a replacement for you. You'll work longer hours but your pay will be triple."

This time Rafael's eyeballs bugged out of his head. "Wh-Why? Why this, and why now?"

"Because I trust you. And if there is anything I've learned after the last six months, it's that trust is a very fragile commodity. So? What do you say?"

"I say yes." Rafael stood, a smile still ghosting his mouth and shock in his glassy eyes. "I say yes because I know that no matter what happens today, you're still going to get the CEO position, and sooner or later, everyone is going to respect you like I do."

Ajay nodded. For the first time, he knew that Rafael was right. He was going to fight tooth and nail to make sure that his future was locked into place, just like it should be.

After clearing his throat, Ajay said, "Now I need you to call in Roshan, Tushar, and our FBI contact."

"Sir?"

"I have a plan."

"Then I'm on it."

Time flew by faster than Ajay could've expected. He rushed through his call with the Napa Valley land developers and spent the rest of his time preparing notes, information, facts, and figures to get everything just right for his family and the board. He was able to verify the three people responsible for feeding information to the news outlet for the article, thanks to some connections, and then called Raj to let her know. She didn't say much except to confirm that she was safe in his penthouse and working on her own fallout strategy.

Rafael popped his head in his office and interrupted Ajay's train of thought at two o'clock. "Okay, they're all here and in the conference room."

Ajay's stomach twisted even as he stood and grabbed his laptop. He handed it to Rafael and asked him to set it up while he started the meeting.

They entered the room together, and the first thing Ajay noticed was the clear divide on either side of the boardroom table. His father, Hem, Mina, Bhram, and Zail sat on one side, while Uncle Frankie and five of the other board members sat on the other. To get that many to agree to come at the last minute to a meeting was incredible.

He'd just have to use their presence to his advantage.

"Gentlemen, and Mina. I'm surprised you've all come on such little notice, but I guess that's neither here nor there. We'll have to use this time wisely."

Uncle Frankie stood on his creaky old bones just as Ajay predicted he would. "I think we all know why we're here, puttar—"

"Frankie, sit down."

Frankie stuttered, his lips smacking with spittle. "Excuse me?"

"You heard me. You may have rallied some of the members here before our year-end meeting—god knows how if all of your calendars look like mine—but as interim CEO I control the agenda. Just because my father is here today doesn't change that. When I open the meeting up for the room, you may speak then."

"Deepak!" Frankie shouted. "Do you see this? Do you see what he's doing?"

Ajay's father shrugged before leaning back in his chair and crossing his arms. "Frankie, Ajay has a point. The CEO and chairman of the board leads the agenda. It's in our bylaws. You really are out of line."

"How *dare* you—?"

"Careful," Ajay said with as much calmness as he could muster. "When you address my father, you speak to him with respect."

Frankie scanned the room and when Ajay's brothers gave him that same, even, measured look, he took a seat.

"Now, as I was saying." Ajay faced his family first. Mina with her encouraging smile. Hem with his serious, concerned expression. His father, who looked at him with so much pride. "Singhs, it appears we're missing a member of the family."

"Your mother assigned me her proxy," his father said. "She has business in the city she needs to attend to. The documentation is with Rafael."

"Fine. Let's start with the easiest and then go to the most difficult." He looked down at his computer, at the notes he'd taken, and the carefully crafted persuasive arguments that he'd anticipated delivering to a room where everyone thought he was unable to do his job.

Well, almost everyone. Ajay smiled at his father, the reason he loved what he did in the first place, who sat patiently waiting for him to speak. The old man's pride, he realized, was enough to help carry the weight of obligations that weighed on his shoulders.

"I know that you all want to discuss the acquisition and the potential nomination by my father to make me CEO of Bharat. I know that everyone is concerned about our stock prices, and whether or not I'm fit for the position."

"I think that's a good summary speech there," one of the board members chimed in. "Are you going to do the right thing, then, and let us source a new CEO?"

"No," Ajay said. He adjusted the silver kara on his wrist so that it rested over the cuff of his shirt. His faith gave him added strength. "I'm not stepping aside, and if my father nominates me, if the family supports that nomination, then I will take it. But for this one time only, I'm going to explain to all of you my reasoning behind the acquisition and the positive result of today's news breach. Members of the board, it has come to our attention that we've had another leak in our company. Another part of our R & D team has been compromised by WTA. We've been looking into this security breach."

Whispers echoed on one side of the boardroom table. The Singhs and Mina remained silent. When the noise died down enough, he continued.

"Today, an article was published about Rajneet Kaur Hothi. Raj is the owner of RKH Collective, a company we are in the process of acquiring. Her services are a natural extension of what we already do, so it's an excellent investment."

More whispering.

"Because she is in the middle of a divorce, the acquisition has been blocked by WTA, which has ulterior motives, of course. The main one being that her future ex-husband is the representative for WTA on our shareholder calls."

The whispers became a cacophony of noise that erupted from the board members. Again, the Singhs and Mina remained quiet, arms or hands folded in front of them.

Frankie jumped up and faced the other board members. "This is an abuse of power when we're supposed to be focused on the new software! Deepak's son is telling us there is a leak but he's too busy with this woman who happens to be connected with our competitor!"

Ajay crossed his ankle over his knee and pointed to the recently vacated chair. "I am not done. You may want to hear the rest of it."

"You can't tell me what to do, puttar," Frankie raged as he paced in front of the windows.

"I sure as hell can," he said. "Now sit down."

One of the other board members leaned over and whispered something to Frankie. Whatever he said must've worked because the old man finally slipped back into his seat.

Ajay scanned the faces at the table, savoring this moment. "An hour ago, police arrested our head of security, Sri."

The conference room hushed until there was pin drop silence.

His father nodded.

"Sri was responsible for personally conducting a background check on Rajneet Kaur Hothi and RKH Collective in anticipation of the buyout. I was aware of her history before the article was published today, but because the acquisition was a good move for us, I proceeded.

"The information in the article is identical to Sri's research and was also shared in tandem with Robert Douglass."

"Wait, you're saying Sri was the one working with WTA, not someone directly on the R&D team?" Frankie said. "Impossible."

"It's possible. We have evidence, as well. We went into his access history and learned that he used Sahar Ali Khan's access keys to pull data after Sahar had already been fired."

Ajay had been told that there were also encrypted messages shared with one Guru Hothi. He hated having to tell Raj that her brother was involved, but he refused to withhold the truth from her.

She was strong. And if she couldn't handle it on her own, he'd be there for her.

"What are the next steps, brother?" Hem asked. "Is Sri locked up?"

"Yes, but we'll most likely have to provide testimony. Hopefully, with the help of RKH Collective, we'll have a more robust security team so this situation never arises again."

The intel had come in barely an hour ago from Roshan. Their FBI contact in white collar crimes, Ms. Hu, had been ready to assist.

"So Raj was right," Mina said. She winked at Ajay. "She told me a while back that if our security team was having such a hard time finding out the mole in the company, we needed to fire them. She knew something was off before anyone."

Ajay nodded with a bittersweet feeling—even though his company had succeeded in ousting the mole, his love was in pain because he'd been the root cause of her secrets being released to the world. "Raj's life story has now been painted in the ugliest way possible in the news because of her dealings with Bharat, despite the positive outcome for us."

Ajay shut the lid of his laptop and stood. "I know some of you blame me for the shit hitting the fan after Bharat went public two years ago. Before we were on the market, we were a growing, profitable business. The rest of you think I'm too young to fill my father's shoes. Well, I'm here to tell all of you that I have no intention of filling anyone's shoes. This is not a damn game of dress up. It's a race, and the only thing that I'm getting from my father is the baton so I can run the next leg of the relay for Bharat."

"Comparisons are inevitable," one of the newer board members chimed in. "You're his son, but you don't program like he does and you stay out of the limelight. People are going to have to use what they know and make assumptions about you."

"And that's going to change," Ajay said. He motioned to his family. "My legacy has been the most important thing in my life, which is why I've been focused internally. After this article about the company we plan on acquiring, I'm going to make major adjustments in the way the Singhs show up. Starting now."

He fixed his tie and the buttons on his suit jacket. "You may have called this meeting out of concern for the decisions I'm making for Bharat. But whether you're family or you're a general board member, I have the same message for you. I'm going to be the CEO of this company. I'll fight all of you for it, because I know I deserve this position. If you don't like it, then get the fuck out. Are we clear?"

There were nodding heads from Bhram, Hem, and his father. The board looked like they'd been hit in the solar plexus.

"Bhai, do you love her?"

The question came from Zail at the far end of the table. He watched Ajay expectantly, as if the other people in the room didn't matter.

"Zail, what does that have—"

"Do you love her? Answer the question."

Ajay let out a breath. "I do. She's a hell of a business-woman, and a lady."

Zail nodded. He looked down at his fingernails, then back at him again. "I'm sorry I misjudged you. You have my support."

Frankie gasped. The old bastard let out a wheezing cough before he said, "What do you think you're doing, Zail?"

"I'm supporting my family, Frankie," he replied. "I made a mistake in bringing you into what should've remained family business."

Ajay wanted to hug his brother, to slap him on the back and say that he loved him and he appreciated Zail's support.

Ajay turned to the man at his right who'd taken his seat again. "Frankie, it looks like the family is voting unanimously. The question is, are you going to continue to be a pain in my ass?"

A knock on the door interrupted Ajay's next thought. Rafael entered and motioned for him to check his phone.

"Excuse me," he said, and pulled out his cell from his pocket.

RAFAEL: Raj is hosting a press conference in an hour. Emailing you the livestream link. We need to get everyone out of here so we can watch it.

Holy hell, Ajay thought. He had no idea what she was up to, but there was no way he was going to miss it. He looked up at the expectant faces. Some were whispering with each other again, and others had blank looks of shock.

"We're going to have to cut this short."

"Hey, future CEO," Bhram called out. "What gives?"

Ajay threw all discretion out the window as he headed toward the exit. "My girlfriend is having a press conference.".

He heard chairs and chatter clatter in an uproar behind him. He grinned as he strode toward his office. His family would be right behind him.

Good, he thought. Rajneet needed all the support she could get, and now that his family knew where he stood, they'd support her, too.

Come on, Raj. Whatever it is you're doing, you have the Singhs behind you.

Chapter Twenty-Three

Rajneet

RAJ KNEW THAT she couldn't hide in Ajay's penthouse forever. She wasn't the hiding type. Furthermore, despite the shame she'd felt when she first read the article, she had nothing to be ashamed of. Yes, her secrets were uncomfortable, but they were hers. She'd made her life choices and reaped the benefits of what she'd sown.

Harnette had just left with instructions about the press conference in two hours. Now all Raj had to do was finalize her statement and wait for her assistant to come pick her up to take her to the location. She'd just trimmed her opening paragraph when she received the one call she'd been dreading since she saw the article.

"Kia," she said with as much briskness as she could muster.

The other woman didn't even bother with pleasantries. "You have some serious enemies, Raj. I'm so sorry about the article."

"I'm sorry that my life is written like a salacious tabloid, but not about the contents." She reached down and picked up Khunda to cuddle. Ajay's view of New York was therapeutic as she stepped up to the glass, phone and puppy cradled in her hands. "Are you calling to tell me that I'm no longer considered for the position of chairwoman and CEO of Gen One?"

Kia let out a sigh. "No, actually. I'm not."

"Excuse me?"

"I'm not going to rescind my nomination of you for the position. I think you're a strong, hardworking woman who has made choices to get the career that you've wanted. I am not judging you, I'm commending you."

Kia's words had Raj staggering into the nearest chair. "I don't understand . . ."

"Honey, what kind of woman would I be, what kind of leader would I be, if I judged the path of other women and leaders in this country? Hell no. I'm not going to do that to you. But the board is a different story. I'm calling to let you know that I don't think they'll support my nomination. I've gotten a few concerning calls this morning, and I've done my best to voice my support, but this position is going to be a bigger battle than even I anticipated. I'm so sorry, Raj. I'll do my best, but I can't promise anything."

Her dog sensed her confusion, her twisted heart, and began licking her cheek. Raj pulled the phone from her ear, buried her face in Khunda's neck, inhaling the fresh puppy scent, and breathed. This was all so overwhelming for her.

She heard a knock at the front door. "Kia, your support means . . . so much. However, if I am constantly going to be defending myself against the board, I don't know if Gen One is the place for me."

"Well, my nomination still stands. What are you going to do about the article today?"

Raj put Khunda down and walked toward the front entrance. "Address it head-on, as I always do," she said. "Thanks, Kia. I have to go."

"Good luck, Raj."

She tucked her cell back in her pocket and opened the door. "Tracey, we don't have to leave for another hour and a half—"

Her brother stood on the other side of the entry, hands tucked in his jeans pockets. She moved to slam the door. His foot jutted out to stop it.

"Wait. I just wanted to talk to you before I leave for the airport."

"I don't care what you have to say," Raj said. "I know you had a part in that article. Ajay found out a little while ago. You've what, come to try and dismantle my life and then leave? Is Mumma even dying? How did you even get up here?"

"It took a lot of convincing," he said. "Just let me in for a minute. Hear what I have to say, gudiya, and then I'll go."

Raj crossed her arms over her chest. "You can tell me what you have to say in the hallway, and then get out."

He hesitated for a moment, and nodded. "Robert approached me for the article. He said he had an inside man who could provide some additional details on you and your relationship with Bharat. I always hated that scumbag."

"Then why the hell did you work with him?"

Guru ran a hand over his beard as if contemplating his next answer. "I technically didn't. I just told him that if a single word was an elaboration or a lie, he'd be floating in the Hudson."

"Dammit, Guru—"

"You spend so much time trying to hide your truth that you are too afraid to live. Raj, when did you become such a coward? You fear that other people will turn you away now, when you were never that girl before."

There was that word again. Coward. It was one thing for Ajay to call her a coward, to force her to be better, to face her fears, but it was another when a man was trying to hurt her.

She wasn't that girl who acted carelessly and recklessly. Nor was she the polished, refined woman who kept people at an arm's length in fear of judgment.

"There is no way you can convince me that hurting me was for my own good. Do you seriously think I'm so blind that I wouldn't see through your pathetic lies? Now, if you're done, I need you to go. You're not welcome."

Her brother shrugged. "I'll go. I'll tell Mumma that convincing you to come was a fruitless exercise. I guess you said your goodbyes to her years ago."

Raj felt tears in her throat, but her eyes remained dry as dust. "I said goodbye to all of you years ago."

"Okay." He put his hands back in his pockets. "For what it's worth," he added in Punjabi. "I really am so proud of who you've become, Rajneet. You were always the brightest star with the most heart and grit in our family. Mom is very proud of you."

The elevator door at the end of the corridor opened and Ajay's mother stepped out. She carried a brown leather tote bag, which clashed with her black walking shoes and black pants. She paused when she saw Guru in the hallway.

"Sat sri akal, Auntyji," Guru said, as he folded his hands in front of him. He motioned for her to come forward. "I was just leaving."

Ajay's mother approached with slow, cautious steps. "Are you a friend of my son's?"

"No, I'm Rajneet's brother, come to visit her from

Punjab. I am headed to the airport now and saying my goodbyes."

"Oh," she said. She turned to Raj, who must've still looked glassy, since Ajay's mother immediately bristled. "Well, have a safe trip."

"Thank you, Auntyji."

He stopped halfway to the elevator. "Auntyji? We're entrusting the happiness and health of my sister to your and your family's hands. Please take care of her. She doesn't think she needs it, but we all know better."

"Guru, I don't need—"

Ajay's mother squeezed her arm. "We'll take care of her." Then she waited for him to leave before facing Raj again.

"He wasn't welcome here," she said simply.

Raj shook her head. She moved back so that the woman could enter her son's home. *I'm getting hit with a one-two punch today*, Raj thought. First Kia, then her brother, and now Ajay's mom. She had a high tolerance for stress and drama, but this was getting a bit much for even Raj to handle.

"Aunty, can I get you something to drink?"

"I'll make it." After toeing off her shoes she put her tote bag on the kitchen counter. She pulled out a foil-wrapped packet and a jar with seasoning in it. "My Ajay usually has masala for chai, but one can't be too careful. I carry some around just in case. I also brought paranthas and mango pickle, too. It's spicy."

Raj hadn't eaten since the few bites she'd consumed

that morning, but she didn't have the stomach for food. She was about to say so when Khunda bounded around the dining table straight toward Ajay's mother.

In Raj's experience, there was a fifty-fifty chance whether or not Indian parents liked pets. Dogs and cats hadn't been common in India when Ajay's parents immigrated to the States, so Raj went to intercept as quickly as she could. Khunda dodged her and pounced on Aunty's foot.

"And this must be Khunda!" She greeted the puppy like a long-lost friend. "My son has sent me a picture of you. I brought you a roti, too, with little oil and no salt. Would you like a roti? Is your mother okay with a roti?"

It took Raj a moment to realize the question was for her. "Auntyji, that is very kind of you to do."

"Nonsense. Now come. Sit while I make this chai."

Raj smoothed a hand down her pants as she thought about the best way to approach her current predicament. If there was one person whose judgment could hurt her, it would be this woman. She'd raised an incredible man and her approval would be . . . no. *No*, Raj thought. She didn't need anyone's approval. She just hoped that Ajay would be okay with that, too. She'd hate to be the cause of widening the wedge between him and his family.

"Aunty, can I ask why you're here?"

The woman pulled out a pot and began filling it with water. "Because I would rather be with you than sitting in a boardroom during Ajay's meeting. My boy can handle it on his own. His father is with him, anyway."

"I know." Raj stepped forward until she could grip the edge of the kitchen island countertop. "That doesn't answer my question."

Aunty paused in the act of dropping a tablespoon of masala into the water. "It does if you were listening."

Well, that put her in her place, didn't it? Raj mused. She slid onto the barstool and decided that it was best to wait and hear what the woman had to say on her own.

"You know, I read your article—"

And there it was.

"—and I didn't think you should be alone right now."

What twilight universe was she living in? Raj picked up Khunda, because obviously her dog was the only thing that made sense right now.

"Aunty, I appreciate your support."

The woman laughed, the sound lyrical to Raj's ears. "It's clear that you aren't comfortable with me. Maybe it was your mother? I don't know how other Punjabi mothers are, but I raised three boys and our life was very different from the moment I stepped foot in the US. That is why I'll tell you what I think."

She pulled two mugs out of the cabinet and then a small canister of sugar. "I think that you need a parent to listen to you. My boys, and my husband, they know I'm no good with business. I'm no good with technology. But I'm good with them. I know them, and I know people. So they've always talked to me. You can talk to me, too, Rajneet."

Raj pressed Khunda closer to her.

"In my limited experience, Punjabi mothers prefer their sons to marry chaste women without secrets in their closets."

The older woman made a dismissive gesture with her hand as she retrieved milk from the fridge. "Bland women are bland in bed and produce bland, boring children."

Raj's mouth dropped. "You're okay with . . . You're okay with me?"

"Now, I didn't say that." She added milk to the pot. "I will judge you, not based on your past, but based on how you respond to your past. After the article today, my son is sitting in a meeting where people are also judging him. Hopefully, he gets what he wants. You are here, sitting in his penthouse. What are you doing to get what you want?"

"I'm going to fight."

"Oh?"

Raj nodded. "In one hour, my assistant is going to pick me up. I'm going to do a press conference where I'll address the contents of the article."

"What will you say?" Aunty placed a steaming mug of chai in front of her, along with a spoon and the sugar dish. "Will you deny the article?"

Raj shook her head. "Not at all. Why should I? It's the truth."

"Will that hurt your business?"

"If it does, then it does. But do you know what, Aunty? I wouldn't have thought that way two months ago. Now, if I fail, I have more than my friends, my dog, my employees. I have Ajay. If I can't figure out another solution, he will."

There was a small smile on Ajay's mother's lips as she rounded the counter so that she could reach out and cup Raj's face. "My soni, soni girl," she said softly. "You're absolutely right. You have family now. I am here."

Raj swallowed the lump in her throat. "Aunty, would you like to come to the press conference with me? I know Ajay will be busy, and I could use . . . I could use some support."

"Of course I can come with you. Now. Will you be wearing something that casual?"

Raj looked down at her slacks. She liked this woman. "No, I'm going to change. I have a lucky black dress."

"Good. Now, let's have some chai. I want to know what your brother was doing here."

Raj smiled. "Yes, Aunty."

Chapter Twenty-Four

Ajay

AJAY: I'm coming down there.
RAJ: No, I'm going to be fine. Your mother is with me.
AJAY: My MOTHER??
RAJ: Yes. She showed up at the penthouse with food. She's been tremendous. You're so lucky to have a family that keeps you grounded.

AJAY SMILED AT the text. His family had a lot of quirks, but Raj was right. They kept him grounded. He stood in front of the flat-screen in his office, watching as the press conference was about to begin. He hadn't spotted

Raj yet, but there was what looked like quite a gathering in front of RKH Collective's office building.

He felt a hand grip his shoulder.

"How are you holding up?" Bhram asked.

"I just want this shit to be over," he told his cousin. "I feel like I got half the battle left to go."

Bhram nodded. "You did great in the board meeting. You put Frankie and those other assholes in their place."

"I just hope it worked. We'll see how next month goes."

Bhram leaned in and lowered his voice. "I have a question for you. Did you know when you asked Sri to look into Raj that—"

"No," he said. "Hell no. I would never do that to her intentionally. It was an unfortunate accident that I had to use to my favor."

"What did she say about it?"

Ajay rubbed the back of his neck, hating that he hadn't been able to talk it out with her before the board meeting. "I let her know the minute I confirmed it was Sri. She wasn't upset, but . . . God, I can't help but feel bad about it."

"You can't take responsibility for everything, brother," Bhram said. "You have to know that."

"I do." Ajay couldn't help feeling obligated, though. Raj was so new in his life, and his feelings for her were raw and fresh. He waited for the press conference to start as his cousin stood vigil at his side.

"Just a few more minutes," Bhram said, motioning to the screen. "Looks like she's arrived."

Ajay surveyed his office, and discovered it was surprisingly empty.

"Where is everyone? They don't want to watch?"

"Your father is talking to some of the employees. He hasn't been here in a while so he wanted to check up on a few people. Hem and Mina are with him to make sure that he doesn't overdo things."

"And Zail?"

Bhram shrugged. "He's been quiet. I think he went to go check with Damany in Finance about our budget restraints."

"No, he's here," Zail said from the doorway. He had bags under his eyes, and he appeared more haggard than usual. He pushed up the flannel arms of his button-down shirt and strolled over to stand on Ajay's right side. "Let's see what she says," he murmured.

Raj appeared on the screen. She wore a slim-fit black dress that hit right above the knee. A cream-colored tweed jacket with a siren-red stripe along the lapels and cuffs completed her outfit.

Always looking like a boss, he thought.

"Good afternoon," she said in her clear, cultured voice. "My name is Rajneet Kaur Hothi, and I am the founder and CEO of RKH Collective." Ajay held his breath as she began.

You got this, Raj. Make them regret every moment they doubted you.

"As all of you have read, an article was released this morning questioning my character, my upbringing, and the way I conduct my business. The article was obviously written by a man."

A flutter of laughter echoed through the crowd. "I've never been one to apologize for my life choices, and I don't intend on starting now. However, because the article made some serious implications about innocent parties, and it could potentially affect the lives of my employees, I am here to provide some context for you.

"The content for this article came from three different sources, all of whom have been confirmed. The first is my brother, an estranged family member interested in . . . interested in bringing to light a past I've kept hidden for far too long. The second is my ex-husband, Robert Douglass the third. Robert is an employee of WTA. He recently acquired a job with them after he sold them information about Bharat that I was personally working on as a part of an RKH–Bharat partnership."

"Holy shit," Bhram, Ajay, and Zail said in unison. They looked at each other, goggling, and then back at the screen.

The audience of reporters rushed with questions. She raised a hand and silence descended. "Questions at the end, please. Now, Robert's activity has been confirmed through video footage. That leaves the last source. This person was working with Robert and is part of an ongoing investigation."

"She went all in," Zail said. "Did she tell you she was going to do this?"

"No, but she has to have a really good reason for it," Ajay said. "Watch."

Raj brushed her hair over her shoulder. She looked strong and confident. Her elegance was a magnet, and she looked regal standing in front of the microphone. "You can try to villainize me when I've lived my life according to my own terms, and you can judge my company while ignoring the tech giant in the room. This tech giant which we all know has affected my business and, in my opinion, is attempting to smother and crush innovative, competitive, and life-altering geniuses like those at Bharat. I have no intention of defending myself against tired stereotypes and sexist allegations. With that being said, I can now take some questions."

Bhram whistled. "She just challenged the big boys."

"Yes, she did," Ajay mused. "WTA is going to come after her now. And I think it's time we step in line and fight them, too."

Zail put a hand on his shoulder. "Bhai." He cleared his throat. "I'm sorry. I can't tell you how sorry I am for fighting you on this. You knew what you were doing and I let my . . . I was angry."

"It's hard being the asshole, isn't it?" Ajay said. He opened his arms and embraced Zail in a bear hug. They pounded each other on the back, and Ajay felt the last heavy weight lift off his heart. Things were back to the way they should be in his family.

Rafael knocked and entered the room. He held a Post-it in his hand. "Sorry to interrupt. Zail? Raj called and left this message for you."

"Raj?" he said, with confusion.

Ajay turned back to the screen. She was still answering questions from the audience. "Raj must've left it right before she got on stage."

"What does it say?" Bhram asked.

"It's an address. In Peoria, Illinois. A remote rental cabin on the lake."

Ajay shared a look with Rafael and then his cousin. He cuffed his brother's neck. "Oye, *duffer*. Whose address do you think it is?"

Zail's face went blank in shock. "Sahar's? She found Sahar for me?"

"If anyone can do it . . ." Ajay said.

Zail shoved the note into his pocket. "I gotta get to Peoria. The jet?"

"At the hangar. Rafael, can you call ahead?"

"Yes, sir."

Zail gripped Ajay in a bruising bear hug again. "You found the right woman after all," he said gruffly in Ajay's ear, and then he was gone.

A few minutes later, Ajay's father, Hem, and Mina walked into the office. "Did we miss it?"

Ajay looked at Bhram and grinned. "You could say that."

He turned back to the screen to listen to the rest of the question-and-answer portion of the press conference. He'd never felt so sure, so determined, about anything in his life as he was about his place at Bharat and how he felt about Rajneet Kaur Hothi.

Now he just had to sell her on the possibility of forever.

Chapter Twenty-Five

Rajneet

RAJ WAS BONE-TIRED and feeling even more wrung out by the minute. She gave a weak smile to the attendant at the security desk as she walked into Bharat's offices. It was late, and most of the staff had gone home for the night, but Ajay had asked for her to meet him there.

As she took the elevator to his floor, she registered every ache and twinge. All she'd done was stand in front of a gaggle of reporters for an hour, then take calls, do interviews and issue statements. Her staff had humbled her with their support. The only person who had been fired up was Robert. She pulled out her cell phone again and read his last few messages.

ROBERT: You bitch!!!! Better prepare yourself for court! You cost me my job!!!

RAJ: No, you cost you your job. Also, our divorce proceeding has been moved up. You violated the confidentiality agreement. Now every penny we have is mine.

ROBERT: FUCK YOU! LIKE HELL! I'll fight you tooth and nail, Raj!

RAJ: Texting in caps is so juvenile, Robert.

She slipped her phone back into her pocket as she keyed into the double doors of Bharat, Inc. The lights were mostly off, and she heard the faint hum of a vacuum cleaner from one side of the floor. She followed the walls to the corner office, but it was dark. Did he forget?

No way. Ajay never forgot things like this. At least, he hadn't in the time that she'd known him. She put her bag down on his desk and, with phone in hand, walked the floor to find him.

He was in the boardroom. The lights were off, and he stood facing the windows with the twinkling lights spread out in front of him. The city was always a breath-taking place. The best part was that every view Ajay shared with her was different and special in its own way.

He turned, his silhouette illuminated by the power of the night sky.

"There you are," he said.

"I am so glad today is finally over." She closed the door behind her.

"It's been quite eventful, although I believe it was more interesting for you than me."

When he lifted a hand, she rounded the table so that she could take it. "I should've told you I was going to attack WTA, but before I went to do the press conference, I had a few visitors."

"Really? Who?"

"Well, I already told you about your mother. She fed me, told me to change my clothes so I looked presentable, and then held my hand the whole way to the press conference. She is so insightful. That's where you get it from, I think."

"Mmm-hmm. Maybe." She fit under his arm and let out a sigh as he brought her close. "Where is Khunda?"

"With your mother, actually. She asked if she could dogsit."

Ajay tilted his head back and laughed. "You're *kidding* me."

"Nope. I was told that if she couldn't have grandchildren, then she'd take the next best thing. Honestly, her backhanded compliments are inspiring. She's ruthless."

"What? You think the hard decisions that made Bharat what it is came from my father?"

Raj grinned for the first time all day. "And that is why her advice was so valuable to me. Because she knows how to make the hard decisions. Ajay, I think I'm going to see my mother."

She registered the surprise on his face.

"Are you sure?"

Raj nodded. After her brother had left, and after she was able to focus on other things once the press conference ended, she had the niggling feeling of regret in her heart. She didn't want to feel anything other than acceptance when it came to her family. Unfortunately, that would mean having to see her brother again, too.

Ajay linked his hands with Raj's. "Do you want me to come with you? We can take the jet and spend as much time there as you want."

Her heart swelled with so much love for him. It was so soon, so early, but that didn't matter. She'd spent years in a loveless relationship, an arrangement, so she knew without a doubt what her feelings were.

"I would like that a lot," she whispered, and tilted her face up to kiss him.

When the kiss never came, she narrowed her eyes. "I think you missed your cue there."

He shook his head. "I need to ask you something."

"What is it?"

He led her to the far end of the table, where one recessed light brightened the table and chair. A manila folder and ballpoint pen sat in front of the chair. Ajay ushered her to sit down. "I have another proposition for you."

"You want to talk business? Ajay, we've both had an incredibly long day."

He rolled his eyes at her, which only made her want to grab the pen and jab him with it. She was about to say so when he opened the folder in front of her.

"This is a personal partnership. I want you to know what the terms are before our relationship continues any further."

Raj tried to focus, tried to concentrate on the words in front of her. They slowly began to take shape, and when she realized what they said, her love grew exponentially.

"This is an employment agreement," she whispered. "To work as part of HAZ Enterprises as president of the Singh Foundation."

"You get to do what you want . . . but you also will be working with the family. You'll be working with me."

"Ajay, I don't know what to say."

"Say yes. Tell me you'll be my family, my future. If you don't like it, then I'll do what I can to help you create your second life, but all I'm asking is that I'm a part of it. What do you think?"

"I think that the terms aren't very clear, and I'm going to need additional information."

His brows V'd. "Additional information? Like what?"

She reached out and unbuckled his belt. "Like do I have any benefits with the role, and will I have to be discrete about using them?"

Understanding brightened in his eyes. "How could I forget?"

They made quick work of his pants and then hiked her dress up over her hips.

She already knew what he wanted, and he gave her what she needed. He tugged her hair, and the tiny prickle of pain and pleasure had her moaning as she bent over the table. She heard him unwrap the condom, and then felt him enter her in one steady push. Her hands spread over the polished wood as Ajay began pumping inside her.

"Yes," she cried, pushing back against him, begging for more, aching for release. He pulled her hair again with one hand, and then reached in front of her to pinch her nipples. She tried desperately not to scream in case one of the cleaning crew came in. "Yes, Ajay, I want it. I want you."

"Are you mine, baby?" He panted as he sped up. "I'm yours, so you're mine, right?"

"Yes, yes, yes," she chanted.

She begged him to fuck her as hard as he could, making promises in the height of her ecstasy. She came in one bright burst of pleasure.

Then, as the night sky brightly twinkled on beyond the windows, Ajay flipped her over and pushed her onto the table. He crawled on top of her and entered her again. This time, Ajay gripped her ankles and held her legs up and wide. It didn't take too long for her to come again, and this time, her love was with her.

He collapsed on top of her, and they lay like that, half dressed, heaving for air, for a long time. Raj ran her fingers through Ajay's hair and told him the only secret that she'd kept from him. The words came from her heart.

"I'm in love with you, Ajay."

"I'm in love with you, too," he whispered back.

She held his face in her hand, reveling in the feel of his beard. "Ajay Singh?"

He looked down at her, smiling with lingering pleasure in his eyes. "Raj Hothi?"

"Let's do business together. I'm in if you're in."

"Always, Raj. With you? Always."

THE SINGH FAMILY Trilogy developed after a series of conversations that occurred between myself and my editor, Elle Keck. Elle, thank you for letting me write about brown billionaires. Your unwavering support has always been a guiding light as I struggle through the trenches of my manuscript. Thank you also to the wonderful women at Avon who support, uplift, and cheer me on. Being a part of the Avon family has been an incredible experience, and you're all the reason I'm so damn happy. Thanks to Joy Tutela at David Black Literary, who is the best partner in crime a girl could have. Thank you to the hubs, who listens to me rant and eats takeout when I am late on edits and desperate to finish. To my friends Smita Kurrumchand and Ali Magnotti Nagel who also listen to me complain incessantly about my novels. To my critique partner, the talented Dee

Ernst. To the RITA Writer's Room class of 2019: Sarah MacLean, Adriana Herrera, Andie Christopher, Sierra Simone, LaQuette, Joanna Shupe, and Alexis Daria. You are the squad that any girl would be lucky to have. Thank you for your shenanigans and your support.

And thanks to all the girl bosses in my career who gave me the tough love I needed to show up and stop apologizing.

Don't miss any of the Singh brothers
finding their perfect matches.
Keep reading for an excerpt from
Hem and Mina's love story,

THE TAKEOVER EFFECT

Hemdeep Singh knows exactly what he wants. With his intelligence and determination, he has what it takes to build his own legacy away from Bharat, Inc., and the empire his father created. But when his brother calls him home, Hem puts his dreams on hold once again to help save the company he walked away from. That's when he encounters the devastating Mina Kohli in the Bharat boardroom, and he realizes he's in for more than he had bargained.

Mina will do whatever it takes to recover control of her mother's law firm, even if it means agreeing to an arranged marriage. Her newest case assignment is to assist Bharat in the midst of a potential takeover. It could be the key to finally achieving her goal while preventing her marriage to a man she doesn't love—as long as her explosive attraction to Hem doesn't get in the way.

As Mina and Hem work to save Bharat, they not only uncover secrets that could threaten the existence of the company, but they also learn that in a winner-takes-all game, love always comes out on top.

Now on sale from Avon Books.

Chapter One

IN SEVENTY-TWO HOURS, Hemdeep Singh had flown halfway around the world, led seven meetings for his client, reviewed hundreds of OSHA guidance documents, and taken a tour of two plants and warehouse facilities. The final contract negotiations were underway, and if he could secure the multimillion-dollar agreement, he'd have another successful win for his new firm.

The hotel he used as his home base for negotiations in the Philippines was a hotbed for tycoons and wealthy families because it provided discretion and luxury. Next to the bar that snaked along one side of the waterfall, where bartenders decorated drinks with exotic flowers, Hem swirled the top-shelf whiskey in his tumbler before toasting Faisal Rao, a magnate in the renewable energy industry. Faisal was also a vicious negotiator and had graduated from a top ten law school before investing his family's fortune in enterprise.

"Section 27.8 won't affect your bottom line, but it'll protect both my client and you from tax concerns."

Faisal hummed and scratched his beard. "I'm likely to agree with you—"

"Then we can sign."

"*But* I want my team to take a look at it."

Damn it, Hem thought. There wasn't a chance in hell of wrapping up the agreement within the hour if Faisal sent it back to his team. They were slow as shit.

"You know your business better than they do," Hem countered. "It's you that's taking the risk."

Faisal grinned. "That's very true." He leaned back in his seat and crossed his arms over his thick chest. "That's why I'm thinking my team should review it. I don't want to make any rushed decisions since I'll be paying the penalty."

"We can go back and forth like this forever," Hem said.

Faisal let out a laugh. "You're right. And on that note, it's nice to see another Indian from the States entrenched in global contract negotiation. We're a rarity, and our conversations have been a pleasure. Are you a Singh from Rajasthan or Singh from—?"

"Punjab. Sikh Punjabi from Chandigarh. My relatives still live there." Hem hated this type of small talk but if he could connect with Faisal on a personal level, then he'd bare his soul like he was talking to a shrink just to close the deal.

"My father's family came from Chandigarh originally," the man said with apparent joy. "My father was desperate to wear a turban and carry a sword in his youth like the traditional Sikh men he saw growing up. So he's said. Honestly, your height should've clued me in. What are you, six-two?"

"Six-four."

"Yes, your height is definitely a trademark quality of a Sikh man. You know, I was surprised that Tevish was using such a young firm to handle the negotiation. It couldn't have just been your height and looks that landed his account."

Pride.

Faisal was dragging his feet because his pride was injured. Hem relaxed in his seat and grinned at his opponent. Here he was, CEO of a successful midsize business, having to work with an outside law firm on a negotiation. Hem could understand executives that were level-conscious. He'd been the same way when he first started working with his father. It had taken him some time to learn that Deepak Singh didn't care what position a person held in his company. They were all treated with respect. That didn't mean executives outside Bharat agreed with the same philosophy, though.

"Tevish's family has deep connections with mine. I worked as an executive for my family business for years after law school so he knew that I could handle something as important as your agreement."

"Oh? What's your family business?"

"Bharat, Inc."

Faisal's eyes nearly bugged out of his head. "Your father is . . ."

"Deepak Singh, yes."

"Why aren't you still working for the company?"

"Because my father's business is growing and I need to expand my experience to help it along. Having the right industry knowledge is important in the technology space."

He'd repeated those words so many times and they felt stale on his tongue. Very few people knew of the heartache, the pain that had triggered his decision to leave. His parents and their involvement in his life were part of the reason why he'd lost his fiancée. Working closely with them was too difficult after he'd gotten his heart obliterated. On top of that, he needed to follow his passion. He'd only ever known Bharat, and it felt too unstructured, too relaxed for him. He wanted more, needed more, and starting his own law firm and investment group had been the best thing he'd ever done.

"Come on, Faisal," Hem said when he was met with silence. "You can't be scared of me now that you know my history."

Faisal's fingers fluttered over the edges of the tablet he'd been referencing. "I'm scared of nobody, kid. I've been at this for a lot longer than you. Honestly, I simply wanted to know how you got so damn good at bullshitting. Now I know. It makes sense why Tevish sent you now."

Hem grinned. He was closing in on the win. He could feel it. "You should've never doubted him."

Hem felt his phone buzz in his pocket and he discreetly reached inside his jacket and silenced the device. "Sign the contract. You'll make a shit ton of money if you do."

"I'm beginning to warm to the idea. Only because I have a feeling you'll never stop bugging me until I do."

Hem's phone began to buzz again.

"Do you need to get that?"

The phone stopped. "No, I—" When it started buzzing again, he took it out and read his brother's name on the screen. "Yeah, actually, give me a second." He didn't spare Faisal another look as he stood from the small table they'd occupied and walked a few feet away for some privacy.

"Ajay, what is it?"

His brother's gruff voice answered immediately. "I'm calling in the troops, brother."

"I'll be back in New York in two days."

"No, you have to come home now."

Hem snorted. "Home? Like the estate? It's better if I keep my distance for a little while longer. Dad still shits himself every time I'm around."

"I'm not fucking around, Hem."

Something in Ajay's voice drained Hem's humor. "What's wrong?"

"Have you checked your email yet?"

"No, was I supposed to?"

"Do it."

Hem opened up his email and saw a message forwarded from his brother. The original message came from Hans Fineburg, CEO of WTA Digital.

TO THE CEO AND CHAIRMAN OF THE BOARD, BOARD OF DIRECTORS, AND LEADERSHIP COUNCIL OF BHARAT, INC.

This missive, adherent to SEC guidelines, constitutes a formal offer of purchase . . .

"What the fuck is this?" Hem snapped.

"That's not all of it," Ajay said. "Dad had a heart attack after the letter hit our inboxes this morning."

Hem felt as if Ajay had sucked all the air out of his lungs. "Is Dad . . . Is he okay?"

"He's in the hospital, but stable. We haven't told any of the extended family or staff yet. We're keeping it quiet. How soon can you be stateside?"

Hem didn't see eye to eye with his father, but they were still family, and he would do anything for family. He checked his Rolex. "It'll take me at least a day. I'm in fucking Manila, Ajay. It's not like they have hourly flights to the US."

"Didn't you take your jet?"

"No, I sold it to pay for overhead costs on my firm."

"Damned inconvenient, Hem."

"I didn't want to dip into my earnings from Bharat or my trust to raise the money."

"It's still inconvenient. I'll check with a supplier to see if we can borrow one of their jets for now. If not, I don't know, chopper to the next largest international airport and book a private jet from there. There is a board meeting in less than twenty-four hours."

"Did Dad make that decision?"

"No, the fucking board chatted with each other like a bunch of aunties and decided to establish a compensation committee immediately to address the offer. They're restless since we haven't met sales targets after we went public. We've got to get them in line before they try to oust Dad."

Ajay was born to be a leader. He'd done amazing work since Hem had left the business and had shark like instincts. If he was worried, things had to be in bad shape. "I'll be there for the meeting. Whatever you need. How's Mom holding up?"

There was a deep, frustrated sigh on the other end of the phone. "How do you think? She's a goddamn rock, man. Yelled at Dad the moment she saw him in the hospital room. Said that he got what he deserved for eating too much mango pickle at night. As if that's the cause of a heart attack."

Hem missed his mother, sometimes painfully. Her predictable reaction made him smile. "Thank god for small blessings. I'm going to get myself to the airport. Let me know what you can do."

"Got it. See you soon, brother."

Hem hung up and walked back over to Faisal who was reading the last set of provisions on his tablet again.

"Everything okay?" he said.

"No. Sorry, but I need to go."

Faisal flipped the cover over his tablet and straightened in his seat. "No problem. This will give me time to review with my team again—"

"No." Hem picked up the tablet which was luckily still unlocked. He scrolled to the bottom of the page, pulled out a stylus, and held it out. "I know you don't want to give up control over this financial aspect, but fuck it, Faisal. You're going to be rich. Stop stalling."

Faisal gave him an even look but he took the stylus and quickly scribbled his name.

Hem did the same for his portion, and they signed six more sections before Hem saved the document and passed the tablet back to Faisal so he could send it through to Hem's email.

"Happy now?" Faisal said.

"Thrilled. It's been a pleasure doing business." Hem picked up his drink and drained the last of its contents before grabbing his coat and his briefcase. He hated himself for wasting those precious five minutes on this guy when all he wanted to do was get home to his father, but he wouldn't get this opportunity again.

As he rode up to his floor, he thought about his father and the bitter words they exchanged the last time they spoke. After Deepak Singh meddled in his life so coldly, so painfully, they had never seemed to see eye to eye again.

This takeover attempt and a heart attack changed everything. He still loved his father and despite everything that had happened, he'd do anything to help salvage Bharat, even if it meant coming back to the company.

Hem keyed into his room and booted up his laptop to draft a quick message to his paralegals, his assistant, and the ten attorneys that worked for him.

I know we're just getting our feet wet, but I need you to divide and take my case load temporarily. I'll sign all the necessary paperwork to transition it to you, but I'll be out of the office for the next few weeks. You can still reach me by email and my cell if it's an emergency.

He gave detailed follow-up instructions to his paralegal and his assistant and then began to pack all of his items in his small carry-on bag.

Dread filled his gut at the thought of letting go of the reins on a business that had been his salvation after Bharat. Hopefully his father could see, after the time that had passed, that he'd made the right choice.

But now wasn't the time to think about old arguments and family politics. His father needed him, his brothers needed him, and there was nothing Hem wouldn't do to protect them.

"The eldest Singh has returned like a Bollywood fucking hero," Hem mused to himself as he zipped up his bag.

Chapter Two

MINA KOHLI LAY sleepless in bed like she did every year on this day. The muted sounds of an early New York City morning filtered through the open window as a backdrop to the drifting memories of her mother. Mina couldn't help but wonder what kind of relationship they'd have if she was still alive. It'd been fifteen years since the accident, but that didn't matter. Every birthday reminded her of the hole in her heart and in her life.

A familiar ping echoed through the bedroom and Mina reached out to pick up her phone.

DAD: You'll get through today.

Simple, short, and to the point. Her father wasn't an affectionate man, nor were he and Mina close, but sometimes he managed to say just the right thing at the right moment. She sent back a response.

MINA: Just like I always do. Hopefully I'll see you at the office.
DAD: No. Working from home. I'll ask my assistant to schedule a lunch later this week.
MINA: Okay, Dad.
DAD: Okay. Happy thirtieth birthday, Mina.

"That's as close to a touching father-daughter moment as we've ever had," Mina muttered. With a sigh, she opened up her photos and clicked through the albums until she found the one labeled 'Mom'.

Pictures filled the screen. Her mother looked like her. Long dark hair, eyes too big for her face, and sharp cheekbones. Mina scrolled through the pregnancy photos, the baby photos, and the pictures of the few times they went to Central Park when she was a child.

Shalini Kaur Kohli had been such a powerhouse her entire short life, with an active career and social life. No matter what, she'd always made time for Mina. She'd been a mother, a wife, a litigator, and a sister who raised two younger brothers to be litigators as well. Her life had ended the day her brothers voted her out of the firm she built from the ground up. She'd gotten raging drunk, then climbed behind the wheel of her sedan. Mina discovered the truth about the accident when she was seventeen. That's when she began her mission to take back her birthright. Nothing was going to stop her.

Except maybe an arranged marriage.

She shifted against her silk pillowcase, thinking about her uncle's offer. If she married Virat, the son of the managing partner at J.J.S. Immigration Law, she'd get the equity partner position at her mother's firm. Her marriage would make way for the union of two of the largest South Asian-owned firms in the country.

The problem was that she wasn't attracted to Virat. He was such a nice guy, but unfortunately, he possessed the personality of a cardboard box.

Mina's phone buzzed in her hand. Her eyebrows rose clear to her hairline when she saw Sanjeev's number. Her uncle rarely called her, and never at four in the morning. Maybe he remembered it was her birthday. Doubtful, but Sanjeev was full of surprises.

"Yes?"

"You agree to the partner position yet, girl?"

Mina slowly sat up. "No, I'm still thinking it through."

"What the hell is taking you so long?"

"You're basically bartering me for an immigration firm. I deserve some time."

His gruff voice boomed in her ear. "There may be another way to get you that equity partner position. Get to the office. There is an emergency board meeting at Bharat, Inc., and you're the only senior associate with patent experience who has the bandwidth to take on another case. If you're here in an hour, that'll give you, oh, three hours to prep on the company, the other board members, and WTA Digital."

Mina's mind raced as she tried to piece together facts. Bharat had recently gone public, but they were floundering, or so the news said. Sanjeev was friendly with the CEO and chairman, which was how he'd been selected to be part of the board. WTA Digital, however . . . Well, their name was as well-known as Google. A tech company that was in bed with the government. They did everything from artificial intelligence and smartphones, to government defense projects and NATO commissioned research.

"Mina! Are you there?"

"I'm here. Let me guess. Offer for purchase?"

"Just get to the office, girl."

Even though Mina hated her uncle, his words made her smile. Once she'd put in her dues, she'd slowly edge out her uncles. Then she'd take the firm to another level, one that would make her mother proud. Cases like a WTA takeover would be the norm for her.

As she showered, she dictated to her digital assistant and drafted emails to her legal assistant and paralegal. She needed to rearrange her schedule, which meant shifting two client calls and asking for an extra day to review a contract.

Mina slipped into a maroon suit dress with matching pumps and a coordinating Chanel bag. Because it took her an extra minute to pile her long hair on top of her head in a sleek updo, she had to call for a car to pick her up in front of her apartment building in Chelsea.

"Looking lovely today, Ms. Kohli," George said as he opened the door for her. "Spring weather at its finest."

"Thanks, George. I may have a meeting with a new client today."

"Knock 'em dead."

"I always do."

The car was already waiting at the curb, and in a practiced move, she folded herself into the back seat and answered emails for the entire drive to Park and 40th.

The lights were on in the building when she scanned her badge and stepped through the glass doors and into the offices for Kohli and Associates. She loved the rows of redwells stacked on top of the filing cabinets that hardly anyone used anymore, the desks for the paralegals and assistances crammed with paper, discarded coffee cups, and personal items. Most of all, she loved that her floor was high enough to get a view of the East River along one row of windows. Sometimes when she was going for a run or binging on movies at her condo, she'd imagine this exact view was spread out in front of her.

"Mina?" her uncle roared from his corner office.

She headed toward the sound, passing empty cubicles along the way. When she reached her uncle's assistant's desk, she paused to admire the woman typing away at the keyboard. Except for the circles under her eyes, Sangeeta was pressed and polished, as if it wasn't five thirty in the morning.

"Good morning, Mina. He's ready for you."

"Why don't you get some coffee, Sangeeta?"

"No, I'm okay."

Mina pulled out her company card and handed it to her. "Get something for yourself. Pastry, too. And if you don't mind, coffees for me and the dragon."

She glanced at his office and then back to Mina. "I shouldn't . . ."

"I'll keep him busy. You look like you could use some fresh air. I think the cart downstairs just opened up."

Sangeeta glanced one more time at Sanjeev's open door before she quickly grabbed her small purse from a bottom drawer in her desk. "Thanks, Mina."

"Anytime. You can always come to me if you need anything. I know that you trusted my mom when you worked for her. I want you to know that you can trust me, too."

"I—I'll be right back," she said before she scrambled down the hall.

"Mina!" her uncle roared again.

She stepped into the corner office, ignoring the smell of stale cigarettes. The space was a pigsty with papers everywhere. There were discarded suitcoats and ties, dirty bowls and mugs, and an overflowing ashtray. She passed the small conference table and dropped her bag into one of his client chairs.

Her uncle turned in his high-back chair, dressed in a black suit and wearing a thunderous scowl. "What took you so long?"

"You said an hour."

"Whatever. Sit down."

Mina pulled her tablet out of her bag and sat in the second chair. "WTA Digital wants to purchase Bharat. The board is going to have to appoint a committee to determine if the value of the offer is equivalent to the value of the company based on forecasting and financials. Depending on the technicality of the patents Bharat has and how well management at Bharat cooperates, it'll take a while to make that decision. This whole thing could take anywhere from ten days to months. WTA's offer is only good for thirty days, but that can be renegotiated."

Her uncle leaned back in his chair, resting his hands on his round belly. "Good. That's very good. I want you to head the committee that's reviewing the offer."

"The committee has to be an impartial party."

Sanjeev ran two fingers over his mustache. "I talked to a friend of mine who handles high profile acquisition cases. Even though I'm on the board, it wouldn't be a conflict of interest if one of my attorneys takes the case. As long as they don't report to me. I also talked to Deepak's son at Bharat. They're okay with my firm's involvement. The remaining members of the committee will be selected by the rest of the board. They'll need to be experts in business intelligence, integrity, and finance."

"Okay. You do realize that I'll have to be on site a couple times a week, right? I do have the bandwidth to take this on since I just closed out a bunch of cases, but court dates, depositions, and meetings for the rest of my workload will have to be rescheduled."

"Fine. Do what you have to do. I want the committee to make a decision as quickly as possible, so if that means you set up a makeshift office there, so be it. Oh, and there is one more thing."

"Shoot."

"I'll make you equity partner, with or without the arranged marriage to Virat, if you report to the Bharat board at the end of your review that we need to take WTA's offer."

Mina jerked in her seat. "What the hell?" She couldn't have heard him right. There was no way he'd just asked her point-blank to commit a crime.

"I know you don't want to marry Virat," Sanjeev continued. "I also know you'll do whatever it takes to become partner. I'm willing to give you another opportunity. One that doesn't include an arranged marriage. Make the WTA deal happen, Mina. If you can't, then it's wedding bells for you. Unless of course, you'd rather be unemployed."

Sanjeev looked too smug, too content. Was he testing her, or trying to get rid of her? She'd do anything to get her mother's company back, except lose her integrity.

"I feel like I'm in an alternate universe. Sanjeev, you aren't seriously asking me to sabotage the vote."

"This is how the real world works, Mina. I shouldn't have to explain myself. Bharat is in the process of registering a patent for software that can locate moving targets traveling over two hundred miles an hour with ninety-eight point eight seven percent accuracy. It's my friend's latest invention in an effort to find missing persons across the world. However, I'm a lawyer and a businessman. I know that they'll never be able to do it. WTA has the resources and manpower to successfully execute the research."

"How the hell did you find this out?"

"Oh, the R&D team presented to the board last quarter," Sanjeev said, waving his hand in dismissal. "Just look like you're doing a due diligence review, but in the end, your report should have one conclusion. It's not only for your future's sake, but also because it's the smartest move."

Sanjeev wasn't telling her the whole truth. That much was clear. He was asking Mina to jeopardize her license and do something unethical for the sake of staying at the firm. Did she appear so driven that he assumed she'd consider risking her future for a chance at a partner position?

Mina should've thrown his proposition back in his face, when something about his expression made her pause.

Bingo.

If she pretended to go through with his plan, it would buy her time to find out if her uncle had waded into anything illegal himself.

She stood and picked up her bag. "Fine. I'll consider . . . all of this. When do we leave for the board meeting?"

"Two hours. Remember, I'm counting on you to make

the right decision for both your career and this law firm. It's about time I get some use out of you."

Her hand tightened on her purse handle. "I'll be in my office."

She left the stifling room, her brain running through legal ethics violations and consequences that Sanjeev could be involved in when she ran straight into Sangeeta.

"Uh, Ms. Kohli? Your coffee and card."

"Oh. Thanks, Sangeeta."

Sangeeta picked up a small wrapped package from her desk and held it out. "And I got you this," she said quietly. "I was reviewing your employment contract for signature and saw your birth date. I know you haven't celebrated it in a while, and a croissant isn't much compared to a cake but . . ."

"No, it's okay. You don't have to—"

"Happy thirtieth birthday."

"Oh. Uh . . . thanks." Mina took the pastry, feeling queasy at the idea of eating anything at the moment. "You didn't have to do that."

"I wanted to. You have your whole life ahead of you, Mina. Don't waste it . . . here with some of these people."

With a sigh, Mina dropped the pastry and card into her bag. "I don't know where else I'd rather be. I feel closest to Mama here. Thanks again, Sangeeta."